Wretched Results

The Outlander Physician Series

Wretched Results

by Barbara Ebel, M.D.

The Outlander Physician Series

Book One: Corruption in the O.R.
Book Two: Wretched Results

Copyright © 2020 by Barbara Ebel, M.D.

Paperback ISBN-13: 978-1-7349847-0-5
ebook ISBN-13: 978-1-7349847-1-2

This book is a work of fiction. Names, characters, places and events are the product of the author's imagination or are used fictitiously. Any resemblance to actual events, persons, or locations is coincidental.

CHAPTER 1

It was the first day of her new anesthesia assignment, but Viktoria was far from excited.

Would women patients, wanting to transform their faces into alluring goddesses, and their bodies into svelte, knockout figures, make up the type of anesthesia cases that bordered on monotony? If that turned out to be the case, it would be safer for them.

Or would her next month of plastic surgery cases be challenging, as when the unexpected occurs, triggering an adrenaline rush and catalyzing the life-saving talented skills she possessed from her years of practice?

Leaving the car motor on, she pondered those questions. She would find out soon enough. Maybe the next few weeks would be far less stressful than the variety of hospital cases she'd originally signed up for and were subsequently changed. Apparently, the plastic surgery center in front of her had called the locum tenens agency in dire need of anesthesia coverage. She didn't know why they had become short-handed, but it was of no concern to her.

Amour Cosmetic Surgery was located in the middle of a Long Island, NY strip mall, and took up most of the length of the entire building. To the right stood a chain sub-sandwich shop and, to the left, a small travel agency office.

Viktoria turned off the ignition of her Honda Accord and realized the marketing cleverness of the business's location before her. Amour was not located further east on the island where it would more likely cater to the more affluent, and neither was it further west where the residential areas were more transient and less wealthy. Situated on the North Shore in its present location, Amour Cosmetic Surgery generated patients from all of Long Island's economic classes.

She gathered her things, locked the car door, and aimed straight for the sparkling clean entrance. It was early, the sun rose not too long ago, and her own reflection greeted her on the smudge-free glass door as she pulled on the handle.

Being her first day, she showed up extra early. The lobby was typical of other surgery centers—up to a point. White floors were polished and immaculate; the front check-in desk was inviting and built of high-end wood grain; and the furniture in the waiting area was as modern as possible. The difference from other centers was the slideshow rolling across a wide screen taking up the length of the side wall. Beautiful faces of women flashing happy smiles and curvaceous figures were shown with their one line testimonials of how Amour Cosmetic Surgery had transformed their image and lives.

The door opened behind her and a woman stepped in. Well dressed, she pulled off her colorful brimmed hat, revealing a dark-blonde braid. She stopped next to Viktoria and nodded towards the wall. "Happy customers."

"I see that," Viktoria said, assuming she was an employee. "Very effective. Usually plastic surgery ads show the before and after surgery pictures of patients, but your waiting room only shows the patients' end results—their transformations after being treated at your center."

"Astute of you to pick up on that. We do, however, highlight what they look like when they first come in for a consultation. We show that in pamphlets, on our website, and other places. Are you here for surgery?"

"No. Luckily I'm not in need of cosmetic changes at this point in my life. I'm Dr. Viktoria Thorsdottir, an Anesthesiologist hired to work here for the next four weeks. Regina, from the locum tenens agency, sent me for the assignment."

"Oh, yes. We are expecting you. Come on back to the meat of the operation and Dr. Castillo can explain our center to you. He'll introduce you to someone in anesthesia who can show you where to find what you'll need." She stepped forward. "By the way, I'm Lucy Murray."

"Glad to meet you." With a door on either side of the front desk, Lucy steered her to the left.

"This side is for consultations and post-op visits. It's the non-surgical side. The whole area straight back from the front desk is our kitchen, the doctors' offices, and workrooms. And on the other side are the operating rooms. I'll point out a locker you can use while you're here."

Lucy veered into a women's changing room and showed her a long vertical locker. "Key's in the door."

They exited, rounded the corner, and entered the kitchenette. The square room housed three round tables and all the makings of a fully-stocked kitchen. By one counter, a short man with sloped shoulders turned around.

"Don't tell me," he said. "This is Dr. Thorsdottir from the agency. Excellent punctuality." He came close, too close, and put out his hand. The black hair of his long sideburns stopped lower than the end of his beaked nose and were meticulously straight. She guessed him to be right around her own age of thirty-nine.

Viktoria obliged his handshake, all too aware that he studied her face. If he was thinking of offering her lip enhancement during her stay, she wasn't interested. Lucy Murray's lips qualified as the big lips seen in pictures of certain fish. No, she didn't want a perfect-pout enhancement.

"Rigoberto Castillo," he added.

"Nice place you have here. I think Regina mentioned you may be the owner as well as a plastic surgeon." She said it with a questioning tone.

"I run this place. Why don't you change into scrubs?" The coffee pot behind him stopped dripping, and he swiveled around. "Bring a cup with you if you'd like."

Viktoria shook her head. "Perhaps later, after I get the lay of the land."

Lucy escorted her out and Viktoria slipped back into the women's room, ready to change into the usual OR cotton blue scrubs. So far, so good, she thought. At least this place had one thing going for it. The first two people she met were hospitable, a far cry from the unwelcoming-welcoming committee she encountered on her last assignment in northern Pennsylvania.

With some help from the anesthesia tech in the anesthesia workroom, Viktoria learned where they stashed supplies. The tech, a young Hispanic woman named Lola, was in the early months of a pregnancy, and beamed like her obstetrician just told her the good news.

"You are in OR number 2," Lola said. "You can check out narcotics from the drug machine outside the workroom. Otherwise, all the resources you'll need are in the red anesthesia cart which I've already rolled into your room. The center is standard fare just like any other place you've worked."

"Thank you so much. Be careful rolling those carts around six months from now."

"Not to worry, Dr. Thorsdottir. I'm pregnant, not crippled."

3

"You make a valid point. A few months ago, on a job down south, I saw a parking space in a normal spot for handicapped parking, right in front of the grocery store. The sign said 'Reserved Parking for Expectant Mothers Only.' I thought that went a tad bit too far."

Lola shook her head. "I go out of my way to walk more while I'm pregnant, not less. Get all that fast blood flow transported to my baby."

"I like your style, Lola, and it sounds like you pick up on medical terminology because of where you work."

Her smile faded, she frowned, and she lowered her voice. "Not only that, but I hear stuff that they think I don't overhear. That's because I'm invisible."

"Invisible?"

"You know. When people think folks like me are not important, they don't 'see' that person. In other words, those people are uninhibited in my presence with what they say."

"Lola, how awful. You are important. Anesthesia technicians are an important part of every anesthesia department in an OR. You better believe that I depend on you to stash the necessary supplies in a cart for every single case I do. What if I need to change out an endotracheal tube and don't have an assortment of tube sizes, or intubating blades, or emergency drugs? A patient's life could be in jeopardy if I don't have what I need immediately."

The young woman stood transfixed by Viktoria's words. Her extra-round glasses on her narrow face slipped a bit, and she raised her hand to push them back up.

"I better get going," Viktoria announced.

Dr. Thorsdottir yanked an OR bonnet out of a box by the door and slid it over her head. The conversation with Lola had been strange, she thought. The woman apparently felt insignificant while working at the center, and heard things she shouldn't. The technician's remarks made her wonder.

Viktoria shook her head. In a way, she would be an unimportant part of this staff for the next month also, but in no way did she want to overhear conversations that she shouldn't. After all, she had landed in a precarious position in her Pennsylvania assignment last month where there was nothing but corruption in the OR. Better to keep her head down, her ears deaf, and her mind glued on her cases.

Focused on finding OR number 2, Viktoria headed into the surgical area, where the hallway was well lit and remarkably spotless. All told, there appeared to be six operating rooms, not too shabby for an independent, non-hospital facility. She passed the scrub sink outside of OR 2 and went straight in. The red anesthesia cart which Lola had provided was well-stocked, allowing Viktoria to sigh with relief. The large anesthesia machine with inhalational agents and accessory machines were all in order as well. She found a bottle of sevoflurane in the drawer and filled the half-empty vaporizer with the agent. Now she needed to go see her first patient.

The preop surgical area bustled with activity as Viktoria stepped in. Staff escorted women into their curtained areas and started IVs. She noticed other anesthesia providers wearing scrubs, but ducked into a cubicle to meet her patient—a forty-eight year old scheduled for a forehead lift.

"Are you Bonnie Sandler?" Viktoria asked.

"I sure am, but at this moment I'm not sure I want to be." The woman had a slight build, her cotton gown wrinkled up all around her torso. Her hand shot up to her brow where she pointed. "You're gonna ask me. I'm getting rid of these because I look like one of those wrinkly dogs who have all those folds above their eyes."

"Yes, a forehead lift. I'm ..."

"I have to. I got divorced a year ago and I'm having a hard time with dating. Guys want to date women younger than them, and I'm striking out because they think I'm in my mid-fifties. I have two kids so that's a deterrent to some guys already and, except for my ex-husband, I like men and can't do without them."

She glanced at the woman sitting quietly nearby. "My friend here had the same procedure and look what it's done for her."

Viktoria nodded, but this time interrupted. "If you want anesthesia, we need to talk."

"Oh, I guess so. I'd like that. Really I would."

"I am Dr. Thorsdottir, the anesthesiologist physician who is going to take care of you."

"That means you have the good stuff. I never had surgery before, and I'm a nervous wreck. I can't believe I actually signed up for this. Maybe I'm crazy, but if I want to start going out on better dates, I don't have a choice."

"Ms. Sandler, when did you last have something to eat or drink?" The way her patient rambled with pressured speech, the more Viktoria thought that she may have drank a pint of espresso before arriving.

Bonnie glanced at her friend and went on with her strong Long Island accent. "She tortured me on the way here, and stopped for cawffee. I'll never forgive her. My belly is empty as a casket waiting for someone to die."

Viktoria twisted her mouth, wanting a more definitive answer than cemetery talk. But it was also refreshing to be back home and hear Islanders "tawk" in their accent.

"Nothing since last night," Bonnie finally answered.

After asking her all the pertinent questions about her medical and surgical history, Viktoria learned the woman so far had a decent bill of health. "Any unusual family medical history?" she added.

Bonnie twisted her mouth. "My poor boys grew up without my dad. They had no grandfather to play ball with, or be scolded by, or to eat junk food with when I wasn't around."

"I'm sorry..." Viktoria waited. "So what happened to him?"

"He died! They said it was a heart attack, but that doesn't make sense because he was younger than me—only thirty-nine years old."

"You must miss him. Did they do an autopsy?"

"I hated that they cut him up, but they did."

Since an autopsy was done, Viktoria felt comfortable believing her father's cause of death, because his heart would have been evaluated by a pathologist. As she often thought, a person was handed down a deck of cards from their parents and forefathers DNA, and there was nothing they could do about it, be it favorable or unfavorable double helixes. Hopefully, Bonnie would not be predisposed to an early myocardial infarct.

"Yes, autopsies are difficult to think about. Two more questions—any family history of problems with anesthesia and are you allergic to any medications?"

"No problems in the family going under anesthesia that I know about, but I had an allergy to some antibiotic once."

"What happened?"

"All of a sudden I had trouble breathing. Went nearby to a walk-in-clinic place and they put a little IV thing in my hand and pushed in some drug. I felt better after that."

"Do you remember the name of the antibiotic?"

"They said to tell anybody in the future it was a Penicillin class."

"Okay, thank you. Now, I'll explain your anesthesia. You should not remember a thing, you'll be well sedated, and I'll take care of your pain. You'll be breathing through a type of mask; I'll try to avoid inserting a breathing tube down your throat and you'll receive adequate IV sedation."

"Sounds great to me."

Viktoria explained the anesthetic risks, and pulled out a syringe with midazolam, a pre-op sedative and amnestic drug. Bonnie's rapid fire talking subsided as her head succumbed back into the pillow after a dose. The well-done red highlights on her hair, matching the freckles on her face, were soon covered up with an OR bonnet.

"The surgeon's here," the nurse said. "Are you ready, Dr. Thorsdottir?"

"Yes, ma'am. Meet you back there."

Since the surgical field in the OR involved the area around Bonnie's forehead, the surgeon and tech stood close to Viktoria's own space at the head of the table. Dr. Ernest Pinto, the surgeon, had shrugged when she had asked him to rotate the table forty-five degrees away from her space, as was more customary, but it was as if he didn't want to bother using up another five minutes.

Viktoria obliged him. She had learned a long time ago to pick her battles with surgeons, and to confront them only when it concerned a patient's safety.

For Bonnie's surgery, Dr. Thorsdottier used a laryngeal mask airway, gave sedation and supplemental oxygen to make her comfortable, and avoided a deep anesthetic state. It was working out just fine as the surgeon was ready to start, and Bonnie's vital signs remained excellent.

"I'm ready," Dr. Pinto informed Viktoria in a low voice, holding a scalpel.

Viktoria noted the surgical start time, part of the official anesthesia record, but then she stared with disappointment at his method. For the apparent prestigious plastic surgery center that it was, the method of the forehead lift she was witnessing could be more modern and less invasive. Of course, it was only her opinion, she thought, admonishing herself. After all, she was no plastic surgeon.

Dr. Pinto made a continuous incision along the top of Bonnie's head slicing from ear to ear. Viktoria injected one more cc of the narcotic, fentanyl, into her patient's IV because it was apparent the surgeon was not going to do an endoscopic lift, the more modern approach. For that method, only a few short incisions were needed in the scalp, a thin scope with a camera was inserted, and another device inserted in another hole to make the needed alterations.

Viktoria knew the endoscopic procedure was not only less invasive, but patients recovered quicker and, more importantly, the anchors which were used allowed the altered tissue to stay in place for a much longer time. Better cosmetic results for a longer time! Wasn't that what beautification surgery was all about?

As she mulled this over in her mind, Dr. Pinto held his scalpel still for a moment. His beady eyes smiled as they settled on the drapes over her chest. "She's really flat-chested."

"You going to do something about that?" the tech asked. Her hands rested on the tray table of sterile instruments between them, and she waited for a reply.

"My breast implant pitch to her is on the tip of my tongue. She'll hear it in a few days when she comes back to see me for her post-op visit. I hope she has money left over after this procedure."

The tech glanced at Viktoria as if they were all in this together. "Cash only," she said.

"In the meantime," Dr. Pinto added, "this procedure is going to do wonders for her because her forehead skin is as botched up as a raisin."

The tech shook her head. "Women can't win. When we get too old for pimples, we go straight into wrinkles."

CHAPTER 2

"Bonnie, your surgery is over."

The woman's eyes fluttered open as Viktoria rested her arms on the handrail.

"Really? No more wrinkles?"

"You'll know soon enough when the bandage comes off. Are you in any pain?"

"No. That's all there was to fixing my forehead?" she asked as Dr. Pinto sidled alongside the stretcher.

"I believe so," Viktoria said.

"Plastic surgery is a miracle to one's self-esteem," Ernest chimed in, "and helpful, since you're in a dating frame of mind. The center is running a special on breast implants in two weeks. Just think, twenty percent off, and you would be more beautiful than you already are."

Bonnie yanked on the sheet, her hand sliding across her chest. His suggestion made sense. Painstakingly aware of her lack of endowment in that department, she had a silent jealously for women well-stacked. But breast implants? Too expensive, she had always thought. This was the first time someone told her that boob jobs could be on sale.

Bonnie bit the side of her mouth in full contemplation of his offer, and he didn't let the opportunity go to waste.

"You'll benefit from a heck of a savings. A fire sale on fixing your body to what Mother Nature should've done in the first place! After all, a woman should grow decent breasts to begin with because she's the one who needs to breast feed her babies."

Ernest Pinto wanted to pat himself on the back. He could practically reserve a surgery spot for her right now before she healed from her forehead lift.

"We'll talk," he said quietly. "I will book extra time into your return visit."

Dr. Pinto turned to Viktoria. "Nice anesthetic. I hope you're doing my next case."

"Dr. Castillo slated me for OR number 2 all day, unless something changes."

His beady eyes narrowed, he patted her forearm, and left through the double doors. After a quick dash to the restroom, Viktoria was back to another forehead lift with her soft-spoken surgeon, except when he was busy drumming up more business with his patients.

Three forehead lifts in a row with Dr. Pinto, and Viktoria was ready for lunch, especially since no one gave her an official break all morning. Dr. Castillo caught her filing her anesthesia paperwork in the staff's office behind the front desk. For being a somewhat modern facility, their anesthesia records were still done by hand, and not electronically.

"I can spare you," he said. "I'm working a full surgery schedule this afternoon myself, but I'm ducking out for lunch. You'll be doing my cases. I'm going to the sandwich place next door, if you want to join me."

"I didn't bring anything to eat. Would love to."

"Most days, everyone brings their lunch and sticks it in the refrigerator. Sometimes we order out and, other times, someone makes a run next door for a group order. We can slip out together. Plus, I can answer any questions you may have. Maybe in another ten years, you'll consider Amour for your cosmetic surgery. There's always Botox in the interim. I am a genius when it comes to taking years off your face with only a filler product."

"To tell you the truth, I am thirty-nine years old, I don't look like a youngster any more, and I am not yet middle-aged. Wish I could stay this way, but I'll pass on your offer."

They headed down the hallway and picked their white, long coats off a hook on the wall. She slid hers on while he opened the door to the waiting room where the scene was nothing like early in the morning. Three people queued up before the check-in desk, and others thumbed through magazines and scrolled cell phones while standing on the sidelines. The seats were almost filled, mostly by women.

"Dr. Castillo," a thin woman said, lurching toward him.

He put up the palm of his hand. "Later, ma'am. Let this famished doctor go eat, or my energy level will be depleted before my afternoon schedule."

She lowered back into the chair reluctantly, as if she lost the opportunity to get the autograph of a celebrity.

Viktoria followed him out, her eyes on his sloping shoulders. On the sidewalk outside, her long legs easily kept pace with his short stride. She stood five-foot seven, and was lucky to be that tall. Being a product of Icelandic DNA, her people traced back to at least a thousand years ago when the Vikings explored the island nation. Those mixed Celtic and Norse people were shorter than their distant offspring of today.

In a few moments, they read the overhead menu in the sandwich store, and Viktoria asked for tuna salad on cheesy garlic bread. After paying, they filled drink cups, and Rigoberto selected a table.

"The only person I met so far regarding anesthesia services is Lola," Viktoria said. "How many anesthesiologists and nurse anesthetists work at your surgery center?"

"It varies. Today there are five rooms going most of the day. One room is staffed by a locum tenens person like yourself, and the other three by regular employee anesthesia providers."

"Temporary fill-in doctors or nurses sent by an agency, a locum tenens agency like the one that sent me, has to be more expensive to your budget."

"Not necessarily. We readjust if we need one to three temporary people based on the upcoming booked surgeries. We are much more monetarily productive that way. Efficiency is my middle name." He generously salted the cold cuts piled in the middle of his bread.

Viktoria stalled, holding her sandwich in her hand. "At some point, I would like to meet your anesthesiologists and CRNAs. I may need their help in finding something in case Lola isn't around."

"Lola is always around. That's what she gets paid for."

"How long have you been at …"

"Where are you from?" he interjected. "You don't have a Long Island accent. Is this your idea of seeing the country by wandering from job to job like a gypsy?"

She swallowed hard. He wasn't the first person to hint about a "gypsy" lifestyle.

"I'm more like an 'outlander,' a foreigner from an unusual nation and culture, who settled on Long Island Sound, but flees the New York area for anesthesia opportunities in other locations."

"Sounds like you're trying to get away from something."

"Maybe so." She bit her tongue. Her marriage and home life in a nearby region was none of his business.

"The lady from the temp agency said this job would be easy for you since your commute time won't be bad. Interesting that Long Island is your home base for your exotic lifestyle."

"Yes. It serves its purpose."

"But what's the strange nation you originally came from?"

"Iceland."

"No wonder you came here. The glaciers, snow, and cold must've been unbearable."

"You're most likely thinking of Greenland."

Barely perceptible, he shrugged his shoulders. "If you say so."

"Not to worry. Many people think that, although that's changing every day. Iceland has become a super tourist destination. I'm afraid my place of birth is being trampled on and spoiled just like every other place on the planet."

"Pity that. Hey, do they do much plastic surgery there?"

"Not really."

"Hmm. Maybe I could start an advertising campaign luring those people to Long Island for their head-turning transformations." His eyes focused on his sandwich as he took a bite, apparently dead serious thinking about the possibilities.

"Is there a prominent national magazine or specific media I could target?" he asked, popping out of his deep thinking.

"How do you make time for marketing and advertising?"

"Not me. Other staff does that."

"There's another perspective on a campaign. Since people around the world google Iceland more than its citizens, your best bet is Icelandic websites that cater to tourism. Those sites bring in heavy traffic. You'd be reaching more people than locals."

"Smart woman. I'll pass that along." His face beamed with pleasure, he sat back, and slurped his drink through a straw.

Viktoria wondered how wise it was to give him new ideas, but she reconsidered her slight disapproval. After all, plastic surgery was a big specialty, and useful as well. Women post-mastectomy from cancer could rebuild their chest walls with reconstructive or implant surgery. People with facial deformities from accidents, cancer, or birth defects, were operated on by plastic surgeons, which made them happier individuals and more able to lead normal lives.

Yes, she thought, like all other fields of medicine, cosmetic surgery had its place. It was a good thing that people like Dr. Castillo and Dr. Pinto trained those extra years in residency and passed those difficult specialty exams which qualified them as Board-Certified Plastic Surgeons.

"Our patient is changing out of her street clothes," Dr. Castillo said after they returned to the center from lunch. "It'll be a few minutes before you can see her." Rigoberto disappeared into his office, leaving Viktoria sipping from her to-go cup inside the doorway of the front desk.

She perched herself sideways on the top of the desk, and leaned against the wall.

A woman scribbled her name in the sign-in sheet and thrust it at an employee through the second glass window. "I've been waiting an hour," she said, "so I'm signing in again. I hope by doing that, I'll spring ahead in line and see a doctor sooner."

"Ma'am," a woman staff member said, "some doctors have afternoon surgeries, and some are evaluating patients. You will leave here satisfied if you wait and are seen. Do you have one of our comprehensive brochures about our services?" She slid over a folded, colorful pamphlet.

"No, I would like to read this one while I wait." The woman inched away, headed for her chair, and another woman took her place.

Closest to Viktoria, Lucy Murray sat tall and straight with impeccable posture. The woman's untouched coffee mug was pushed out of reach, and she listened attentively to a middle-aged female who leaned over a large purse she had set on the counter.

"This isn't fair, and I'm tired of waiting. I need my money back. It's been almost three weeks."

Lucy tilted her head. "I hope to help you, Mrs. ...."

"Walters."

"If this is a billing or payment issue, have you talked to our business office?"

"I'm here because Amour Cosmetic Surgery owes me money, not the other way around."

"Who contacted you about that?"

"Nobody! You're not listening." Her voice carried further into the room and Lucy leaned forward. "Three weeks ago, my surgery was cancelled. That was a disappointment and wrench in my schedule and, on top of that, the deposit I paid up front hasn't been returned."

"I'm so sorry to hear you haven't had your surgery yet. Would you like to reschedule?"

"No, I can't. Not now. Something else has come up and I need my money back."

Lucy nodded. "Our staff here at the surgery center does not balance bills, manage refunds, or anything like that. We are not the billing office. There is a professional service that takes care of those matters. I'm sure you have their number from the initial literature you received."

The woman thumped her hand on her black bag. "I called that number twice and it's busy or I get put on hold. There's only so long I can listen to elevator music, so I came by in person."

"I learned a trick which helps me when I'm put on hold. Tap your iPhone on audio speaker and grab yourself a cup of cawffee. In addition, I'm going to make note of your name and problem." She wrote the woman's name on the tiny pad in front of her while spelling out "Walters."

The woman maintained her stance. Lucy finished writing and tapped her hand on the notepad like Mrs. Walters' problem was of the utmost priority.

"Okay, then. Between the both of us working on this, I'll expect my deposit to be returned soon. Let's hope the United States postal service can deliver the check to the correct address."

Lucy Murray swiped her braid to the front of her shoulder and smiled. "For sure. Enjoy the rest of your day."

Mrs. Walters clutched her bag to her chest and marched out.

"It's always something," Lucy said, reaching for her mug.

"Do you even know why her surgery was cancelled?"

"Sure don't, and she didn't say."

"Must everyone advance a deposit for their surgery?"

"Yes, that's standard practice for most cosmetic surgery. And we take no credit cards. It's cash only."

"I hate to say this out loud, but I wonder if some people don't have the money for their out-of-pocket real medical expenses over and above what medicare or their insurance companies pay, but can come up with the cash for plastic surgery."

"I wouldn't know anything about that and I don't ask. People from all walks of life come in here—both the lower-middle class and the rich, and the healthy as well as the sick. We don't discriminate." Lucy chuckled. "One-hundred dollar bills are green no matter who forks them over. That goes for everything."

Lucy sipped from her mug and frowned. "Cold. Stone cold."

"I'll pop it in the microwave for you."

"Would you? I think another problem patient is headed my way."

"I'd be glad to." Viktoria slid off the desk. "Too bad your billing office isn't on site. That would make things easier for you, and that poor woman would have gone home with her much-needed money."

Wanting to be helpful, Viktoria took the coffee cup from her. As she stepped through the open doorway, she could swear that Lucy crumpled the note paper she'd written on, and threw it in the wastebasket.

CHAPTER 3

Vikotoria Thorsdottir's husband, Rick Richter, spent the Fall afternoon in the backyard of their Long Island home. Since he pieced together two different jobs to fill his resume, which didn't amount to a normal person's part-time position, he secured the luxury of filling his days the way he wanted. Especially at the age of thirty-seven. How fortunate for him that he had married a workaholic physician.

The two red maples in the fenced-in yard were ablaze with color, one of them more magnificently scarlet, and the other one displaying orange and yellow like it mimicked pieces of fruit. Another one on their property, on the front lawn, was beautifully broad and the fastest grower. Particularly fond of them, he had secured a hammock between the two in the back.

He stood with a rake, his early efforts paying off. Recently, the deciduous leaves had started to fall, and he wanted to prevail with stuffing them into trash bags in a timely fashion. There was no other significant yard work he needed to do all year, except to mow the grass and trim a few bushes in the front. He did enjoy the outside yard work and, in addition, his efforts were noticed by his wife, and that counted for something.

Of course, there was another reason why he spent his afternoon outside. He qualified as a heavy marijuana smoker, so much so that it made his head spin—literally. Viktoria was home for a month, a rare occurrence, and he wasn't used to that. Most of the time, he could smoke in the house, but with her coming and going, it would be difficult to mask the odor and the evidence. And she would be home soon.

It wasn't that she didn't know about his habit, because she did. However, she knew nothing about his addiction when they first married. In essence, he had kept his pot stash and smoking from her, and only over time did she come to know. It threw a wrench in their marriage.

It bothered her immensely that he was breaking the law since marijuana was still illegal in New York. When she would argue with him about it, he would tell her that the day would come when that would change. As reported in the papers, the governor was already thinking about a future law which would decriminalize people for possessing small amounts of weed.

That was not her only problem with him using it, however. His moods went up and down like a teeter totter. Although he tried to deny it, he could get quite nasty while on a smoking binge. At some level, he wondered if the purity of his grass from his dealers was getting more doctored with other additives, but he was no weed pharmacist.

He wanted to hurry and get in another fix before his wife came home, so he pulled out his pipe, lighter, and baggie of ground weed from the pocket of his light jacket. After putting some marijuana into the pipe, he engaged the lighter to the edge and inhaled lightly. With a nod to himself, he praised the heat distribution, airflow, and how efficiently he mastered the technique. However, he liked to mix up his methods simply for the variety of it all. No question, he rolled his joints damn well too.

After another drag, he blew out, and stared at the trash bag. It should be fuller by now, he thought. He could swear he stuffed it already and was ready to make a knot in that bright yellow drawstring.

His head spun with a beautiful buzz. Later in the day, he was scheduled for a therapy session to begin treatment to kick his habit, a recent decision he made before his wife had come home from her last assignment. Knowing he may be finished with marijuana for the foreseeable future, he wanted to ramp up the afternoon and smoke more, rather than less. Make it a cannabis good-bye party!

Rick chuckled out loud and laid down in the pile of leaves which were on the grass, rather than in the bag. The last time he stared up at the passing clouds against the blue sky was when he was probably eight-years old.

For Viktoria, the afternoon sped by, one case after another with Rigoberto Castillo. Like other surgery centers or hospital ORs, the more a facility and a surgeon performed certain cases, the more well-oiled and slick the process and procedures.

Viktoria left her previous case in the recovery room, and scurried into the preop holding area where she found her next patient, Mr. Robinski, a man in his sixties with a growing concern. Each year added another fraction of an inch to his sagging eyelids, so that one of these days, he was afraid all he'd be able to see were his shoes. His lids drooped down, obscuring his vision, so that every day he wanted to spear them with a safety pin, and pin them up to his eyebrows.

He glanced skeptically at Viktoria while wiggling his feet which jutted out of the blanket keeping him warm. Since he stood very tall, he didn't fit on the stretcher.

"Greetings," Viktoria said. "I'll be with you the whole time. I am Dr. Thorsdottir, the anesthesiologist."

He let a smile form, and said, "Just who I want to see, if these damn eyelids weren't in my way. But that's why I'm here. My wife says the reason I'm having this surgery is so that I can ogle over pretty women again. But that's the half of it. I can't be baby-sitting the grandskids if I can't adequately see what trouble they're getting into. Like the other day, I missed the toddler picking up a thumbtack on the floor. Had my wife not walked in, that little bugger would have swallowed that thing."

"Horrors," Viktoria said. "I'm glad you scheduled this surgery. Dr. Castillo should be able to fix you up and eliminate that veil over your eyes."

"Can't wait."

After asking him his full medical history, Viktoria explained the anesthesia. He asked no questions, but chit-chatted his way back to the OR while enjoying the ride.

Gowned and gloved, Dr. Castillo soon sat near the head of the table and, every once in a while, rolled his stool closer to the area of Mr. Robinski's eyelid he was working on. His afternoon was jammed with blepharoplasties which were plastic surgeries on eyelids to remove excess or fatty tissue. His patients were getting either their upper or lower lids done, or both.

The table was turned ninety degrees from Viktoria, her equipment within arm's reach. And although the present patient's airway was a slight distance away, she gave safe, appropriate anesthetic care and monitoring.

"Mr. Robinski is the first male patient all day," Rigoberto said as he sat straight for a moment. "It figures that his blepharoplasty is for more medical reasons than cosmetic like all the women have been. Everybody has different concerns."

"His upper eyelids sure did sag," Viktoria commented. "Never seen someone that bad. His vision must have been severely impaired, to the point of not being able to see and drive safely."

"He should not have waited to come see me as long as he did. After all, medical insurance is covering his case."

"Isn't this a cash-only practice?"

"We are. He still had to pay up front, but when insurance money comes through and, if we somehow get the payment, we'll reimburse it to him."

"That may be his reason for delaying right there. Perhaps it took him time to scrounge up the money."

"I've learned that everybody has cash on hand for a rainy day or a New York major highlight. If tickets go on sale at night for the US Open in Flushing Meadow, they're usually gone by the morning. Same thing with buying plastic surgery procedures, especially when we advertise 'reduced rates.'"

Dr. Castillo rolled closer to the other eye. "Most likely, the women you gave anesthesia to today, stole the funds from their household money used for food, or their kids school supplies, or vet visits for their dogs. They want to improve the appearance of their eyelids, or whatever, and revive their face. Just by removing the bags under their eyes, which are xerox copies representing their droopy lives, they are rejuvenated into their younger selves. That alone is worth a fortune to them and worth every penny."

Viktoria hated to hear his explanation about the financial side of plastic surgery, but she couldn't fault him. The field was meant to be a lucrative business as well as a beauty or medical enhancing one, and she could not deny that. Again, she knew, it was a recognized medical specialty, one in which doctors thoroughly trained just like her years in anesthesia residency. Most doctors in good facilities were also board-certified and, in that case, they were experts in the needed knowledge. The only disparity would be if the person or persons somehow lacked the 'hands-on' skills. After all the residency training, however, that would be rare.

Rigoberto started on the next eye and Viktoria injected another ml of midazolam and fentanyl into the man's IV in his forearm, resting and secured on the arm board next to her. His oxygen level remained in the high ninety percentile, and his blood pressure barely budged.

Viktoria thought of Mr. Robinski's eyelids as heavy window shades which obscured most of his vision. As she watched with interest, Dr. Castillo removed a horizontal sliver of eyelid tissue, but she hoped he took enough so that he didn't have to come back for the same procedure all over again.

With her first day at Amour Cosmetic Surgery behind her, Viktoria changed into street clothes, and said good-by to Lucy and the staff at the front desk.

She stepped outside to the wide parking lot, the landscaping less manicured than the front, opposite side of the building. Except for three entrance paths, the perimeter of the sidewalk was lined with hedges. One bench and flower pot sat outside Amour, a nice touch for patients bored with waiting inside.

After slipping into her white Honda, she noted the time. With no stops to make along the way, she'd be home before four o'clock. Working locum positions at forty-hours a week or less was a God-send. Most doctors worked far longer and became burned out with the grueling pace. For her, she went home tired enough after eight hours, and became anxious to enjoy the rest of the day.

From Amour to her house was a fifteen-minute drive, half of which she drove on a four-lane road, and the rest a two-lane road. Their address was "Harbour Village," Long Island, New York, but in essence, what used to be a small, quaint village now sprawled east, west, and south and merged into the next towns, or mini-cities as she thought of them. After all, each area had its fill of shopping malls and fast-food restaurants.

The only charm left to the place, in her opinion, encompassed the historic, older part of the Village. A lovely place to walk on foot, the streets ended at a marina, a boardwalk, and little stretches of beach on Long Island Sound. When she needed to clear her head, she would brave the parking spot scarcity and head that way.

Arriving home, she eyed the front of the house as she veered her vehicle into the double garage. The aging home wore a new coat of paint—a soft earth tone with white trim around the windows—and the red maple was lovely with fall colors. On the ground was a full scattering of leaves.

She sighed with pleasure. Maybe it wouldn't be so bad being home for a month after all.

After turning off the ignition, she decided. Yes, the rest of the day would be wonderful, especially since she had practically planned it in full. Awakening earlier than usual, she had cut up chicken tenders, onions, and carrots, and tossed them in a storage container with seasoning and a home-made sauce she conjured up the night before. She also set out her largest crockpot on the counter. After being on the road the last month, she looked forward to some home-made food.

Before she left the house that morning, she went back into the bedroom where Rick had gotten up to use the bathroom, and she told him, "I put together our dinner for tonight. It's in the large container in the refrigerator. All you have to do is dump the contents in the slow cooker on the counter and turn it on at nine a.m. Voila! We'll have a scrumptious chicken recipe at 5 p.m."

"Tender slow-cooking," he said with his thumb up. "Will do."

To make doubly sure that he wouldn't possibly forget, she wrote a bold note and left it on the kitchen counter.

In addition to her pre-prepared dinner, she began watching a DVD movie the night before, and enjoyed what she had seen already. She had decided to save the rest of it for tonight and paused it. All she had to do after dinner was resume watching it wherever she had left off.

Viktoria walked alongside Rick's car and fumbled for her keys. She went inside, where the first floor was the only modernized area of the house. The big room had hardwood floors and a bay window, and double doors exited to the backyard. They were likely going to redo the three rooms upstairs as well.

After dropping her bag on a chair, she went straight to peek in the clear plastic cover of the crockpot. Thank goodness, she thought. The cooker was almost full to the top with her preparation. Without looking away, it dawned on her that a sumptuous aroma of hot chicken should be engulfing her nostrils. It wasn't.

"Uh-oh," she mumbled under her breath. As the realization set in that the poultry appeared to be raw, she placed a fingertip on the outside of the pot. *The temperature should be a finger burner,* she thought. The slow cooker was room temperature. Peering to the front, the dial was set on "off."

Tonight, her savory meal was not to be. *Damn,* she cursed, again to herself. The work and planning she had put in around her work schedule was an ironic joke on her. Theoretically, her husband should have been the one to prepare the whole one-pot meal, and now a healthy dinner was not to be had.

Her disappointment ramped up, and she gritted her teeth and pursed her lips. It wasn't only that her unfocused husband had not turned on the pot to cook their dinner, but all the ingredients would now go to waste. All they had now was poultry a-la-bacterial contamination. Salmonella chicken stew, she thought.

Where was he anyway?

Perhaps he was getting ready for later. He had surprised her when she came home on Saturday and told her about his plan to see a therapist—to try to kick his marijuana habit. A habit which he had kept secret from her for a good long time—even so much as during their dating and early marriage. Even now, he tried to camouflage his menacing, pitiful addiction.

In general, Viktoria voiced no problem with weed use, but when it came to disrupting a person's lifestyle, their ability to work, and their very personality, that was another story.

And, hell, the guy she dated had pulled a number on her. Had she known of his addiction, she would have never married him. After all, he pretended to be someone he wasn't and how could she trust or love a spouse after that?

CHAPTER 4

Viktoria finally removed the clear see-through cover of the slow cooker and continued to sulk over the waste of both the vegetables and chicken, and the time she spent with the meal's preparation. She couldn't just throw it all in the garbage to let it stink after a while, but she needed to discard it into a plastic bag big enough to hold it.

As she took a step away to look under the sink for one, her gaze roamed to the back of the big room where the TV was turned on, and the sound muted. Ironic, she thought, her husband could remember to turn on and watch TV in the middle of the day, but forgot to turn a simple button to "on" on the crockpot.

Something struck her as odd, however. Instead of a television channel playing, the characters from the movie she began watching last night were on the screen. Rick must have resumed "play" on her movie, but now she had no idea where she had stopped. Darn, she thought, she just can't win. As far as she was concerned, it would be too much trouble to try to find out where to resume. Starting the flick over was an option, but forget it, she thought angrily.

As the outrage against her husband ramped up she began looking for him. She marched into the bedroom, and then her small office next to the kitchen, to no avail. Hustling to Rick's office and the two bedrooms upstairs, she found them empty.

Since his car was parked in the garage, she knew he was home, so she stormed back downstairs and to the double doors facing the stone patio. Outside, the gorgeous day filled her with yearning to go plant herself in the hammock and rid herself of the present malevolence she felt towards her spouse.

To throw gas on her fire, her husband was in the middle of the yard. With a rake on the ground, and a lawn bag nearby, his sleeping body lay on the ground.

Viktoria charged over and stood above him.

Rick's mind—dreaming and loaded with the effects of weed—soared in a blissful state as he felt himself drift in the middle of a canoe on a waterway, which he could only fathom existed deep in a southern swampland. Although he lived in the north, his euphoric state dredged up his two memorable, extended visits to Louisiana.

Since the murky water below him moved south at an imperceptible rate, he concentrated on the stately trees, wildlife, and topography of the swamp.

The bald cypress alongside his craft rose out of the wetland soil with such a magnificent height and width, that at first he dreamed it was a wood building. But a building, he fathomed, could not have the protrusion which he spied to be sticking out of the water and growing from the tree's roots. No, what stood next to him was definitely an old, stately swamp tree, maybe hundreds of years old.

He lowered himself off the bench in the watercraft and stared up and over. Past the cypress beauty stood a tupelo tree, boldly dazzling him with shiny, large leaves full of autumn color. He smiled at the tree and chuckled when a leaf twirled like a paper airplane past his nose.

Even as magnificent as the surrounding foliage, a great blue heron soared silently above him and landed on the bayou. Rick nodded at the bird, allowing him to enter his tangible yet euphoric state of dreaming. The heron made not a peep and blended into the blissful silence and serenity.

Rick could stay like this forever. People he knew thought the coolest thing to do entailed chanting mantras and meditating. But they were missing out. All they needed to do was to grab a small watercraft or flotation device and go to a down-south swampland. No meditation needed. A person's mind would drift to fantastic heights.

Shifting his focus back to studying the sky, he stared at the deep blue color and a wispy streak of a cloud.

But all of a sudden, the sky dimmed less blue, and the cypress and tupelo trees looked more like the red maples in his yard, and the heron had disappeared. Next, he detected a jostling, a tapping right through the sole of his sneaker. More than that, a cantankerous voice interrupted him.

"Rick, what are you accomplishing today?"

Focus. His eyes needed to focus. He nailed down the voice before recognizing the individual standing irately above him as his wife.

He propped himself on an elbow to try to sit up. The surrounding leaves were crisp and playful as he righted himself. Too bad for the disruption, he thought, but he better scramble to get up. Her majesty is irate.

"You failed to turn our dinner on to cook all day," Viktoria said.

"So let's go turn it on."

She shook her head. "Start cooking raw chicken that's been sitting out for nine hours? Only if you want food poisoning and/or you want to eat tomorrow, be my guest."

"What are you getting so mad about? All I did was fail to turn on a button."

"Jeez. And thanks for scrambling up the DVD movie—where I was going to resume watching it."

The gaiety from his afternoon pot and antics stayed with him, and he smiled as he stood. "See, I'm not being all bitchy, and you just jarred me from the most wonderful dream."

"Are you for real? High as a kite. And this is how you're going to start therapy?"

At some subconscious level, he dared not push the envelope with her, but he couldn't refrain from blurting out his next words as they flew from his mouth. "You need DNA genetic testing."

"What's that supposed to mean?"

"To verify the fact that you carry the 'bitch' gene."

Rather than stand there and engage further with her potted husband, Viktoria spun around and went inside. Avoiding fights with him was one reason she stayed away from home, but how she could handle one month of this was beyond her. And a few minutes ago, he had put no filter over his mouth, and let her have it—what he really thought about her.

She always gave him the benefit of the doubt when he flung insults at her, because usually it entailed his mind being messed up with cannabis. He was the nicest, most thoughtful guy when he was straight, like when she first met him while launching her kayak, and subsequently when they dated and married, and he kept his habit secretly segregated from their relationship.

But how much was she going to take?

Viktoria stood over the crockpot and shook her head. She had been through it a million times. A divorce would be as unpleasant financially and emotionally as the burden she now lived with. She did not want to see most of what she'd worked for go to him with a divorce, nor did she want to pay him alimony, legal bills, etc. because his tax return would show a minor income and a judge would feel sorry for him.

No, she thought, enjoy the month at home as much as possible. She called up her Icelandic strength from her gut and vowed not to let him stress her out. Being a talented and smart lady, she would control her own thoughts and reactions to his behavior.

From under the sink, Viktoria grabbed a sizable plastic bag, lined it in the sink, and tilted the contents of the pot. The cascade of chicken and vegetables slid in, she tied a knot, and put it aside as she washed the slow cooker.

Behind her, the door opened, and footsteps approached.

"Viktoria! I was only kidding about the 'B' word. Really! I heard someone else say that on television today, so it happened to come right back out of my mouth. And cooking the food today? Yes, I didn't turn it on, but that was a simple oversight."

"Do you mean you heard 'bitch' on the movie that I was going to resume watching tonight?"

He stared at her with a blank expression.

"Never mind," she said. "Don't you have an appointment at five o'clock? What was this afternoon about? You're not earnest about therapy to quit marijuana when you load up with it on the same day you're supposed to free yourself of its wretched hold."

"It was my idea to get help, wasn't it? So I'm going."

Before Viktoria responded, he hurried off to fetch his wallet and car keys. He left for the psychologist's appointment without changing his pants, which still wore remnants of the leaf pile he'd napped in.

Viktoria retreated to her office next to the kitchen and fell into her comfortable desk chair. She massaged her wide forehead and dark eyebrows, and then let her shiny, black hair out of the elastic tie she often wore. It draped down, slightly further than her shoulders. Resting her head back against the leather, she contemplated the white plastic container on her desktop.

That piece on her desk, in the sunlight through the window during the day, held the cremated ashes of the dog she had just lost in Pennsylvania on her last job. Not only did he die there from the horrific circumstances of having ingested, unbeknownst to her, rat poisoning, but it was also where she had rescued him from a terrible fate. All in one month, she had come to love and to lose a Border Collie dog she had named Buddy.

Now Buddy's remains rested in her home hundreds of miles away from where she'd found him but, at least in the end, the dog knew a human being had loved him, and now he had a permanent resting place. Since she had enjoyed the short-lived relationship so much, a question lingered in her brain. Should she get another dog?

A dog for her would entail being on the road, traveling with her—going from place to place where she rendered anesthesia services. In one way, she thought it selfish to do that to a dog, yet dogs were buddies to all sorts of people with different lifestyles. Also, when she was home on Long Island, a dog would have the enjoyment of a fenced-in yard.

She placed her hand on the holder and closed her eyes. Concentrating on the memories of Buddy, she let his spirit sink into her mind and body, and his remains did more to comfort her and settle her nerves than the man who just left the house.

Only ten minutes from home, Rick pulled into the psychologist's driveway, followed the sign for "patient's parking," and stopped next to one other vehicle. The door to the back, lower entrance of the house opened, and a couple emerged. He nodded as they got into their vehicle and backed up.

A bell chimed as he stepped inside the entrance and sat in an empty waiting area. The mental health professional he sought out, doubled up using her private home for her business, but Rick thought it could use a face lift. Magazines sat on tables and in a rack, and a bowl of fake fruit and real hard candies were on the main cocktail table in front of him. He sorted through berry drops and popped a strawberry flavored one in his mouth, especially after considering that he may smell like weed.

The therapist's office door opened, and she stood in the doorway. "Mr. Richter?"

"That's me."

"I'm Paula Spinner. Come on back." She waited for him and shook his hand. Like the rest of her, her hand was long and slender. Except for her soft voice, which he thought to be part of her act—the act of pretending to care about her patients and what they told her—she appeared to be vibrant and satisfied with her work situation. In her late 50s, she wore silver-dyed hair and tear-drop earrings which bobbed along the side her neck.

"Have a seat."

He eyed the three available chairs; one in front and two on the side of her desk. "I bet there's a psychology profile to a patient, depending on which chair he or she chooses. If I choose the 'right' one, I'm going to quit being a pothead. If I choose the left one, I'm going to hell with a joint in my hand, and if I choose the one in front of you, you and I are going to butt heads like I do with my wife, and then I'll give up on this whole idea and won't be returning."

"Why and when do you think you butt heads with your wife?"

"We got into it right before I came over here."

She nodded with understanding, relaxed in her chair, while her checkered-unbuttoned blouse opened a bit more over a pastel tank top. Rick sighed, thinking his first-time-ever therapist seemed pleasant enough.

"Tell me about that," she coaxed him.

"I spent the afternoon raking up our back yard. Some thanks I got when she arrived home after work."

"Did you expect her to thank you after she also worked?"

Rick shrugged.

"What does she do?"

"She's a physician. An anesthesiologist."

"She must put in demanding days. You told me on the phone that your marijuana use has become excessive and you would like help to tone it down. You mentioned your behavior is causing strife in your marriage."

Rick crossed his legs and wiggled his foot. "I smoked quite a bit this afternoon, so I may not be too clear-headed. If I told you that, it's true. She's mad because I'm flying off the handle these days. She says I have a 'see-saw' personality anymore, and she never knows if she's up or down with me. She says she tiptoes around me not knowing who's present—Dr. Jekyll or Mr. Hyde."

"Sounds like you are hard to live with."

"That's why she goes away to work all the time."

"Oh my. This is serious, Mr. Richter."

Rick propped his elbow on the armrest and nestled the side of his face into his hand.

"This will be hard work on your part. You have an addiction problem which has spilled over into a marital problem. Calling me was the first step to repair your indiscretions, but getting high before your wife came home, and your coming here, is a bad sign. If you are not able to commit to taking at least baby steps to not use weed, then there is no point in starting therapy."

Rick twisted his mouth, realizing she was a tough therapist, like a tough-love parent. "I hired you, but I wonder if somehow my wife picked you out."

"Give yourself some credit. You made the call."

Rick looked at the round clock on the side wall. It seemed like it only started ticking then. He was ready, and he could do this.

"Now let's buckle down and get to the bottom of this," she said.

CHAPTER 5

Bonnie Sandler woke the next day with a bright attitude and renewed interest in the whole cosmetic surgery industry. With her forehead lift behind her the day before, she had sprung over the scary hurdle to take the plunge, and she had made it happen. Now she was convinced that rejuvenating surgery was not so bad, especially since the anesthesia had worked like magic. The specialty medication took care of her anxiety immediately beforehand, it kept her unconscious throughout the procedure, and she remembered nothing painful or disturbing in the recovery room or on the drive home with her female friend.

During the night, she had also slept soundly with two of the pain pills Dr. Pinto had prescribed, and had even slept to 8 a.m., later than normal. The only important thing she had on her agenda now was to intermittently apply an ice pack during the day over her forehead bandage.

She stepped into the bathroom, washed her face below the bandage, and brushed her teeth, all the while contemplating making a call to Amour Cosmetic Surgery. In yesterday's cloudy anesthetic state, she thought she remembered Dr. Pinto mentioning a "deal" on the most magnificent of all enhancement procedures—breast implants.

After throwing on a pair of jeans and a warm cotton blouse, Bonnie overlooked the coffee pot and stirred instant granules into a mug of water and set it in the microwave. It came out piping hot, so she let it sit, and glanced down at her flat chest. The only time they had appeared magnificent was when she had breast fed her babies twenty-four and twenty-seven years ago.

At forty-eight years old, and in the dating market, two things made the most sense. If she was going to eventually end up with enhanced breasts, she should do it soon to gain the most mileage in the foreseeable future to help attract male companionship.

And, secondly, make use of the monetary enticement she believed Dr. Pinto offered her. After all, she earned not much more than minimum wage as the front desk receptionist at a certified public accountant's office. Maybe she could turn heads as the curvy red head who greets people with the news of their yearly tax return next April.

Bonnie stepped over to the make-shift folding table under the family room window, and sprang her computer to life. She Googled the cost of breast implant surgery. Biting her lip, the cost dampened her mood. The straight fee, without consideration of the facility or anesthesia's charge, was anywhere between $3,800 up to $12,000. Since Long Island wasn't cheap, the higher number was probably more accurate.

"What the hell," Bonnie said out loud. She grabbed her cell phone and dialed Amour Plastic Surgery. As she remembered from a month ago, she navigated a complex telephone answering recording. The option she chose was to press number seven: "To find out more about a beautifying procedure, or to schedule an appointment or surgery, please press lucky number seven."

"Amour Plastic Surgery. How may I help you?" Subtle, soft music played in the background of the woman's voice, and Bonnie was grateful not to be put on hold to memorize loud elevator music.

"This is Bonnie Sandler, a patient from yesterday. Dr. Pinto did a forehead lift on me."

"Excellent, Mrs. Sandler. I take it you are doing well today."

"Yes, thank you. I believe he mentioned something about a twenty percent off upcoming sale on breast implants?"

"A Halloween special. Yes. It was Dr. Castillo's brilliant idea. Take advantage of his kindheartedness before you are too late."

Bonnie thought of used car salesman tactics, or what she heard about them anyway. Before she committed, she needed to hear the financial outlay for this fire sale. "How much are we talking about? I already found out the going rate on Long Island." She felt pleased that the internet was able to tell her everything, although she never admitted to herself the validity of what she read.

"Mrs. Sandler, you're going to love this. First of all, we charge less than most. A mere six-thousand dollars. With this big deal, we're talking only four-thousand eight hundred."

Way better than the top price of twelve grand, it was still a big chunk of change for her. She slumped her shoulders as the two women on the call remained quiet. In the meantime, Bonnie heard other phone calls in the background, where it sounded like a busy room with many operators taking and placing calls. So much so, that the background sounded like a telemarketer's business.

The other woman broke the silence. "I tell you what. Dr. Castillo would back me up on this. Since you are a recent patient, we'll deduct another ten percent, for a thirty percent reduction. Think of it as a super frequent flier bonus. Thirty percent off of six-thousand dollars if you schedule your surgery before Halloween. That makes the total a skimpy four-thousand-two-hundred dollars. You will save eighteen-hundred dollars!"

Bonnie wrapped her head around eighteen-hundred dollars. That was too much money to save or spend, but she *was* going to do this.

"Yes, yes. Put me down. But," she stammered, "how should we do this since I'm still recovering from yesterday?"

"I will talk to Dr. Pinto and get back to you today at this number. Meanwhile, let's put you down for breast implant surgery in seven days, so that your spot doesn't disappear, taken by someone else making use of the Halloween special."

"Thank you so much. I'll listen for your call back today."

Bonnie disconnected her call. Next, she needed to announce her plastic surgery idea to her two sons. They may give her flack to undergo medically unnecessary surgery, but she was determined to win them over. Other than that, the truth of the matter hit her squarely in the gut. For her, forty-two hundred dollars was still a lot of money. On her strict budget and little savings, how was she going to come up with the cash?

Impulsively, wanting to break the news before she changed her mind, Bonnie called her oldest son, Andrew.

"Hey, Mom," the twenty-seven-year old said, "any problems overnight? How's your pain?"

"I'm taking the pills the surgeon prescribed and I'm feeling pretty good. I've decided to have another procedure right away. By doing so, they are giving me a huge discount. I hope you and Jack can be open-minded about this. Secretly, I have always wanted breast implants, so I'm going to do it."

The silence hurt her ears, and she grimaced.

"Mom, it's one thing to have a forehead lift, but it's a totally different matter to have a surgeon cut into the front of your chest."

"Andrew, please. Remember when you were a kid, and absolutely wanted a basketball hoop in the driveway? You hinted about it all the time, and the sunshine on your face was worth it when I finally made it happen."

"I remember, Mom. Then you were annoyed when I was dribbling and shooting baskets, and I wouldn't listen to you when you would call me in for dinner."

"That's how much you loved it. That's how I'm going to feel with a perfect chest shape and size. You know how I enjoy getting out and dating. After this, I promise you boys, I'll leave myself alone."

"No more cosmetic surgeries?"

"Exactly."

"What's it going to set you back?"

"Forty two hundred dollars, but I'm saving eighteen hundred dollars from the regular price."

Andrew grimaced. His mother had a hard enough time paying the affordable residual mortgage on her small home. "Sounds like your mind is made up, so I won't try anymore to talk you out of it."

"Thank you. Let me call Jack and fill him in as well."

"I'll call him for you, if you'd like. No sense in having him try to talk you out of it as well. I may be calling you back."

"Thanks, Andrew. Love you."

Andrew clicked on his brother's number, and caught his twenty-four year old brother on the way to work.

"Hey, bro," Jack said. "I'm eating a breakfast biscuit, and dodging traffic. What's up?"

"I just talked to Mom. That surgery she had yesterday went fine, but she wants to go back for breast implants. Who knew she would want such a thing?"

A piece of egg went down the wrong track, and Jack coughed. "Certainly not me. Where'd she get that idea from?"

"I don't understand most women, but our own mother apparently wants to be curvy and look twenty years younger."

"Did you talk her out of it?"

"I tried, but instead, she made me understand her point of view. She rarely splurges on herself, so I kind of gave her my blessing."

"Oh great. When's this going to happen?"

"Really soon, but here's the thing. It will cost her over four thousand dollars. I was wondering if you and I could split the cost. It could be an early Christmas present to her, and maybe the biggest and most memorable gift we ever give her."

"You want to actually promote this crazy idea? Andrew, they call that 'enabling.'" He stopped at a light and nibbled another piece off the biscuit.

"Look, we don't like the idea, but she does. And it's her body. And when was the last time we really did something incredible for her?"

"I gave her a charm bracelet two years ago, and she keeps adding to it."

"Come on, we can both choke up the cash."

"All right, already. Okay, if it'll make her happy."

"Thanks. We won't regret it. She'll be happier than that buxom bombshell on that news channel you're always watching."

Bonnie Sandler put down a cup of coffee and answered the incoming call from her son Andrew. "That was fast. Did you get a hold of Jack?"

"Sure did. He's on his way to work. We have a huge surprise for you, mom."

"Are one of you getting married?" she asked, knowing that was highly unlikely at this point in time.

"No, but hear me out. This is a weird thing for sons to spend money on for their mother, but this is what you want, and that's way too much cash for you to worry about scrounging up, so Jack and I are going to pay for your surgery."

Bonnie placed her other hand on the warm coffee cup as if to keep from flinging it up in the air with excitement. She couldn't believe her ears.

"Are you sure? We're not talking twenty bucks here."

"We know, Mom. It will be our early Christmas present to you, and birthday present, and we won't foot a dinner bill for a while."

"You boys are the best." She crinkled her face, ready to spill a tear. "I don't know what to say except thank you from the bottom of my heart."

"You're welcome, Mom. We're happy to give you something that means so much to you."

In the middle of the afternoon, Bonnie's forehead began throbbing, and she realized Dr. Pinto's pain medicine had worn off. She decided to avoid taking the half-narcotic pill again if she could avoid it, and reached for a nonsteroidal anti-inflammatory pill instead. After all, she considered, the area between her eyes and her hairline was inflamed!

Since lunchtime, Bonnie wondered when Amour's office staff would call her back when finally her cell phone rang.

"Mrs. Sandler, this is the plastic surgery center calling you back. Do you have a few moments?"

"Most certainly. I've been waiting."

"I spoke to Dr. Pinto in detail and our center can accommodate your every wish. If you would like, he has availability on his schedule to do your breast implants on Friday."

Bonnie reeled back from the news. "That seems mighty quick since my forehead is still recovering."

"Not at all. Bigger surgeries than yours often happen within one week. Some major back surgeries these days are split up into two days, two days apart. Haven't you taken some time off from work, and now you could kill two birds with one stone?"

"Yes. And my employer certainly wouldn't let me take four weeks off again soon like this."

"Are you having any problems with your forehead?"

"No, I'm taking something for pain."

"Good. Dr. Pinto said you wouldn't need to come in this week for a postop visit, because he can check your forehead on Friday when you come in for surgery. And your record is so fresh, we have all the medical information needed for us and for anesthesia."

"Wow. This is too good to be true. Yes, for sure, put me down for Friday."

"Excellent. Come on in tomorrow to pick out the implant size that you want and to make your full surgery payment of our agreed upon, super deal of a price."

"I'm excited already. I'll have to pick up the money from my two sons. They are buying me this present!"

"You are a lucky lady. You may come by tomorrow at any time you wish."

"See you then," Bonnie said and hung up. She could hardly believe it. Last week, her forehead was wrinkly, and she had flat breasts. By the end of this week, she would be transformed. Who said advancing into middle age was so bad?

CHAPTER 6

Tuesday morning, Viktoria was out of the house before Rick stirred. She was quite happy to pull into a drive-through coffee venue and not deal with making coffee at home. Being extra early, there were no lines, and she was not pressed for time. After all, she had not made the mistake again of gathering the ingredients at home for making dinner and depending on her husband to help out in any way, even to turn on a button.

"I'll take a decaf," Viktoria said, "and pour in a little mocha."

A bangle-wristed hand reached out from a young woman, and they exchanged cash for coffee. Viktoria gave a nod and slid forward. She drove the short distance, sipping occasionally, and wondering about her husband's comments when he arrived home last night from therapy.

"The therapist said I'm going to do just fine," he had announced. "I was motivated enough to call her, and the first step is to make up your mind that you're going to quit doing something."

To her, that didn't seem promising, and it sounded like the same old rhetoric from him. But, people who want to change for the good need support and, unless she witnessed him cheating on his new goal, she would not voice her skepticism.

She pulled into Amour's strip mall, finished her coffee, and stepped out of her car. Clouds formed billowy pillows in the sky, and the overnight air had dipped down below fifty, making the morning feel crisp and invigorating. It was the type of day when she could steal the rake from Rick and do every bit of yard work without so much as a complaint. And, of course, she wouldn't need to "smoke" to do it. The outdoors was her high.

Since it was only her second day at Amour, there were many more procedures she may encounter, as well as surgeons, and individual techniques. This was her first time spending a length of time doing anesthesia for only plastic surgery cases. She was curious about both ends of the spectrum: the surgeons doing them, and the interesting women and their reasons for going under the knife for mostly beauty enhancement. In a way, the women must be pretty brave and optimistic.

She yanked on the door, and slipped through the waiting room of advertising, early patients, and their significant others.

"Good morning, Dr. Thorsdottir," Lucy Murray said, her dirty-blonde braid swept to the other side of her shoulders than yesterday.

"Good day as well."

"Your first patient is bright and early, and she can't wait to meet her surgeon and anesthesiologist."

"Excellent. I'll go set up my room and see her in a jiffy."

"Call on Lola if you can't find anything."

Viktoria changed into scrubs and checked the OR schedule board. Her first anesthetic of the day was for a patient having an abdominoplasty which, in layman's terms, was called a tummy tuck, and the surgeon was another new name to her—Victor Reed.

"Lola, you're a doll," Viktoria said ten minutes later after the anesthesia tech rolled a fresh cart in her room. "How's that baby today?"

"Growing like a weed. Can't say that I blame her. I feed her first and then the leftovers go to me. It's the time of year for candy, but when I eat that junk, I say a prayer to Mother Mary so that the chocolate and candy corn doesn't go through the umbilical cord to her. That sugar stays with me."

"I see," Viktoria said as she drew up anesthetic drugs into her syringes. "I hope the prayers work." She tilted her head and grimaced. "That's not how I learned blood flow works in a pregnancy. Your circulatory system won't discriminate. Luckily, it sends your blood flow everywhere—to your brain as well as to your baby."

"Shucks, doc. I'm trying to sneak a couple of candies."

"In moderation, Lola, in moderation." She patted the younger woman on her back. "Just think. In a year from now, you may be dressing up your infant in a Halloween costume."

Lola pushed her glasses up, her eyes growing wide with delight.

"The surgeon in my OR room today is Dr. Pinto. Anything you can tell me about him?"

"I bet he's over there brown nosing his patient right now." She turned and slunk out the OR doors, without another word.

Viktoria heard the chatter before she parted the patient's curtain in the preop holding area. She slid the drape and three people turned their heads. "I'm Dr. Thorsdottier, the anesthesiologist."

"I'm Dr. Reed," the man standing said. "And Dorothy Flores here is our patient, all decked out and ready for her tummy tuck. I have told her she's in excellent hands, surgically and anesthetically, and she can't wait for the end result."

The surgeon's thick arms waved the whole time as he talked with his hands. He was a broadly-built man with tanned skin and engaging brown eyes under thick eyebrows. Pointedly, he smiled at Viktoria and then back to Dorothy and a woman sitting beside her.

"Nice to meet you. Are you finished? May I ask Ms. Flores my questions?" Viktoria returned his smile as she held her clipboard with the preanesthetic form.

Victor Reed backed up with a bow and waved his hand gracefully. "She's all yours."

After he exited the cubicle, Viktoria drew closer to the two women. By the information listed on the chart, her patient was five-foot-five inches tall and weighed one-hundred and sixty pounds. Her dark complexion was smooth and flawless and her eyes twinkled.

"This is my sister, Marilyn," Dorothy said.

Her older sister sat by her side, a smaller version of Dorothy, with a head of curls like her sibling.

"Nice to meet both of you. May I ask you a few questions?"

Dorothy nodded and soon Viktoria had a clear picture of the woman's medical and surgical history. Except for her obesity and occasional cigarettes, she had no known problems.

"I'm ecstatic about today," Dorothy said. "I've been planning this for months."

"Good for you. This surgery isn't for everyone."

"What do you mean?"

"The procedure is a bit more risky if a patient has heart disease or diabetes, or if they are extremely large, with what we call a body mass index over thirty. And I'm assuming you are not considering future pregnancies?"

"I'm not finished having kids. I haven't even had my first one yet."

Viktoria shifted her weight. She hoped Dr. Reed cautioned, or mentioned to her, the possible negative consequences of becoming pregnant after the multiple incisions and tightening of her abdominal tissue with the abdominoplasty she was about to undergo.

"Well, I hope everything goes well for you. I will see you shortly back in the OR."

With soft music soon playing in the background of the OR, the orderly wheeled Dorothy's stretcher in, and she scooted over to the surgical table. Viktoria hooked up the blood pressure cuff, pulse oximeter, and EKG on her patient, let her breathe oxygen through a mask, and slowly gave sedation and induction drugs through her IV which caused Dorothy to sleep with a beautifully safe anesthetic. Viktoria inserted a breathing tube down her trachea or windpipe, and soon had her anesthetic continue with an inhalational agent through her breathing circuit.

After scrubbing at the sink outside the room, Dr. Reed appeared. Mandy, the scrub tech, helped him don sterile gloves.

"You are going to reshape your patient for Halloween," Mandy said. "In a week or so, she'll be able to dress up as a princess."

"So true," he said. "That's because right now she's shaped like some kind of vegetable, a butternut squash to be exact."

Viktoria distorted her face with disapproval. She held the ability to keep a person unconscious, but she hated it when disparaging remarks were made about any patient on her table. An anesthetized person couldn't speak up for themselves and, to Viktoria, to make those remarks seemed like a violation of an unwritten trust between the caretaker and patient.

A thorough prep of Dorothy's entire abdominal area was soon completed and, after a modified liposuction, and separating the umbilicus or belly button from the skin, Dr. Reed slid his scalpel across her lower abdomen from right to left. Yellow, fatty tissue was now clearly exposed—the globular, moist tissue unsightly—and was the reason why the patient was here.

Mandy handed him the cautery to sear tiny vessels that bled. "Location, location, location," she said, affirming the placement of his lower abdominal incision.

"I'm not in the real estate business," he said jokingly. "What's more important now is 'exposure, exposure, exposure.' Digging in and pulling up, I need to clearly see this blubber. Isn't it amazing that this tissue is going to be garbage pretty soon!"

"Yes, sir." She handed him a lap sponge, and he patted the area under his hands without looking.

Viktoria sat down on her rolling stool as the surgeon and tech continued with small talk.

"In case anyone asks me," Mandy asked, "what does one of these procedures cost?"

"Rigoberto charged her thirty-five hundred dollars. A steal."

"No kidding."

Their chit-chat silenced, and after twenty minutes, Victor asked for different music. The circulating nurse piped up the volume as well, while Viktoria scanned her monitors. Dorothy handled the surgery well so far, her vital signs stable, and she only needed anesthetic IV drugs based on her calculated lean body weight rather than her total weight with the extra pounds she carried around.

Dr. Reed sighed intermittently and glanced over at the round wall clock more frequently. Viktoria stood, flexed her shoulders, and peered at the surgical site where the distracted Victor made a more obtuse angled incision. Rather than before, he parted the yellow mass more quickly this time, almost ready to connect the previous incision and lift out the surgical mass. Still pressing, it seemed like the resistance let up and his hand easily went forward into the surgical site.

Viktoria furrowed her eyebrows and tilted her head forward, but she couldn't see the area straight below his eyesight. She continued to stand, the informative noises from the monitors more important to her than the modern pop music now playing on the boom box.

Dorothy's tummy tuck finally came to an end. Making clean lines and reattaching the areas he'd worked on, minus the slices of skin with attached fat, Dr. Reed had her abdomen all sutured back up. He stood back and flicked off his gloves.

"That was a productive morning," he said. "She'll be deliriously happy with her results."

While Dr. Reed headed out, Viktoria concentrated on reversing Dorothy's anesthesia and took out her breathing tube. She tucked one of the thirty-four-year old's gorgeous head curls into her bonnet as her patient tried to smile and mumbled, "How did I do?"

"Your anesthesia went fine," Viktoria reassured her as they rolled her out of the room.

As they hooked her up to the monitors in the recovery room, Dorothy gently placed her hands over her surgical gown and slid them up and down her abdomen. Despite her grogginess, her lips formed a smile. "Sometimes people say that a huge weight was lifted from their shoulders. Not me. A huge weight was just physically lifted from my belly thanks to Dr. Reed."

Still wearing pajamas, Rick Richter strolled in from the bedroom and studied all the kitchen counters. He suppressed a yawn as he made sure that his wife had not left a note like yesterday, giving him any kind of instructions for their dinner preparation. Although it appeared he was off the hook from any kind of 'honey-do' list, he wondered if she had a plan for dinner at all. When she was not around, he opened soup cans, made sandwiches, or ate out.

One of these evenings, he should take his wife out to dinner, he thought. He still cared for her a lot, way more than he believed she cared for him. But the relationship had turned sour in the last few years, and they had drifted apart. There were causative factors which Rick could not deny, but they were so far embedded into their lifestyle, turning them around was impossible.

After all, he worked less, she worked more. He turned to marijuana more, she hit the road more. He took less of a role in maintaining the upkeep of their house, inside and out, and she cared less and less.

In essence, both of them had silently agreed to live separate and independent lives.

However, he couldn't face the idea of a divorce. He did care for her and wanted her to stay a part of his life, no matter how distant their behavior was to each other. Plus, he wasn't born yesterday. Their income was almost solely due to her. Why jeopardize that? He had no clear understanding of the divorce process and whether or not he would be left out to dry. He didn't spend a ton of money, yet maintaining real estate on Long Island was not cheap, nor was his marijuana habit.

Rick made a cup of coffee and went upstairs to the bedroom which functioned as his home office, mostly for the art auction work he did. For the entire day, he only planned on going into the small insurance office he ran in the afternoon to check on one of his employees and a property damage estimate. He had gathered much of the preliminary information from a client, so he believed the visit shouldn't take too long.

But standing over his desk, he felt an urge, like a hex or a spell calling out to him to open the top drawer. What difference did it make if he simply took a better look at the new product he had bought last week before his wife even came home from Pennsylvania?

He sat in his rolling desk chair, slid open the drawer, and put the product in his hand. These things were popular these days, so why hadn't he bought and made use of one of them before? Being behind the times was like only listening to sixty's music when the musical variety these days was so much more lively and entertaining.

Turning over the vape pen in his hand, he smiled at the choice he had made. Better yet, after making lots of inquiries, and also checking with his usual marijuana 'dealer,' he believed he found the best damn oil cartridges in the region.

Rick changed into blue jeans and a long-sleeved t-shirt, and went outside to the backyard. If vaping proved to be as great as he thought it would be, he would immensely and secretly enjoy the thrill of it and continue to appease his wife by going to a therapist. Plus, in the afternoon, he would even go to the office like a working stiff.

CHAPTER 7

"I'm checking on you again," Viktoria said two hours later. She had delayed discharging Dorothy Flores from the recovery room because her patient needed a bit more hydration through her IV. Dorothy now leaned against the stretcher and her sister Marilyn squatted, assisting the nurse in pulling up her trousers.

Dorothy smiled with her eyes. "Thank you again for putting me to sleep. This is a happy day for me."

Marilyn shot Viktoria a glance. "My sister has been given a new lease on life."

"Will you be the one spending the night with her?"

"Yes. We're tight as stuck ticks. I'm staying at her house until tomorrow."

"Dr. Reed wrote a pain prescription for her." Viktoria held her patient's arm to assist them. "Your operation was no small matter. He excised a lot of tissue and you are going to be uncomfortable."

Dorothy moved her hand between her abdomen and the inside of her trousers. "Look at this empty space. That was my fatty tissue filling that gap. I can't believe how fat I was. This is freaking magic!"

Marilyn and the nurse both laughed, and Viktoria gave her patient a gentle, one-sided hug.

"All the best to you," Viktoria said," and enjoy buying some new clothes." She scooted out from the closed curtains.

"It's close enough to three o'clock," Dr. Castillo said, standing at the counter. "You're through for the day. You and Dr. Reed did a nice job for that big lady. I love satisfied customers."

"Patients, sir. Yes, she's about the happiest patient I've taken care of in a long time."

"Most of your plastic surgery patients will leave here satisfied. Ever consider just doing this type of anesthesia? If you continue to fit in here, I could always tack on another month for you through the locum's agency."

"I'm an outlander. I tour operating rooms in different locations, providing anesthesia services in an endless round of surgical gigs." She paused to laugh. "I'm kidding but half-serious. Thanks for letting me leave

early. Makes me want to follow through on something I've been ·
contemplating doing."

"If you change your mind about giving us another month of your
service ..."

In the locker room, Viktoria changed into her street clothes, sat on the
bench, and whipped out her cell phone. She had a vague impression of
where the regional pet shelter was located, but she nevertheless pin-
pointed the address on her browser and sighed. It was now or never.

The memory of the Border Collie she had rescued in Pennsylvania was
still fresh, and she had grown accustomed to the idea of bringing him on
the road with her. Buddy, or any dog that comes into a person's life, could
not be replaced, so his death, she believed, was a portal for her to go rescue
another in his place.

She turned on the radio in her car, stayed north on the island, and
headed east. With the sun shining down unobstructed by clouds, and a
gentle breeze filtering in a northeast direction, the cards were in her favor.
The beautiful day would emblazon today's memory of selecting the
particular dog waiting to go home with her. He or she would be her best
friend.

Passing through an intersection, Viktoria glimpsed at a large retail store
on the southeast corner. She was still a half mile from the shelter, but she
decided to sidetrack into the chain store which not only sold agricultural
and lawn maintenance items, but home improvement and pet care supplies.

Although she still had a few items left over from Buddy, she needed
fresh dog food, and a few more toys wouldn't hurt. Viktoria parked and
scurried straight in.

With a wide smile, a male employee leaned over the check-out counter
as a customer and her dog passed, but then glanced at Viktoria.
"Welcome," he said.

"Hi," she replied. "Where are your dog food choices and supplies?"

"In the back of the store, in the middle."

Another, older employee wearing a store smock, walked past and
pointed. "Holler if you need help."

Viktoria passed the shelves of equipment geared for farmers, and came to the domestic pet area. Not knowing what kind of dog she would end up with, she picked a small bag of the best food for a young dog. After circling the aisle, she found an assortment of toys, and grabbed a bag of plush toys with no dangerous stuffing and no squeaky plastic parts.

At the front of the store, she placed her items on the counter and the male with a generous smile scanned the bag of cloth animals first.

"These are one of my dogs' favorites, besides their balls with the holes in them. Plus, the toys in here are safe and I don't have to supervise their play."

"You have more than one?"

"Sure. Three right now. How about you?"

"None at present. That may change within a half hour. That's why I'm getting ready with these purchases."

"Picking up a puppy?"

"I'm headed to the animal shelter."

"I am fostering one of the dogs in my possession. She is waiting on her forever home." He scanned the dry dog food and tilted his head. "She's beautiful, nine months old, and housebroken. I will hate to part with her, but that's what I do. I foster Miniature American Shepherds." His hand held on to the top of the item, giving her time to soak in his words.

Viktoria squinted her eyes. "A Miniature American Shepherd?"

"People really know the breed as a Miniature Australian Shepherd. The AKC has successfully renamed the breed." He slid his cell phone out of his back pocket and pressed on photos. "Here she is. Her name is Millie."

A merle-colored dog sat in profile, the sun reflecting off the long hair on her neck. "She looks intelligent and calm."

"Intelligent she is, and calm sometimes, but she's a bundle of energy which is characteristic of the breed."

Viktoria saddened. "Looks similar to the Border Collie I recently lost."

"I'm sorry to hear it. Maybe Millie is your Border Collie's gift to you."

She inserted her credit card in the swipe machine. "Guess this is too circumstantial that I walked in here. I suppose I should see her, huh?"

"I would say so. I'm eight to four today, so I get off in a little while. Follow me to my place and meet Millie."

"I'm here to nine," the older employee said, stepping into the aisle between the cash registers. "Take off now, Jerry, and show this lady your foster pet."

"How far away do you live?" Viktoria asked.

"A distance that will be worth every square inch if you and Millie are meant to be."

Jerry lived in a modest home, and they met his wife inside the door. "This is Viktoria," he said. "She's here to consider adopting Millie."

His wife threw her hands up. "I call her my little Millie Muff. When she finds a new home, I'll cry, yet sing for joy." The woman turned to mix up an iced tea for Viktoria and slid a lemon wedge on the lip of the glass.

"Come to the window," Jerry said, "and spy on them in the backyard."

Viktoria followed him past a worn sofa and standing lamp, and circled around two dog beds on the floor. Several balls of different sizes dotted the square fenced-in yard, and two trees stood on one side.

"There they are," Jerry pointed.

Below the trees, were three long-haired dogs. Two stood at attention and the other one seemed fast asleep. As if they knew they were being watched, the two standing raced towards the house.

"Tinker is our couch potato. But here comes Millie and Wally."

Viktoria's heart seemed to nestle in her chest, warmed by the sight of them. "Oh my," she mumbled. "May I?" She inched to the door, and he opened it for her. Instead of racing in, they allowed her to step out, and a flurry of activity ensued.

"Millie is a tad smaller than Wally." He stooped and picked up the thirty pound female. Viktoria studied the dog's bluish gray color mixed with splotches of reddish-brown. "Officially, she's a blue merle with white points," he added.

With only inches between them, she stroked the dog's coat—long and fine, and soft as velvet. Her reward was a blue-eyed, alert stare back from Millie.

"I'm speechless," Viktoria said.

Jerry smiled and placed her down with Wally. He opened the door again, and their third dog also came bounding over.

Inside, Jerry guided Viktoria to sit down on the sofa and his wife set her iced tea to the side. He guided his own dogs to their crates. "Now you can visit with Millie on her own."

Millie faced Viktoria and raised her paw. "Thank you very much," she said and looked at Jerry. "Do you know the story with her? Why does such a beauty and a sweetheart not have a permanent home?"

"We do know what happened, which is not always the case. She came from an older, vibrant woman living by herself, who was killed abruptly in a hit-and-run. It was a windy day, and the woman had a long, slim tree branch dragging under her car. Cops think she stopped to evaluate what was making all the noise under her vehicle. They think the other driver was texting, hit her, and kept going."

"That's awful. No family member wanted her dog?"

"She has one son, and he's overseas in the military and couldn't take the dog. But the best news, after all that, is that Millie ended up cared for by a rescue group and sent to me."

With moisture accumulating in her eyes, Viktoria took Millie's face in her hands and kissed her. "If it's okay with you, and her, and the rescue group, may she become part of my family? How does the adoption work?"

Jerry and his wife grinned. "Wonderful! The foster family actively tries to find a home for the dogs they take in, but the final paperwork comes through the rescue company."

At their kitchen counter, and after answering many questions about her home environment, Viktoria told them how Millie would be her traveling buddy. She filled out the preliminary paperwork which Jerry promised to drop off at the rescue group's office the next day, then he handed her the dog's health record, pointing out which shots were due next.

She raised her eyebrows at Jerry. "May I leave here with her or do I need more vetting?"

"We feel very satisfied with you, and I believe the rescue group will too. We can always fetch her back if there's a problem, or even if she doesn't somehow work out for you."

"I am a physician and an animal lover; she'll be in fine hands. I will take care of her until her dying breath."

"That's beautiful of you to say that, and I believe you." Jerry kneeled on the floor and gave Millie a hug. "Bye, girl." He swiped a tear from his eyes. "That's the hardest part of fostering dogs. I fall in love with them and then part with them."

"But you provide a caring home, rather than having a dog stay in a kennel with a concrete floor, or in a dwelling that is not a no-kill shelter."

Jerry nodded as one of his own dogs nestled next to him after being let out of his crate.

Viktoria stood, looked down, and exclaimed, "You're coming home to your forever home, Millie!"

The dog cocked her head. The pretty pup soon rode home in Viktoria's Honda Accord.

Viktoria pulled into the garage next to Rick's car and, with little prompting, Millie jumped out of her vehicle. She grabbed the items she had bought where she met Jerry, and opened the door to the house. With reluctance, the dog entered.

After sniffing the entrance mat, Millie trotted ahead on the hardwood floor, while the sound of a game show blared from the flat screen TV. Viktoria hustled behind the dog.

She caught up, and scooped the dog in her arms. So manageable, her size was perfect for loving on her. Since she didn't see Rick in the big room, she glanced in her office. He wasn't there, so she peered out the back door. But unlike finding him in a pile of leaves like the day before, the back yard was devoid of her flippant husband.

"Let's go introduce you to the upstairs," Viktoria said. She carried the dog for the fun of it, especially not wanting Millie to race into Rick by surprise.

It became a lot quieter as she stepped on the top landing. Hoping he was doing a bit of work at home, she peeked into his bedroom office to the right. His computer and piles of papers on the desk appeared to be as untouched as when she'd returned from her out-of-state locums job.

"Come on, Millie," she whispered in the dog's ear. She squeezed the dog with a hug and went downstairs into the master bedroom to find Rick fast asleep on top of the Queen bed's comforter.

CHAPTER 8

To Viktoria, the first day of bringing a new dog home was sacred. In no way would she let Rick spoil it for her and Millie. She didn't care much about what her husband did in his spare time, as long as his weed addiction was being curtailed or eliminated, and that he stayed active working in the two fields he knew about. She wondered if he'd done anything useful all day.

Holding a small, pliable Frisbee, she opened the back door and introduced the young dog to the backyard. Millie cautiously investigated the middle of the lawn and then followed a course along the fence line. Her examination was systematic, so Viktoria gave her credit for making sure the area met with her approval and that it was safe from critters or rodents.

The door creaked open behind her, and Rick sidled next to her. They let the moments tick by, not saying a word, as if pretending she had never gone into the bedroom.

"Is it a she or a he?" he asked.

"Her name is Millie."

"Where'd you get her? I guess I'm the last to know."

"She's a rescue. I stumbled on her from someone who fostered her." She clutched her hands in front of her chest. "For me, she's 'meant to be.'"

"Didn't think you'd get one so soon," he said, his baritone voice plunging deeper. "Especially if you cared for the last one as much as you said."

"I'm grieving inside about Buddy, but I can't change that he's gone. Life goes on."

"A client said that to me recently."

"What client?"

"What's that supposed to mean?"

"Exactly what I said."

"Are you insinuating that I don't have a client?"

"My two simple words asked you about the client you just mentioned. There are no voodoo words or foreign language in that question."

"So you say." He lowered himself cautiously, so she wondered if he had been spicing the herb.

"The client who said 'Life goes on,' wanted a print I sold online at my last auction. The picture went to someone else, but he got over it." Rick tucked his legs in, clapped at Millie, and hoped she would come over.

"Maybe he'll spot something he likes during your next auction."

"Yes, I'm lining one up this month because I have a dozen stellar pieces to turn over."

"If your auction goes well, I bet they'll sell."

Rick nodded. "Thanks."

Millie darted over, satisfied with her exploring, and sniffed and considered Rick. "I guess she'll be with me while you're working. At least when I'm home."

"Can you handle all thirty pounds of her?" Viktoria asked lightheartedly.

He ruffled the hair streaming in front of Millie's neck. "No problem. We'll be playing together with that Frisbee before you finish your Long Island assignment. After all, after that, I'll only be privy to her once in a while when you're home."

On Wednesday, Bonnie Sandler had so much to be excited about, she thought she would burst. Standing over the bathroom sink, the figure staring back at her from the mirror was her own, with a much improved, smoother, and wrinkle less forehead. Despite the bruising, the purplish color after the surgery, she could tell that the forehead lift had dropped years off of her face.

Getting dressed and buttoning her blouse, she looked down and began to hum. Within one week, she thought, the cotton top she was wearing may not fit. Her timing was uncanny—a Halloween special on breast implants.

She was on her way into Amour Cosmetic Surgery with a check in hand for forty-two hundred dollars. Like they had discussed, Jack and Andrew had pooled their resources and delivered the check to her the day before. How she had raised the two most magnificent, thoughtful sons she ever heard of, was beyond her.

The humming continued as she drove in an easterly direction to the surgical center. Her body improvement plan was like a dream come true!

When she arrived at Amour, and entered the facility, she halted her humming as she stared at the moving pictures in the waiting area. The pictures said it all.

"Hi," Lucy Murray said, as Bonnie stepped forward. "What can I do for you today?"

"I'm Bonnie Sandler from two days ago. You know, the forehead lift." She pointed to her face.

"Yes. Dr. Pinto did a fine job. You are also healing fast!"

"Really?"

"Yes. Quicker than most."

"I presume that should help me with my next surgery as well. Here's my check for the breast implant surgery scheduled for Friday."

Lucy's slender hand reached over and searched the schedule on their computer. "Ah, yes. A breast augmentation at a super-cut rate deal."

Lucy pulled the check behind the glass partition and scanned the details. "Would you like to go pick out your implant size?"

Bonnie nodded wholeheartedly and followed Lucy to a small room with a leather couch, two chairs, and a glass topped table. Several silver-colored boxes sat on top.

Lucy pointed to the couch and methodically took the cover off of each box. "There is a wonderful assortment of sizes. Take your time. As you know, however, the fee you just paid does not include the type of breast implants."

Bonnie's expression faded into disappointment. "Somehow, I missed that detail."

"It also does not include anesthesia's services, or the operating facility's cost."

Staring at small, yet shapely implants, Bonnie frowned. Her brain scrambled to figure out how to make all of this work. Originally, she was going to scrape up some money herself, before her sons had chipped in. There was no way she was backing out now. Her heart was set on it.

"I hear you. I'll deal with my finances later."

Lucy nodded, took out the most popular sized implants and cupped them in her hand. "What do you think about these?"

Bonnie put them in her own hands. "Way shapely," she said. "I don't see extra big ones here, though. Like the country music singer wears."

"Breast implants are evaluated by the United States Food and Drug

Administration. They watch out for patients' safety and make recommendations regarding saline and silicone gel-filled implants. We would not sell or implant a non-approved size—those extra-large sizes come from outside the United States."

"Don't worry. I was curious if they look like a miniature soccer ball."

Lucy laughed and nodded at what she held in her hand. "Those would suit you fine. Your blouse would be filled out nicely."

"I agree. Please tell Dr. Pinto this is the size I want."

Viktoria passed through the recovery room doors after leaving her last patient, and Rigoberto caught up with her. "There's a lull before your next case. Grab some lunch."

"I would be happy to."

"You have enough time to splurge next door," he added, swiping his beaked nose. "I'll text you when your next patient arrives."

She grabbed her purse and small MAC computer from the locker room and slipped off her OR cap and shoe covers. In the hallway, a door opened and Lucy and a familiar patient stepped in front of her.

"Dr. Thorsdottir, remember me, Bonnie Sandler? You did my anesthesia on Monday." She bounced her index finger off her forehead and smiled.

"Yes. My presence must have been extremely boring because you were asleep."

Bonnie squinted her eyes. "Ohh. That's very funny."

Lucy chuckled and slipped behind the front desk, and Viktoria opened the entrance door.

"What a beautiful day," Viktoria said, passing the bench and flower pot.

"And I'm starving," Bonnie said, as both women headed towards the sandwich shop.

"Make a tuna salad on that tasty cheese bread and I'll buy a drink," Viktoria said inside to a man at the counter.

"Make me a hot ham and cheese on wheat," Bonnie said, "to go."

Hair fell over the employee's eyes as he grabbed two loaves of bread and sliced them in half.

"Dr. Thorsdottir, patients pick out their surgeons. Is it possible to do the same thing regarding being put to sleep? To request a particular anesthesia doctor?"

"Fulfilling such a request is more likely to happen if the patient makes the inquiry ahead of time. That's because OR rooms and cases are usually scheduled with anesthesia providers the day before, depending on who will be available. For instance, an anesthesiologist that a patient may want for their surgery may be post-call or on vacation, and won't be working on a certain day. Why do you ask?"

"I'm having surgery again this week." She turned her head and lowered her voice. "Dr. Pinto is enhancing my chest on Friday."

"Really? You are a brave woman to go back to the OR again so soon."

"You are shapely, if I may say so, but if your chest was board-flat like mine, you would want to do it too. The center offered me a cheap price. Or part of it is cheap." She frowned. "I'll have to dig up more money, but at least that didn't have to be paid up front today, like the rest of it."

Viktoria slid over in front of the cashier, and dug out her credit card. "Can you pay any of the fee by credit card?"

"Nope." She turned on a big smile. "My sons choked up the money I paid them today."

"Wow. You are a lucky woman."

"Yes. Anyway, can you do my anesthesia on Friday?"

"I will talk to Dr. Castillo, the doctor in charge. I think that can be arranged."

"Awesome." She paid and grasped the brown bag the cashier handed her.

Viktoria selected a table, and placed her computer behind the food tray.

"Bye," Bonnie said. "See you on Friday. I'm as happy as a tornado in a trailer park."

She watched the bubbly woman from the window, pleased that plastic surgery can make a significant difference in peoples' lives. The whole submarine sandwich was too much, so she folded the waxy paper around half, and opened her computer.

Every time she walked through Amour Cosmetic Surgery's waiting room, the number of patients impressed her, as well as the number of cases booked ahead on the computer schedule at Lucy's desk. Cosmetic surgery worked well by word of mouth, but Amour's advertising and marketing must be quite sophisticated, she thought.

She sat pondering. If the President of the United States used Twitter, what about Amour Cosmetic Surgery? She brought up her home page on the social media site and clicked on the search box. After trying a couple of possibilities, she stumbled on @AmourBeautificationonLI.

The tweets were classy, with split screen pictures of before and after patients transformed by the surgery center. Or so they said, she thought. They were thoughtfully crafted, some rhymed, and they added every useful hashtag imaginable:

"Beauty IS in the Eye of the Beholder.

Transform yourself and become the apple of HIS eye."

#loveyourself #plasticsurgery #surgery #healthandbeauty

#beauty #gorgeous #amour

The next one read:

"Look for a #cosmeticsurgeon who shares your aesthetic sensibility.

Beauty is not equal for everyone!"

#happylife   #surgery   #amour   #giftyourself   #plasticsurgery

#LongIsland

Dr. Thorsdottir kept scrolling as she gulped down her iced tea, and noticed that they kept on a schedule of every two hours. Other users retweeted their messages also, so the platform gave them excellent exposure.

She switched over to her Facebook home page and also plugged in a search for Amour Cosmetic Surgery. Their public group page came up without any alteration of their name and, again, she noted a professional presentation of the services they offered.

"Turn the clock backwards!

Amour Cosmetic Surgery offers Long Islanders, as well as those from afar, a chance to do just that.

How young or shapely do you want to be?"

Viktoria didn't use Pinterest very much, but she took a stab at that as well. A 'board' showed up for the center and, since pictures were the platform's specialty, there were too many to look at. Instagram was no different.

One more, she thought. What about YouTube? Surprised not to find Rigoberto Castillo featured in one of the videos, she recognized one of the other surgeons.

"The procedure here at Amour Cosmetic Surgery may be called a face lift," the surgeon said, "but our technique is pure magic—facial rejuvenation at its finest."

Viktoria sat tall. The advertising and scope of the social media blasts she'd just seen were somewhat of a surprise, and she thought back to the medical field before the 1980s. In those days, doctors built their practices by word of mouth. Their good doctoring skills and reputation defined them and it took years for that to happen.

Now it was a different story. In 1982, the Supreme Court made a major decision—they lifted the ban previously in place and now physicians could advertise!

The transformation for physicians and their practices sped up overnight via the internet and other venues. The business aspect of medical care, especially plastic surgery, became—who posted the better advertisement, the better before and after surgery pictures, the better sex appeal, and a leg up on prices.

Viktoria sighed. In essence, Amour's reach to potential patients was global. She wouldn't be surprised if an Icelander had come to Long Island for their services!

A ding sounded and she read Rigoberto's text. *"Your patient is here."* She closed her computer, grasped her left-over sandwich, and headed next door.

Dr. Castillo and Lucy were at the front, so she sat against the desk next to them. "Rigoberto, can you schedule me in Bonnie Sandler's room on Friday, for her breast augmentation?"

He glanced questioningly at Lucy.

"Yes, she paid this morning," Lucy assured him.

"Sure," he said back to Viktoria. "You will be her personal anesthesiologist."

"Thanks. By the way, I'm totally curious about how Amour maintains a media advertising and marketing presence. Do you hire an outside agency or does someone in this little front office do it?"

"Something like that, but not quite," Dr. Castillo said, turning away. "Your next patient is waiting for you in the holding area."

CHAPTER 9

Dorothy Flores stared up at her bedroom ceiling, frustrated at her uncomfortable night in bed. Her preferred position to sleep was on her stomach. Certainly, she thought, she could not expect to be belly down after having surgery on her abdomen. But, nevertheless, she never expected to be *this* sore after Dr. Reed had performed her tummy tuck.

Would she ever be able to cuddle face down into her pillow again, she wondered. This cosmetic surgery she went through was not for the faint of heart. She inched her torso to the side of the bed, carefully placed her legs on the carpet, and moved upright.

Dorothy went to the bathroom and brushed her teeth while placing her other hand on the vanity. She needed the support, but she expected that. After all, her whole body shape and weight had been changed. It must take time for her brain to acquaint itself with new muscle memory—her new body was no longer shaped like some kind of squash.

She put her toothbrush in its holder, and glanced at the shower stall, yearning to take a warm, invigorating shower. But the bandages couldn't come off yet, or at least that was her impression. The folder with post-op instructions was sparse, and she wasn't good at understanding medical instructions anyway.

After washing her face, and brushing out her head of curls, she ambled out to the kitchen without changing her pajamas. The day before, she had done the same thing—lived in a nightgown all day. She turned on the coffee machine with a few scoops of dark roast and, as the water dripped into the pot, she peeled a banana. The thought of eating her usual breakfast of a bowl of cereal or crispy toast with honey butter did not appeal to her.

She considered the thought of calling her surgeon, Victor Reed, but he had better things to do than listen to a whining woman after what he had done for her. After all, he was busy making more women beautiful.

Relieved to see a call come in from her older sister, she answered her cell phone. "Hey, Marilyn."

"Good morning. How are you feeling?"

"I'm grubby and sleep deprived. Didn't sleep a wink." She pressed the palm of her free hand over her forehead. "I wonder if I have a touch of fever."

"You do own a thermometer, don't you?"

"Yes, but finding where I put it years ago will be a chore. It's not like that is a readily accessible object which sits on my sink every day with my soap dish."

"If you can't find it, call me back. I would be happy to bring you one and check on you at the same time."

"Really?"

"Of course."

"Then please do. I don't feel up to rummaging through bathroom drawers for a buried item. And maybe you can bring me a container of broccoli cheddar soup from the bread place along the way?"

"Consider it done, sis." Marilyn hung up and bit the inside of her mouth. That was not like her sister at all to ask for help. Especially for something as simple as her delivering soup compared to her sister heating a can up in her kitchen.

After lunch and evaluating her next patient, Viktoria settled into an easy case on a healthy person. A focused female surgeon stood at the head of the OR table and performed an otoplasty on a twenty-two-year-old named Pamela Rodriguez. Viktoria had no problems giving the general anesthetic and admired the skill of the surgeon, Dr. Kippy Saliner. The patient had been self-conscious by how far her ears stuck out from her head, and Viktoria had a hunch that her patient was going to end up being pleased with the results.

At the end of the case, she woke her patient up like clock-work and pushed her stretcher into the recovery room. The woman gave her caretakers a groggy smile after touching the bandages on her ears.

"Now I won't look like Alfalfa of the Little Rascals," the woman said.

"That was a television show even before my time," Viktoria said. She pulled the blanket up around the woman's shoulders and wrote down her vital signs. "How did you go back in time to watch America's most iconic nerd and those lovable youngsters?"

"The bank I work in redecorated the tellers' area and next to it is a sitting area and television. The branch manager sets the TV on the old black and white programs. I now love those shows. Better than any of the junk they show today."

"Dr. Thorsdottir has you wide-awake and alert," the recovery room nurse interjected. "You were blessed today with the best surgeon and the best anesthesiologist, and you are gifted with fine taste in television."

"Lucky me," she said, and pulled in a long, full breath.

Viktoria pushed through the double doors and noticed her name was off the schedule board. It was almost three o'clock, so her day was grinding to an end. Voices still percolated from the front, and she slid into Lucy's area to be inquisitive and assure herself that Rigoberto was finished with her services for the day.

"Any significant plans for tonight?" Lucy asked, switching her braid to the other side of her shoulder.

"I have a new dog, so I'll probably give her a super walk."

"Is she a baby?"

"Not yet a year old."

The front door opened and a woman and a man stomped straight up to the desk. Viktoria recognized the disgruntled woman from the other day as she stuck her head through the open-glass partition.

"Mrs. Murray," she said, "I am still being ignored by the surgery center, so I am here again to demand my money back."

Women in the waiting area glanced away from their cell phones and magazines and locked onto the newcomers. One man leaned forward and narrowed his eyes.

Lucy stood quickly. "I assure you…"

"You assured me last time, but this time I brought my brother. He's an attorney. Maybe now we can resolve this issue without him sending you a nasty letter."

"Renee," he whispered, "I'll do the heavy lifting." He gently directed her away from the window and stepped into her spot.

"This matter will be simple for me, but a nightmare for you. I am a pit bull when it comes to businesses cheating my clients. Plus, she's my sister. I understand my sister had a face lift scheduled here, and then changed her mind and cancelled. The problem is that she paid ahead of time and has not been refunded her money. When I get through with you, you'll pay her what you owe her, you'll pay her interest, and you'll pay her a big award for being such pricks."

Lucy twisted her hands in a ball and wanted to reach out and muzzle the man. The patients in the waiting room heard more than they needed to, and as the tension mounted, she bent forward. "Sir, I am not the department …"

"I don't want to hear the excuses you already told my sister."

"If you would let me finish, I will personally see what I can do about this. But, please, let's simmer down. Come and wait in our private patient room."

He nodded. Viktoria watched as Lucy escorted them into the room where Bonnie Sandler had picked out her upcoming breast implants. Ms. Murray hurried down the hallway again and, surprisingly, opened the front door and went outside.

Viktoria stepped around into the waiting area. A male visitor shook his head at her, and others went back to what they were doing. She glanced out the front door. Perhaps Lucy went to her car for something—her checkbook?

The advertising scrolled across the side wall and Viktoria was getting sick of the same pictures. She glanced at the wall on the other side. Two calming beach pictures of Jones Beach hung on either side of a framed certificate. The type of document was familiar and prestigious. She had one herself—for her accomplishment in Anesthesiology. The matted certificate read:

"The American Board of Plastic Surgery

Hereby certifies that Kippy Saliner, A licensed Graduate of Medicine, having complied with all the requirements of this Board, is qualified to serve as a consultant in Plastic Surgery."

Dr. Saliner's board certification was not a surprise to Viktoria because she had just witnessed the woman's skill doing an otoplasty. Plus, Kippy acted very professional in her pre and postop dealings with her patient.

However, it was what was missing from the wall that suddenly bothered Viktoria. Instead of the water color artwork of Long Island's beach, why weren't there more Board Certification documents on the wall? Even if the originals were not available, it was possible to post copies.

What about Rigoberto Castillo, Ernest Pinto, Victor Reed, or the other surgeons who rotate through Amour Cosmetic Surgery center? Their Board certifications were not hanging. It seemed strange to only highlight one of them. Of course, not all doctors are board certified, and many are decent physicians despite that fact.

However, to maintain a practice with mostly board-certified physicians was the norm, not the exception. She shook her head, and gave Amour the benefit of the doubt. Patients in a waiting room, she thought, probably prefer beach scenes rather than inquiring about, or staring at, dull doctor's qualification documents.

The door swung open and Lucy again crossed the entrance. Her hand clutched a piece of paper, and she hurried to the room where Mrs. Walters and her attorney brother waited.

Dr. Thorsdottir acted interested in a magazine rack, and selected a beauty publication with too many suggestions of unwise products to smear on one's face. After a few minutes, the two disgruntled visitors pranced through the waiting room, and Viktoria noted the man slipping a folded paper into the pocket of his sports jacket.

A customer sitting by the door stared at them with a questioning look.

"I wouldn't go here if I were you," Mrs. Walters advised her.

It was time for Viktoria to leave as well, so she headed towards the locker room.

"Glad that's resolved," Lucy mumbled as Viktoria passed her in the hallway. "Some people!"

"They seemed happier than when they entered," Viktoria commented.

"Yes, I rustled up her surgical payment. She should have heeded our cancellation policies more carefully, and been more proactive about getting in touch with us."

Viktoria decided not to respond, especially since she'd witnessed the woman trying to personally get a refund two days ago. The legal clout must have worked on Lucy.

While changing out of scrubs, Viktoria could not make sense of one thing she had just witnessed. Had Lucy Murray written a check to the woman while sitting in her car in the parking lot?

Surely, Amour was a lot more sophisticated than that and plus, the check and check receipt must have been typed out.

Viktoria grasped her computer and her bag, tipped her hand good-bye at the front desk, and stepped out into the sunlight. Deliberately, she sat on the outside bench where the manicured hedges helped camouflage the asphalt parking lot. The sandwich place was to the left, and a small travel agency office was situated to the right. She leaned forward and glanced that way. A door was situated between the travel place and Amour. Without any sign of a business there, she had overlooked it.

As she stared up, she realized she had missed that detail about the strip mall—there was a second floor level.

Her curiosity took hold, especially since Lucy had come and gone. And in that interim, a business check had materialized.

She walked over and, trying the door, she found it unlocked. The passageway was ill-lighted, and she glanced between the handrail on the right and the steps. Another door greeted her upstairs on the landing, and she pulled it open.

The cacophony of noise made her reel backwards, and the sight in the open, large room took her breath away. Women and men, mostly in their twenties and thirties, sat in front of computers and telephones, and each person conducted their own agenda.

Luckily, no one glanced her way. It was as if time was their most valuable asset as they placed calls and scrolled the internet.

She slid to the side wall and lurked at the end of one of the long tables, which was actually multiple tables lined up in a row, and keyed in on the nearest man's conversation:

"Ma'am the plastic surgery center I am calling about is Long Island's most prestigious get-beautiful center for all your health and beauty updates. We are running a special for Halloween, only available a few more days."

The man spoke quickly and astutely. If the person on the other end of the phone line wanted to interrupt him, that was impossible. He read his prepared sales talk from a written script, trying to persuade the person in his most heart-felt tone of voice.

"Yes, Ma'am, I would be happy to. I will text you some pictures right now."

He used the phone like a wizard, through the MacBook Air's computer message center, and zipped off two face lift before-and-after pictures. "Those results are phenomenal," he said. "I can schedule you with the same surgeon who was responsible for that surgery. All I need is a commitment and a small down payment, and then we can talk in the near future as to when you want to come in, talk to him, and schedule. We can be flexible."

Viktoria moved along the wall to the next aisle where the nearest woman's hands sped along a keyboard and she handled a call through the computer before her:

"I would be happy to explain our products, services, and prices in more detail. We aim to please. I am shooting you pictures of shapely women who have breast implants—done at our very talented surgical center.

"It is fortunate that I caught hold of you today because we are running a discount in the next week for those patients who sign up for surgery in the next month or so. Our doctors would love to see you for a presurgical assessment. They want to make sure you qualify."

"Oh gosh," the woman on the line answered. "I hope I meet their qualifications. In the back of my mind, I suppose I've always wondered about getting breast implants. After all, half the women in Hollywood and in the Music City, seem to grow their chests. I don't see pictures of them in social media for a while, and then when they reappear, their chests are different! If they can do it, then why can't I?"

"Exactly, especially since we're the best at what we do."

Viktoria moved along the wall, not being scrutinized by anyone. A nearby woman stood and stretched her legs with earbuds in her ears, the wire dangling down to her cell phone.

"Look, I'm not asking for credit card numbers," she said. "But we're willing to pay your standard fee for names and telephone numbers from your sources."

A delay ensured, and then she continued. "That's right. Give me your potential customer names from your telephone directories, magazine reply cards, and the lists you've purchased from other organizations."

Viktoria's blood simmered. Knowing that telemarketers existed and hounded people was one thing, but seeing them in action was alarming. Solicitous and arm-twisting, they carried on with their calls and lists.

In the back of the room, the tables disappeared and a line-up of private desks took their place. Personal items of pictures and nick-knacks graced the wooden tops and women were not on the phone. She was convinced they were not carrying on telemarketing like the others.

Viktoria approached one of the desks. "Hi there."

The woman furrowed her brow and stopped flipping through a file. "I'm sorry. Do we know you?"

"I am one of the doctors working at Amour. Am I correct in assuming this is the business office?"

"Yes, it is."

"A client just complained about a down-payment not being refunded. I assume her refund was just rebated through one of you."

"Yes, her check came through us. But that should not concern you. We thoroughly separate the different aspects of our business. You don't need to bother your pretty head about it."

"Don't speak to me that way."

"Sorry." She placed her hands on her lap. "I am leaving to take a small break. May I walk you out?"

"I know the way."

"It was nice meeting you …"

"I'm Dr. Thorsdottir, an anesthesiologist. You are paying the locum tenens agency for my services.

"Oh, yes. Regina is the go-to person at the agency. I'm glad she sent you. We appreciate our anesthesiologists."

"Yes, well, I have never seen a medical practice having such a detailed sales and business office. Seems a bit like high-pressure sales tactics."

"It's called surviving in the practice of plastic surgery, Dr. Thorsdottir, just like other businesses trying to survive. In the end, people make their own choices—how much money they want to spend and on what. We don't make their decisions for them."

CHAPTER 10

Rick looked down into Millie's blue eyes, took off the slip lead around her neck, and threw the tennis ball. The day had taken on a new meaning, a new purpose, he thought, as he moved away from the park bench and tried to coax her to drop the ball. She dropped it, more interested in what went on behind him, so she darted that way.

An occasional car pulled in and out of the nearby parking lot, and Rick paid no attention to the area. Millie, however, was quite interested in cars, as well as the leashed dog who jumped out of a CRV.

The Miniature American Shepherd bolted to the Labrador Retriever and ran circles around him, engaging the leash, making the two dogs a tangled mess. "Stop! Stop!" the driver of the car said. She leaned down and grabbed Millie by the neck.

"Hey," Rick yelled. "Let go of her."

"Are you crazy? If she's not trained off leash, why do you have her running wild?"

"Excuse me." Rick laid sarcasm on his remark, and replaced his own grip on Millie.

The woman untangled her dog's leash and shook her head as he watched. She grabbed the end of the leash, closed the back door, and glared at him. "Poor dog," she mumbled.

Rick fumbled with the green leash and slipped it back on Millie. He looked around for his vehicle, momentarily wondering where he had parked. "There we are," he said, and tugged on the rope. At the car, he let her jump in, tossed the ball behind her, and scrambled into the driver's seat.

Glancing at his watch, he smirked. He had an appointment in a half hour with his psychologist. Now it was simply a matter of appeasing his wife, keeping her aware of the fact that he was seeking treatment and would quit marijuana. All because she thought it made him passive aggressive and nasty. Lots of people smoked, he thought, so her understanding of his habit was unwarranted. He'd been through the thought process a hundred times. There was no getting around it. He needed to 'appease' her.

There was enough time before Paula Spinner's appointment, however, and it would be best to do his THC vaping right here in his car, at the park. He turned to the passenger seat, his items packed in a black vinyl bag, and set up the cartridge. For a glorious twenty minutes, he enjoyed every moment of his addiction. His head leaned on the head rest and his thoughts became dreams. Dreams of flying over the Grand Canyon holding onto some kind of parachute. An eagle caught up with him and flew beside him. All was fine at first as they flew neck to neck, but then the bird glared at him like the woman at the park, and he began pecking at Rick's parachute. "This is my life support," Rick hollered. "Leave me alone."

The great bird of prey ignored him and became more aggressive. With the vinyl glider torn in too many places, the vehicle for gliding failed to support Rick anymore. He plunged to the depths of the red-brown cliffs and said good-bye to his maker.

The blare of a horn sounded and jolted Rick back to reality. A car passed behind him, and the woman driver with the Labrador Retriever shook her fist at him. "I guess she was angrier than I thought," he said to Millie who was flat on the back seat and paid him no mind.

Rick turned on the ignition and let the motor simmer. He plucked his cell phone up to text his wife. Prove to her that he was following his commitment.

"Goin now to the therapistt. Millies in the car cuz I gave heer a park walk. She's fine but,, come get her if you want."

He tried to focus, but it didn't matter if he was stoned. Typos or weird text messages could be blamed on the damn phone's auto-correct. He zipped the message off to Viktoria.

Viktoria stayed at work longer than necessary. Her last patient, an older woman trying to turn back her years, was slow to wake up, and she wanted the woman's blood pressure to be lower before discharging her.

"Why are you still here?" Rigoberto asked her, eating a pack of crackers in the kitchenette.

"I'm watching someone in the recovery room. I'll be out of here soon." She selected a cookie and tore open the plastic wrap. "I stumbled upstairs to the second floor today. Excuse the double meaning, but you have quite an operation here."

"I've worked hard to create Amour," he snapped.

"I'm sure you have. How long has Amour been in operation?"

"I wish longer. There are aspects of running a business that you cannot even contemplate. What it takes…" He faced the counter, and topped off his mug with more coffee. "But I don't expect you to. You are not here to help my business staff."

Rigoberto shifted his stance and met her eyes. "I am paying you to provide anesthesia services, and anesthesia services only. You are a high-end doctor that I am paying more than usual."

"Are you inferring that I represent a pearl in an oyster among a bunch of snails?"

He laughed and then caught himself. Wiggling his sloped shoulders, he said, "Snails, you're being a bit harsh, don't you think?"

"Perhaps. Maybe what you mean is that I am board certified in my specialty, and that makes me stand out compared to some other doctors working here. That's why you're paying me 'more than usual?'"

"Board certified doesn't mean a thing if a doctor doesn't have hands-on physician skills. Perhaps it only means that he or she has book and test-taking skills."

"You started this. Yes, so true. But, being board-certified these days is more the norm for doctors in a practice than not."

"Dr. Thorsdottir, I never said that most of the doctors here are not board-certified. You inferred that."

"Well, are they?"

He rolled his eyes and walked to the door. "Have a nice evening."

Viktoria finished the chocolate chip cookie in her hand. It left a better taste in her mouth than having a discussion with Dr. Castillo. What was his problem? she thought. When she made small talk about Amour Cosmetic Surgery, he always became defensive. Even answering a simple question like how long they'd been in operation, she didn't get a straight answer.

Her phone played a train whistle sound, and she looked at the incoming text message from her husband:

"Goin now to the therapistt. Millies in the car cuz I gave heer a park walk. She's fine but,, come get her if you want."

She walked to the recovery room to hopefully discharge her patient.

Rick's message had a few too many typos and errors. Auto-correct could botch up a text, so she stopped and read it again. But her suspicions were aroused, just like her wariness about Rigoberto Castillo's business practices.

After signing out her patient and changing into street clothes, Viktoria left. Turning on the ignition of her Honda, she glanced up at the second floor of the strip mall building and thought of all the telemarketing calls being made from there. They were effective, she thought, otherwise that business practice wouldn't exist.

She placed her iPhone in its holder on the vent of the dashboard. It would be useful to swing by Paula Spinner's office and pick Millie up from Rick. Apparently the dog was having a successful first day in her new home, and her husband had included her in his day's activities. She couldn't ask or wish for more than that!

Bypassing the turn-off to Harbour Village and their subdivision, Viktoria kept going and pulled into the neighborhood area of Rick's psychologist.

She wondered if she should bother going into Dr. Spinner's office because Rick should be in there discussing or readjusting his mindset for his marijuana addiction. It would be better not to wait for him or interrupt them, she figured, so she made sure she carried one of his car keys. She began scouring the vehicles on the street, looking for a Mazda convertible with the top up. His vehicle didn't count for being dog-friendly, so she hoped Millie had behaved herself and not shred any upholstery.

She slipped off the light sweater she wore and draped it over her arm. The temperature had risen, and the sun's rays smacked her cheeks, enough that she wished she had sunscreen in her moisturizer. Spotting Rick's car a distance away at the periphery of a close parking lot, it was parked in the striped loading zone for a handicap vehicle. She hated that. Why had he done that?

Viktoria trotted over, peered in the back seat, and swallowed hard. Poor Millie's tongue hung out as she panted and not a window was cracked. Good thing it wasn't the dead of summer, otherwise the dog would be dead. Nevertheless, she knew, the inside of a car heats up even if it's sixty degrees outside with no fresh air or ventilation. Quickly, she unlocked the door with her key, grabbed Millie's slip leash, and put it around her neck. She huddled the young dog in her arms and placed her on the ground.

"Come on, Millie. We're going home immediately, so I can give you some water."

"My wife is leaving me her dog to mind while she's at work," Rick said, his legs crossed, his eyes avoiding contact with his therapist.

"Do you have a problem with that?"

Rick dodged the answer in his mind. He couldn't figure out the answer. He disliked his time being managed by something that was due to Viktoria, yet the dog was more fun than any effort on his part.

"I guess I don't mind it."

"Are you referring to the dog as an 'it,' or does it have a name?"

"Millie."

Paula Spinner fiddled with the earring dangling alongside her neck. She suspected her patient was not abiding by the whole purpose why he was there—to quit marijuana. So, she artfully talked generalities with him at first, testing his mental cognition.

"The right dog can be a superb form of therapy. Millie would serve you well by absorbing some of your time outside of working your two jobs. When you feel like hitting the weed, take the dog for a walk. Consider her the absolute substitution. Make that firm commitment. Just a thought."

He straightened up, his broad shoulders flexing, and he flashed his ultra white teeth. "I suppose." He figured it was the best way to appease her. Actually, he could do both things at the same time—walk the dog and vape, like today.

"Unlike what you've been doing already today. Mr. Richter, we're trying to make progress here. We are only in the beginning of our sessions, and if you can't take this serious from the start, there's not much hope."

"I tell you what, why don't you add group sessions as well? You can meet people who are dealing with addictions like you, and build a support network besides me."

"Sure," he said. Viktoria would praise him for the effort, he thought, and next month when she leaves for a new job assignment, he can cut back on all the therapy. She'd never know the difference.

"Here's the information. Call the group leader ahead of time, so he expects you." She leaned forward and handed him a business card. "Now, what made you reach for marijuana today?"

At home, Viktoria set down a fresh bowl of water for Millie, and she lapped up the liquid like it was underground water feeding a desert oasis. The blue Merle shepherd sat and thanked her master by making sharp eye contact.

"Now it's time to eat, sweetheart." She fed Millie and conjured up a grilled sandwich on the indoor electric grill and tossed a salad for herself. By the time she washed the dishes, she heard the garage door open.

Rick came strutting in with a pleasant smile and patted Millie on the head. "My appointment went well," he announced, "and I see you grabbed Millie from my car."

"Yes, I did. Next time, perhaps it would be better if you bring her home and not leave her in the Mazda."

"Why's that?"

"The windows were not cracked, and the heat inside built up. And with unpredictable weather approaching, it could be more dangerous for her."

"More dangerous? More dangerous than what?"

"Than today."

"Damn, Viktoria! I took care of her, didn't I?"

"Rick, have you been smoking today?"

"How dare you. I went to therapy today and I'm on the road to recovery."

"You scare me, Rick. Do you realize where you parked in the mall's parking lot? In the loading zone of a handicapped person's space."

"I don't know what you're talking about."

"Let's drop it."

"Happy to." He put his hand at the base of his neck, grimaced, and slunk into a dining room chair against the wall. Millie backed away from him and stood next to Viktoria.

Viktoria opened the refrigerator and poured a glass of iced tea. "Do you want some? Maybe you're as thirsty as Millie was hanging out in your car without water."

"I thought we were going to drop it?"

"I couldn't resist."

"I feel too nauseous to drink, or eat."

She eyed him. He did look a bit green around the gills.

He stood and rubbed his upper chest. "Whatever I ate last is about to come up," he said, and made a dash toward her.

Viktoria stepped out of the way as he brushed against the sink and vomited. He stood waiting and a minute later, upchucked again. He ran water, splashed some over his lower face, and rinsed his mouth.

"I wouldn't have made it to the bathroom," he explained, turning around.

"Did you eat some food that went bad?"

"No. I guess therapy doesn't agree with me," he added, forcing a smile.

"I wouldn't doubt it."

"You'll be happy to know I'm going to try more options—a group which meets for addiction recovery."

She glanced into her glass, at the ice cube sitting on top, which would soon melt into oblivion. "I hope the sessions help you."

CHAPTER 11

After another restless night, Dorothy Flores reluctantly put her feet on the carpet. She noticed the clump at the bottom of the bed, the comforter in a wad after she became too hot and wiggled it off with her legs. She seemed warmer than the day before. Yesterday, her sister had given her a thermometer and they learned that she had a slight fever. But they didn't worry about that because the medical staff at Amour said a slight postop fever may be normal at first.

What concerned her the most, however, was the stomach pain which ramped up during the night. "Damn," she groaned, as she leaned over to scoot her feet into her slippers. She glanced back at the bed, not wanting to get up. The pain was much less, she realized, while lying still.

But, there was no way she could stay seated because a queasiness took hold of her abdomen and the urge to vomit was too strong. Dorothy flip-flopped in her slippers, taking hold of the bathroom doorway on the way, and pitched forward over the toilet bowl.

Her stomach felt like nothing was left in it when she finished, and she held onto the seat like a steering wheel. She carefully rose, wiped her mouth at the sink, and palpated her resized abdomen. Touching it made her shudder because that made the pain worse. Twitching her mouth, she realized she also had a case of the shivers and was a bit dizzy.

Dorothy ran her hand through her droopy curls and ambled to the kitchen. Opening the folder from Amour, she flipped through the paperwork. There was no specific phone number for her surgeon, Victor Reed, but that shouldn't matter, she thought. She called the surgical center and let it ring and ring, but no one answered. Not even a nameless recording.

She dialed again, her sister Marilyn. "Morning, sis," she said.

"Morning yourself. Are you doing any better today? You're up early."

Dorothy grimaced about making the call while her sister readied for work. "I suppose I'm having normal postoperative nausea and fatigue. I'm sure not ready to drive on the L.I.E."

"Few of us are. That is the only route for me to get to work, so I don't have a choice. But back to you. Maybe you should contact your surgeon to be on the safe side."

"I called Amour. They must not be open yet."

"Okay, try again later. I'll call you back this afternoon to check on you."

Dorothy hung up and twisted her mouth at the thought of drinking a cup of coffee.

Late in the morning, the recovery room buzzed with the first round of patients getting ready to go home. Viktoria signed out her last patient, almost as alert as when she arrived at the center hours ago.

"Viktoria," Rigoberto said, "go take a break, get coffee, or whatever. I'll preop your next patient when they arrive because I have a pause in my morning Botox appointments. But first, a patient is here to see you. She's waiting at the front desk."

Viktoria stepped past the front desk and opened the door.

"Dr. Thorsdottir!" Pamela Rodriguez exclaimed. The twenty-two-year old with gauze taped over her ears, stepped forward. "I live close by and decided to come by and thank you and Dr. Saliner personally."

Viktoria's expression softened from a question mark to gratitude. She could count on one hand how many people had ever made *a point* to thank her for their safe anesthetic. After all, she held their lives in her hand while they were 'under.'

"I changed the surgical dressing this morning," Pamela said, "and my ears look terrific. Dr. Saliner did a terrific job, and I slept like a lamb during the procedure because of you." She shoved a small plastic, ribbon-tied bag into her hand. "This is for you, and I have one for her too."

"Thank you," Viktoria stammered. This was a first, a gift from a patient, and she felt uncomfortable about accepting it.

"The surgeon is busy in the operating room. Would you give this one to her?" She placed a second bag in Viktoria's hands.

"I will echo your 'thank you' to her too. We don't expect to be acknowledged like this. We are just doing our jobs."

"Sure, but people do their work in different ways. You can strive to be the best at whatever you do, or not give a damn, and just trudge through the actions. Right?"

Lucy Murray's ears were as big as elephants as she eavesdropped on the conversation going on in front of the desk. She pushed out her rolling chair from the desk and stood.

"Well," Viktoria said, "we were happy to take care of you, and I'm glad the result will give you satisfaction."

Wearing a pants-suit with sleek lines, her figure tall and slender, Lucy now stood next to them. "Ms. Rodriguez, I overheard your satisfactory comments about your care and outcome from Amour Cosmetic Surgery." She gestured towards the wall and broke out in a wider smile.

"I would like to write down your comments and use them in our advertising. You would be a hit. So many of our outstanding results and reviews from patients come from breast augmentation, tummy tucks, and butt lift procedures. But, as your life now became more exhilarating—your ears now made more naturally flatter and not sticking out like God didn't intend—you can be a spokesperson for otoplasties."

Pamela glanced between Lucy and Viktoria. "I would love to! Do you mean you would use my picture too?"

"After your bandages come off, and there is no tissue puffiness, and you look gorgeous, yes! Your before and after pictures will be stunning, just like you."

She was never gorgeous, Pamela thought, all because of her ears. Now someone was actually considering her looks good enough to be a model. "How terrific."

"Come inside, so we can talk about it further. I will also give you our social network sites so you can post reviews on the internet." She guided Pamela inside to the comfortable consultation room.

Viktoria followed them and broke off into the kitchenette. She poured coffee, sat down, and untied the ribbon on her bag. Grasping the item and pulling it out, she found a string of navy blue beads, those used in counting prayers. She had not seen Catholic rosary beads in a long time. Not being faithful to any one religion, she still smiled. This was her patient's idea of a wonderful gift to give someone, and she clutched it with appreciation.

After toasting a bagel, Dr. Saliner walked in. "Kippy, just who I wanted to see. Our otoplasty patient from yesterday, Pamela Rodriguez, came back today to personally thank you and me for the care she received yesterday. She left you this."

Kippy opened the bag. "How sweet—a backup pair of rosary beads.

I'll keep these in my purse." She looked at Viktoria. "This is the first time someone gave me something over and above the payment for my services."

"Same here. It's heartwarming."

Kippy nodded and held the rosary beads. As she silently joined Viktoria over coffee, Viktoria wondered if the surgeon's fingers moved from bead to bead on her lap. The health care workers, the business personnel, and the patients at Amour Cosmetic Surgery kept surprising her with their diversity.

Viktoria pulled into an empty garage, Rick's vehicle gone, and she wondered if he'd taken Millie somewhere. When she went inside, the dog wiggled standing on the other side of the back door.

She opened the door and Millie greeted her, circling her legs. "Try this," Viktoria said. She spread her legs and directed the dog in and out, side-to-side between her legs. At first, her puppy acted confused, but within two tries, she weaved like she'd done the trick her whole life.

"Awesome, Millie. You are quite the girl!"

Viktoria grabbed a bottle of water and some treats in her pocket. "Let's go downtown to Harbour Village, and walk along the North Shore. Have you seen Long Island Sound yet, or experienced the salt air hitting your nostrils?"

The dog stared, and popped up when Viktoria grabbed her leash.

They set off in her car, and soon were near their destination. The breeze picked up as they slowed through the tourist-clad downtown, and crept over the speed bumps. Parking in the lot near the small beach area and pier, all she could think of was that this place was where she had first met her husband. How polite he was to help her, a stranger, launch her kayak into the choppy inlet. That encounter seemed like a lifetime ago. Who and what was he when she met him? As she learned later, he had camouflaged his addiction from her.

No way, she thought. That had set the stage for a cursed marriage to begin with. After all, he had *hid* his habit from her. Her marriage could be defined in one word—distrust.

As her mind wandered, Viktoria barely passed one person who did not smile and ask to pet her dog. "Surely," she said to each person. "Dogs are social lubricants. Pet away!"

A little girl clutched her mother's hand, her pony tail bobbing at the back of her head, and her eyes grew big as Millie trotted toward her. She let out a delightful sound and patted the dog's head. Her mother, a grown look-alike, shook her head. "I can't fight it anymore. I think a puppy is in our future."

"Best of luck," Viktoria said. "You will round out your daughter's life with a four-legged friend."

They continued in opposite directions, and Viktoria finally sat on a steel bench, facing the sound. She pulled her cell phone out of her pocket to check if Rick had texted about his whereabouts. But it wasn't her husband who had left a message, but another adult male.

Viktoria's heart jumped, sending a rush of blood through her veins. The words came from Jeffrey Appleton, the Director of Surgical Services from Masonville General Hospital, a man she had met during her anesthesia position in Northern Pennsylvania last month.

"Hi Viktoria. How was your drive back to Long Island? How is your new locums position working out?"

She absentmindedly stroked Millie, staring at her phone. When she left, neither one of them mentioned whether they would contact, or meet each other, again. Distance was a factor, but the unspoken issue was her marital status. She was married and he was not. Because of her marriage, she never dreamed of having an affair, and it only happened at the very end of her trip while there. Too many issues had come to a head, causing her and Jeff to connect emotionally and physically, like salt and pepper sprinkled on a tasteless omelet. Her fingers started to text and then they continued the 'dialogue:'

"Like PA, not exactly run-of-the-mill. I'm working at a plastic surgery center. I hope the place is unlike any other, because they concentrate on advertising a lot!"

"Part of a business plan, I suppose. How are you?"

"Falling into a routine back at home. It's been awhile since I've been here for any length of time. My new news is that I took in another dog. Her name is Millie."

"That's wonderful. I still feel terrible about what happened to the dog you befriended up here. Did you bury Buddy's ashes?"

"No. I can't part with them."

"Tell me about Millie."

Viktoria's fingers zoomed across the letters and soon had Jeff smiling as he read her account. *"She's here with me now,"* she added.

After some time, he bridged asking her, *"How are things at home with your husband? Don't tell me if you don't want."*

"The hole is getting deeper."

"I'm sorry. I truly am."

Staring at his last words, she realized she believed this man more than she trusted her husband.

"If I were to manage a business trip to L.I., would I be able to see you again?"

A gentle breeze stroked her cheeks and ruffled Millie's coat. It felt invigorating, but contemplating seeing another man in the area where she lived gave her the jitters. She paused her fingers, not wanting to commit and make a hasty decision via a text message, and she suspected that Rick was going nowhere with his therapy. What if the group sessions he announced to her would also have the same worthless results?

The chance of Jeffrey Appleton landing on a business trip to NY were probably slim, she thought. But being honest about it, she would love to spend time with him again, and gaze into his light brown, smiling eyes. Maybe even from the standpoint of being together in bed.

Ha, she thought, perhaps she was being as bad as her husband to think about such a thing, but this was new to her, not like Rick's long-standing secretive history.

Once making up her mind, she darted her fingers across the letters. *"That would be nice, and you can meet Millie."*

"I'm looking forward..."

She grinned at his pronouncement, and when she and Millie left the waterfront, they hustled back to the car with vitality to their steps.

CHAPTER 12

Her cell phone rang, and Dorothy Flores reached over from the brown ottoman where she sat. A round serving bowl sat on the floor in front of her, ready to catch any vomit she needed to upchuck.

"Hello? Sis?"

"Yes, it's me. Dorothy, you sound terrible. What's going on?'

"I'm worse, not better. Lying down is better for my stomach pain, but I'm stuck sitting up, just in case I need to vomit. This is terrible." She hunched over simply to alleviate the discomfort, but her abdomen stuck out farther than normal and felt hard.

"What the hell is your surgeon doing for you?" she asked, losing her temper.

"I haven't talked to him."

"I'm coming straight over. I just walked in from work, but I'll be there as soon as I can. I'm taking you to the emergency room."

Dorothy didn't resist her younger sister's suggestion, and waited with anticipation.

When she arrived, Marilyn used her own key to open the front door. She would have preferred to see her sister's kitchen strewn with dirty dishes but, instead, she found remnants of a person's illness—dirty wash cloths, soiled gauze pads, a used thermometer, and a pan with evidence of old vomit. A slight noise came from the living room, where Dorothy glanced up with surprise.

"Come on," Marilyn said, grabbing her sister under her armpits and hoisting her up. "Let me grab your purse with insurance information as I steer you to the door."

Marilyn situated her sister in the front passenger seat and placed the pan she had been using in her lap. She kept her mouth shut, not wanting to make her sister feel worse than she already did. They pulled into the region's only hospital, a tall tan building, with an impressive front entrance, but Marilyn veered around to the back ER entrance.

Parking at the curb, Marilyn popped out and grabbed a wheel chair from inside the door, and wheeled her sister into the registration desk. After parking her car, she went back in and sat beside her sister. The waiting game was on. Maybe a doctor would give her some answers. Why would a cosmetic surgery outside of Dorothy's abdominal cavity cause an upheaval in her well-being?

"Good evening," a male RN stated two hours later. He laid his eyes on Dorothy and Marilyn inside the room where the two women had finally settled.

"I wish so." Marilyn shook her head. "I understand people were here before us, and that the registration office must confirm a person's insurance coverage, but a patient could die out there waiting to be seen."

"Don't bark at him," Dorothy mumbled. "My issue stems from another medical facility, not this place."

"So true," Marilyn said. "I'm sorry young man."

The RNs name tag said "Bruce Wilson." He attached a blood pressure cuff around Dorothy's upper arm, and when he finished taking her vital signs, he patted her shoulder. "It is frustrating to wait outside, but we do our jobs as carefully and as methodically as we can. The doctor will be in shortly."

Soon enough, a Dr. Cantrell walked in wearing scrubs and a white jacket, as well as shadows under her eyes and large-rimmed glasses. She took her new patient's history, her face turning glummer by the minute, and examined her. Dorothy's pain worsened when the woman palpated her abdomen.

"First, we need to draw some labs, and while they're cooking, you need an X-ray of your abdomen. In the meantime, in the interest of time, I'm going to consult a general surgeon."

Dorothy narrowed her eyes. "What for?"

"Let me gather your study results, and then we'll talk."

Viktoria pulled into the garage, her escapade with Millie after work over, and noticed Rick's car. The walk downtown and by the water always invigorated her, and it was one of the few things she missed by not spending more time on Long Island.

More importantly, she carried a pleasant feeling after Jeffrey Appleton had contacted her. The memory of him, as well as the dog she had befriended while in Pennsylvania, was still plastered in her brain. She was not a person who smiled much for she was more of a serious person, but before she turned the door knob to enter the house, a glint of a smile crossed her lips.

Millie bounded into the house first, her docked Shepherd tail area moving as she raced in search of Rick. Viktoria opened the refrigerator and poured an iced tea while her husband came down the stairs.

"Hey," Rick said.

Viktoria pointed to the pitcher. "Can I pour you some?"

"Sure."

"Have you been working upstairs?"

"For a few hours. I received a tip that I may use some artwork from Georgia to put up with my next online auction."

Viktoria handed him the drink as Millie waited for his acknowledgment. Rick grinned and patted her head. He took the glass, but kept it on the counter.

"You doing any better after that GI upset yesterday?"

Rick twisted his mouth. "Still nauseous."

Viktoria stirred sugar in her tea, and set her eyes on him. His well-developed shoulders slumped as he ignored the dog. There were non-specific changes about him, she decided, and realized he was losing weight.

"Are you eating enough these days?"

He shrugged. "Why?"

"You look like you've thinned out, especially your face."

"I've had diarrhea along with the vomiting and, I agree. Perhaps I'm forgetting to eat."

"Forgetting or don't have an appetite?"

"Both."

"You don't believe in going to the doctor, and you don't see a primary care physician like I do, but you should go visit one."

"Alright. Tomorrow I'll set foot in one of those ambulatory places. See a doc-in-a-box."

His ready consent came as a surprise. Not only did he not make appointments with doctors, but he thought poorly of them. How the two of them married in the first place was a mystery to her.

But like his "addiction," she didn't know his true feelings about doctors and medicine when they courted. He thought her job as an anesthesiologist was awesome, and he respected the responsibility she carried of having someone's life in her hands while they were undergoing surgery. That was as far as it went.

"I'll hold you to it," Viktoria added.

Rick gave her a distinctive nod. In his mind, he made a snapshot of a sparse things-to-do list for the next day, and besides going to the immediate care center, he needed to meet his marijuana supplier for a supply refill—or he wouldn't be vaping in a few days.

The ER doctor yanked open the drapes. It was midnight, Marilyn's head drooped over, and she startled when a woman strutted in.

"Dorothy, I'm back," she said.

Dorothy opened her bleary eyes, but the light in the cubicle caused her to flutter her eyelids. At least Dr. Cantrell stood over her, and not a surgeon. She must be better than she thought. Maybe she could go back home.

"Ms. Flores," the ER doctor said, "the surgeon on call is swamped, but I consulted him an hour or two ago to see you. He should be here any minute. Your white blood cell count, which is an indicator of an infection, is high. You have a fever, your heartbeat is fast, and your X-ray shows air in your abdominal cavity. You have a gastrointestinal perforation and peritonitis."

Having evaluated Dorothy's ER chart, and stripping off an OR blue bonnet from his head, a man stepped in behind her. "I'm Dr. Woodson, may I join in?"

"I'll leave Ms. Flores to you," Dr. Cantrell said. "You can explain what needs to be done."

"I heard your update. Thanks."

Dorothy's heart rate sped up even more, the blood flow thumping rapidly in her wrist. Her eyelids no longer fluttered, but were wide open. "I don't understand what she just said."

"Apparently your abdomen was nicked open during that tummy tuck you had. Obviously, you're not supposed to have an open entrance into your abdominal cavity, so there is a blatant infection inside there. Your condition is serious. Peritonitis means that the entire covering of your organs inside, your stomach and intestines, are swollen and infected."

Marilyn reached her arm over, grabbed Dorothy's hand, and squeezed. Dorothy shot a glance at her sister, and crushed her hand longer.

"Am I going to die?" Dorothy asked.

Dr. Woodson shook his head, his kind eyes settling her nerves. "I need to bring you to the operating room because surgery is necessary to close the hole. Regardless, treating your condition will involve prescribing antibiotics. During the procedure, I may need to remove a piece of your small or large intestine which could result in a colostomy or ileostomy. We don't want to delay. A life-threatening bacterial infection called sepsis could ensue."

She didn't know what half of that meant. "It sounds like I could die. Please, Dr. Woodson, do what you must as soon as you can."

Dorothy signed papers the next half hour, many of which she didn't read. She mostly thought of one thing. All she did was try to look better, younger, and like magazine models, female newscasters, and weatherchannel women and own a flat stomach. What she'd done to herself was certainly not worth it.

But, what happened can't be normal or the usual outcome, she thought. That damn surgeon and Amour Cosmetic Surgery was to blame. Dr. Victor Reed with the engaging brown eyes punched a hole in her, a surgical mistake, and he hadn't given her the opportunity to talk to him or be examined by him afterwards.

They took her money and, so far, assumed no responsibility for the botched-up procedure they performed on her.

Marilyn sat at the bottom of her stretcher as they waited for her to be wheeled upstairs to the OR.

"Do you know any good lawyers?" Dorothy asked.

The anesthesiologist greeted Dorothy as medical personnel shifted her from the stretcher to the operating room table. Here she was again, going to be cut on, in less than a week. Okay, she thought, trying to be strong and adult-like, no big deal. It seemed like scrub and mask-clad people came at her from every direction, and she was soon wearing monitors`on her chest, and arm, and finger. A mask came down on her face, everything become a blur, and she went to sleep.

It seemed like seconds later that the anesthesiologist above her was waking her back up, but then she drifted back off to sleep. When she awoke the next time, she was in the recovery room. No one was in her cubicle, but voices sounded around her outside.

Dorothy was groggy, but realized that residual anesthesia and pain medicine were the cause. Her abdomen was sore, particularly in one spot, where it felt like something was sticking out of it. She shuddered and stared at the small opening in the drapes, both in anticipation of finding out how her surgery went.

She waited what seemed a half hour, and then the drape slid open and her short, compact surgeon with the kind eyes appeared.

"You definitely came into the ER in the nick of time. Your abdominal infection was simmering like a kettle of water on a stove. I needed to do a colostomy. That procedure allows intestinal contents to drain or empty into a bag attached to your abdominal wall."

Dorothy's eyes flew more open. Her fingers palpated across the sheet, touching her tender abdomen, and settled upon a bulky protrusion. She inched the sheet down and moved the hospital gown to the side. Horrified at the continued decimation of her skin color, now more purple, blue, and black than ever, she gasped.

Her lips trembled when her eyes settled on a plastic tube and the bag Dr. Woodson mentioned. Dorothy had no background in medicine, nor had she or a family member ever been involved in any significant medical problem, so laying her eyes on her belly terrorized her.

"Do I stay in the hospital with that thing? What am I supposed to do with it? You mean my food goes in and comes out in a bag?"

"No, you will go home, but we're keeping you here today until you are medically cleared. You will also receive detailed instructions about your colostomy bag." He sat on the chair beside her and pulled forward. "Basically, your stool will drain into the pouch."

"Oh, heavens! How gross. I went for plastic surgery to look fantastic and now the waste of my body is draining to my outside. This is unbelievable."

"I'm sorry this happened to you, Ms. Flores."

She wrinkled her face. "It's not your fault."

"Once the nurse starts giving you care instructions, you'll hear the term 'stoma.' That is the opening from your abdominal wall, where I stitched the edges of your colon to your skin. The team will answer all your questions. You can invite your sister to learn about these matters as well. She's very worried about you."

"Thank goodness for Marilyn. I would be lost and alone in all this if it were not for her. One good friend or one close sister is worth a thousand so-called friends."

"I will swing by on rounds later today."

"I'm better off staying here, I suppose."

Dr. Woodson left, but not before giving her a pat on her shoulder. Maybe she could grab some sleep in a hospital room, she thought. After all, it was morning; her surgery had been an emergency during the night. She watched the IV bag above drip into the chamber and the fluids move into the catheter in her forearm. Her eyes weren't twinkling like usual, and she snarled her lip thinking about the cut-rate price of $3,500 Amour Cosmetic Surgery had charged her for a "tummy tuck."

Her tummy tuck had cost her a lot more than that.

CHAPTER 13

The two curly-headed sisters sat in Dorothy's room with a TV weather briefing repeating the same northeast weather pattern over and over again.

"Guess the cloudiness is here to stay for a day or two," Marilyn said, "but I don't need that information hammered into my head."

"Those meteorologists can't control the weather. It's better they aren't reporting tornadoes, floods, or hurricanes."

"Yes, sister, you are right. I'll shut up. I can't help but be livid about what happened to you. You asked me if I knew any good attorneys, so here we go." She rummaged through her purse for her cell phone and placed a call.

"Stewart and Klein," the voice said on the line.

Marilyn put the call on speaker. "Jonathan Stewart, please."

"Just a moment."

The call was transferred and a loud, deep voice came on. Dorothy watched the antibiotic dripping through the chamber going into her arm, but heard the voice on the speaker.

"Mr. Stewart, this is Marilyn Flores. You handled a small matter for me a year ago."

"Successfully, I believe. What can I do for you?"

"I'm sitting in a hospital room because my sister got butchered by a plastic surgeon, is having complications, and she couldn't even reach them after surgery to ask for help. Can you handle this as a case?"

The small, impeccably dressed man swiveled around to his one-cup coffee maker and didn't miss a beat. "My secretary has blocked in a lunchtime for me today. Why don't I use it to gather all the needed information, in person? Someone needs to pay for your poor sister's predicament."

"Mr. Stewart, thank you so much."

Marilyn gave him the hospital's name and room number and hung up. "We're in business. He is a cut-throat, stubbornly determined attorney, who hates it when someone is blatantly wronged. Wait till you see the dogged determination he'll have against Dr. Reed at Amour."

"He sounds fine, or perfect, but I'm not in it for the money. I just want my life back."

"When your life gets back on track, you'll be a lot happier with a truckload of money in your bank account. Which is what you deserve."

Seeing the last antibiotic drip drop into the chamber, she nodded. "So true, I'll have this behind me before I know it, but Victor Reed won't get off the hook faster than me."

"There you go, sis, and unless Stewart settles your upcoming lawsuit quickly, Reed will be dealing with it for some time."

"My beautiful girl," Viktoria said, holding Millie's snout in her hand. She opened the back door, the dog sprinted into the backyard, and she turned to pour her first cup of coffee for the morning.

Having looked at the printed schedule for Friday from the day before, Viktoria knew her first patient this morning was Bonnie Sandler, back for breast implants after her forehead lift on Monday. She had gotten a kick out of the forty-eight year-old divorced mother of two because she still wanted so much to plunge back into the dating scene. Looking like a younger version of herself, or like a beauty queen, was the woman's objective.

Although Amour was running a price discount on implants, Viktoria still wondered how her patient drummed up the money for surgery, especially since medical insurance wouldn't cover it.

She took a sip of the hot coffee blend while Millie's little face peeked through the door window. Letting the dog in, the little Shepherd pranced excitedly across the hardwood floor looking for her breakfast. As Viktoria set it down, she heard water running in the back bedroom.

"Bye, Millie. Enjoy that breakfast. You are all set for now. She glanced at the back, but Rick was still in the bathroom.

Taking her coffee to the car, she doubted her husband would skip going to the doctor in the next few hours. Marijuana couldn't be very pleasurable right now with a GI bug going on, but she doubted he'd spent the last few days without smoking it.

She didn't know where the week had flown when she pulled into the Long Island parking lot. Although she loved practicing anesthesia with a passion, her dislike for Amour Cosmetic Surgery had grown.

The issues which had popped up during the week, and from what she had learned on her own, made her leery of the professional credibility of the place, as well as some medical and business staff working there. Sometimes she thought working locums was a blessing in disguise. She did not need to return to a place ever again, or she could repeatedly rebook a medical facility she liked.

Amour Cosmetic Surgery was one place to cross off her future work schedule, she thought, as she stepped out into a brisk breeze which emanated over from the Long Island Sound. She hurried past the bushes and bench and into the front door.

"Morning, Lucy," she said. "Morning, Rigoberto." They nodded back to her from the front desk as Dr. Castillo slipped an OR bonnet on his head.

"Your first patient is in the holding area," he said.

"Thanks. Nothing like a repeat customer."

"Yes, and if you had not given her an excellent anesthetic, I'm sure she would not be redoing a procedure with us."

"Thanks, but I'm sure Dr. Pinto contributed to her satisfaction."

"Dr. Pinto does a wonderful job," Lucy chimed in. "I always say that anesthesia is the appetizer and the surgery is the entrée to a fabulous meal."

Viktoria chuckled. She slipped into the dressing room, put on scrubs, and went to preop holding to evaluate Bonnie Sandler.

"Dr. Thorsdottir," Bonnie said. "I asked the staff if you were here yet. You're putting me to sleep again like I requested, right?"

"Yes, I will, but I will change it up a bit for today's longer surgery."

"My oldest son, Andrew, was able to come with me today." She pointed to an earthy, tanned man wearing short boots. His strong, weathered hand extended for a handshake.

Viktoria grasped his hand. "Your mom is going to appreciate you driving her home."

"Both my boys are loves," Bonnie added. "Knowing how much I wanted this surgery, they coughed up the money for me. This is a weird surgery for sons to pay for, but that's how considerate they are to me." A watery film gathered in her eyes, and she rubbed one of them with the top of the sheet.

"How lovely, and your forehead looks quite remarkable after your plastic surgery lift. It is healing quite nicely."

Even Ms. Sandler's freckles seemed to smile as her lips broadened into a wide grin. "I agree, and I can't wait for today's results too."

"She's like a little kid," Andrew said, shaking his head. "You'd think she was gifted a hefty Amazon gift card to do with as she pleases."

"You have made her happy, and I am delighted to take care of her again."

"Dr. Thorsdottier, you would not understand because your figure is a lot nicer than mine. Getting this surgery will help boost my self-esteem which, I'm sure, is not as high as yours, being a doctor and all. People call it a 'boob job,' but I don't care. My new chest will be my secret as well as my family's, and it's going to make me feel sexier."

Viktoria smiled. "Then I am happy you are getting the implants sooner than later. Now, let me refresh my memory from last Monday and look at your anesthesia and surgical record."

Viktoria read the previous preanesthetic and remembered Bonnie's clean bill of health, and her allergy and family history—her reaction to some 'penicillin,' and her dad having an early-aged, lethal heart attack. She also checked over her intraoperative record. The case had gone smoothly.

She looked over at Bonnie, in her hospital gown and tucked under a sheet, except for one arm where her IV was in place. The red highlights in her hair shined like they'd been rubbed with a glistening oil. Viktoria reached in a box on the shelf behind the stretcher, handed her patient a head bonnet, and Bonnie slid it on.

"Has any of your medical history changed this week? Any new medications?"

"No, and I didn't take any of those pain pills Dr. Pinto prescribed for me. I didn't need them."

"When did you last eat or drink?"

"Last evening. Nothing since then."

"Excellent. This time, since your surgery will be longer, I will put a breathing tube in your windpipe after I put you to sleep."

Bonnie gave her a thumbs up signal as the curtain parted and Ernest Pinto appeared. He nodded towards each of them.

"Ready for your final transformation?" he asked Bonnie in his low monotone voice.

"Yes. More than ready, and I can't thank you all enough." She reached over to Andrew and squeezed his hand. "But, for some reason, I'm a bit nervous. More than last time."

"I will take care of that now," Viktoria said, pulling out a syringe of midazolam. "Anything else you need to talk to her about?" Viktoria asked Ernest.

"No." He focused on Bonnie. "Next time you see me, you will be a more stunning red head—more beautiful than Dolly Parton, and sized more appropriately."

Viktoria injected one cc of midazolam to let Bonnie relax, an orderly came in, unlocked the foot pedal, and wheeled her back to the OR.

The quietness of the OR ceased once Viktoria hooked Bonnie up to the monitors and her heartbeat pranced across the EKG machine with a steady rhythm. Her patient intermittently opened her eyes to look around, but closed them once the oxygen mask was placed over her nose and mouth.

"Pick out a fun dream," Viktoria said, "and we'll see you in the recovery room." She injected a cc of fentanyl, the white anesthetic induction agent, propofol, and then manually breathed for her patient when she went to sleep. After following with an IV muscle relaxant, she opened Bonnie's mouth with a laryngoscope, and inserted a breathing tube into her trachea.

As she listened to her patient's breath sounds to make sure the tube was in the correct place, she second-guessed her decision to use an endotracheal tube versus the laryngeal mask airway she had used for her patient's forehead lift earlier in the week. It struck her that surgical cases at Amour Cosmetic Surgery seemed to take a lot less time than the same procedures elsewhere.

Dr. Pinto pushed open the OR doors. After being gowned and gloved, he stepped to the table. "This won't take long. Let me see the implants she selected."

Across from him, the gloved and gowned tech handed him one from the overlying tray table. His beady eyes glued onto the object in his hands, and he rolled it around in his hands.

"The other one." He handed it back to her, and she slipped him the second one.

He evaluated the implant, making sure it was without defects. Viktoria thought that a smart move.

Ernest chuckled. "I should put a squeaky toy in every breast implant."

"Oh my God," the tech said. "That's hilarious.

"Some guy making love to her would have a canary if he massaged her breasts," Dr. Pinto added.

Viktoria continued catching up with her chart work and watching over the drapes. Sometimes OR humor, she knew, gets carried away.

But, she thought, what happens or gets said in the OR, stays in the OR.

Ernest made his incision, starting with the left breast.

"Did you want Ms. Sandler to have a presurgical antibiotic?" Viktoria asked.

His hands worked fast. "Not at the moment," he quipped. "I have quite a few of these augments in this room today, so let's keep this assembly line moving."

"I noticed that. My turnover will be quick too."

"At least you have the anesthesia tech to help freshen up your cart with new materials for your next case. Lola needs to be snappy, or she'd be out of here."

The poor pregnant tech, Viktoria thought. Hopefully they weren't making her job harder than it should be. "I am curious how the center keeps afloat. After all, the surgeries here seem to be dirt cheap compared to most cosmetic centers."

"Dr. Castillo learned a long time ago. This business runs on quantity or volume."

"Quantity versus quality?"

"I never said that. And there's incentive for a doctor like me. Castillo makes ends meet by hiring doctors willing to work on commission. I receive thirty percent of the business that I generate."

Viktoria rose from her stool and put her clipboard on top of the cart. Rigoberto Castillo's business methods were different. She adjusted the anesthetic gas, the sevoflurane vaporizer, upwards, and pondered Ernest's total statement—all of it disconcerting. What did he mean by "a doctor like me?"

"Well, at least Bonnie was satisfied with the forehead lift that you did."

He beamed over the drapes at her. "Have you seen me whip through those butt lifts?"

Now he really had her attention. She had not done the anesthesia for what was called a "Brazilian butt lift" all week, but one thing was for certain, they were considered the most dangerous procedures in cosmetic surgery.

"You set a record last week," the tech said.

Ernest straightened his posture. "Twenty five in five days."

"I accidentally overheard Lucy say your commission last week rounded out to thirty-three thousand dollars doing those. Because of one week, you could buy a nice new car."

"I already have one. I may take a trip to Vegas one of these days. Maybe I can double my money."

"That's what gamblers think. Don't do that. You can put it to more philanthropic causes and buy *me* a new car."

He waved off the tech's comment, picked up the electrocautery, and stopped some bleeding from Bonnie's left breast.

CHAPTER 14

For some reason, Bonnie's vital signs were more labile during the case than during her last surgery and anesthetic. Of course, the breast augment was a lot more painful than a forehead lift. Viktoria carefully adjusted the woman's anesthetic needs as she mulled over what she'd previously read about the "Brazilian butt lift." Without a doubt, before her assignment ended at Amour, she would be in one of those cases since they did so many of them.

The rear-end lifts were one of the fastest-growing plastic surgeries in the United States. Driven by a pop culture fad, movie stars, TV celebrities, and rap stars, they had caused a tsunami of desire for the procedure which augments the shape and size of the buttocks without implants.

Viktoria contracted her brow, not understanding how someone could do that to themselves. Basically, it was a fat-transfer procedure. Surgeons removed fat from areas of the patient—their hips, abdomen, lower back, or thighs—and strategically injected it into their buttocks. The liposuction procedure entailed using a long, thin tube to suction fat out and then inject it into the buttocks to enlarge them.

She thought that living in Iceland as a child must have been another planet because, there, women didn't desire big butts!

What people did to their bodies was constantly surprising her in the United States, but this potentially perilous procedure carried an estimated death rate of one in three-thousand operations. Someone may be one of the two-thousand nine-hundred-ninety-nine patients, but if you are the 'one' patient, then your chances of death were one-hundred percent. Not good, not good at all.

Luckily, safe procedures were being done around the country in the hands of well-trained physicians, but the problems arose if doctors accidentally injected the fat they procured from somewhere else and injected it into muscle instead, and accidentally tore open a vein.

Once a vein tear occurred, the fat injected would be carried along the vessels to the heart and lungs where a deadly blockage could ensue. Even lay persons have heard of embolisms. One of those racing straight for your lungs, a pulmonary embolism, could be deadly!

Being a totally non-needed, non-medical procedure, why would anyone electively undergo a procedure subjecting themselves to the potential for death? Albeit, maybe the risk was small, but it still made no sense to her at all. Why play Russian roulette with your own life?

Viktoria sighed as an OR door swung open and an older man walked in, weaved around the cords in the back of the anesthesia equipment, and introduced himself.

"I'm Mick, one of the permanent anesthesiologists who work here." The older man's OR cap sat flat over his bald head, and his mouth was a string of dental implants underneath his mask. "Hope you're enjoying your stint with us. Dr. Castillo sent me in to give you a break."

"Thanks. We have not had the pleasure, so I'm pleased to meet you." Viktoria nodded towards the surgical field. "This is Bonnie Sandler, obviously undergoing breast augmentation. This is the happiest person I've ever met to undergo a procedure."

Mick shrugged. "That is one reason I love doing anesthesia here. The patients are so happy coming in here. It's not like being in a hospital OR and dealing with people undergoing procedures for medical illnesses, broken bones, traumatic car accidents, or whatever."

"You are spot-on about that," Ernest interjected. "They are a different breed, these frequent fliers having these operations. Do you know what the infamously famous Dolly said about implants?"

"You've told me," Mick said. "It costs a lot of money to look this cheap."

"She should know," Viktoria said, "but I love that woman's philanthropic nature." She deviated the conversation to Bonnie and gave Mick a full report for him to handle the anesthetic.

The man sat on the stool and rubbed his knee as Viktoria slipped out. The coffee pot in the kitchen was almost full, and Rigoberto's beaked nose was pointed into the wide-brimmed mug he had raised to his lips. He sat at the table, and looked up.

"Dr. Thorsdottir, take a seat. Coffee's fresh."

"Thanks for the prompt break." She helped herself and positioned herself across from him. "You sure gave Bonnie Sandler a surgery discount she and her sons couldn't refuse."

"I aim to please, but I also need to pay salaries, and utility bills, and taxes, so part of the secret is to not have any 'down' OR time. I throw out the cheap prices like bread crumbs to a flock of birds. The patients, well, they look at themselves—and if something is saggin', baggin', or draggin', they're gonna have it nipped, tucked, or sucked!"

"I understand. One thing that bothers me about medicine is that the docs who create long-term relationships and detailed care to their patients—the primary care and internal medicine doctors—earn less and less these days. I also know obstetricians who closed their doors, given up their practices, and could not make ends meet. It's a shame. I wish the tide would turn *for them.*"

"You are a smart woman to go into anesthesia. Your field has expanded to areas outside the OR, such as GI suites doing colonoscopies, X-ray departments where sedation or general anesthetics are needed, and cardiac procedure rooms. All of us can't do without you people."

"So true. Seems like you have a long-term employee with Mick. Where did he do his residency?"

"Are you kidding? That was a long time ago. I don't remember his educational background or work history at all. He's an old timer, and he is capable of making mistakes."

"He may have known old providers that used open drop techniques, ether, or the Copper Kettle. Anesthesia has come a long way. It would be nice to pick his brain some day."

He reached over to a name-brand box and pulled out a white dusted donut. "Doubt if he would give you a history lesson. He's jumped around before in his career."

"There are doctors who do that, just like in everything else. Sometimes people don't know what they want to do in life. Or they are on an unremitting search to find the perfect job which doesn't exist."

Rigoberto wiped the edges of his small mouth, and chewed in a hurry. "Better get back to my case. I really needed to step out, and they are waiting on me. Take a fifteen-minute break, not ten. Make use of Mick's presence today. Sometimes, breaks can be few and far between."

"Since I'm going to sample one of these donuts, don't mind if I do." Watching him leave, she shook her head. It was not the norm for a surgeon to leave his ongoing surgery for a cup of coffee. Their breaks came between cases while anesthesia was waking their patient up, or wheeling them to the recovery room, or while their next patient's case was being readied in the preop holding area.

Viktoria relished the freshness of the fried dough and then texted Rick. *"Don't forget to go to the doctor today,"* she wrote.

"I still plan on going," Rick responded. *"Getting ready now. My GI symptoms are slowing me down, but I may have also developed a cold. I'm coughing a lot."*

Viktoria bit her lip. For someone who manages his own work hours and takes time for himself, her husband was presently not the epitome of health.

"Keep me posted."

Viktoria swallowed the last bite and, after using the rest room, went back to her case. Mick stood with an expression of disgust on his face.

"Well," Dr. Pinto said, "can I get on with it? I don't have all day."

"Go ahead." Mick cranked up the sevoflurane vaporizer as Viktoria stepped between the anesthesia machines and the head of the table. The two anesthesia providers bumped shoulders as she gasped at Bonnie's blood pressure.

"One-hundred-ninety over one-hundred-ten? What's going on here? She's going to stroke with pressures like that." She reached for a syringe with a vasodilator to bring down Bonnie's pressure.

"No," Mick said. "I just gave her neosynephrine to bring her pressure *up*. That's why she's so high. I kept giving her a cc at a time, and she didn't respond. But she finally responded."

"Why? How hypotensive was she and why did her pressure plummet?"

"It was pretty low," the tech inserted. "I saw seventy over thirty."

Viktoria gulped. Her patient's roller coaster blood pressures were dangerous. She wished she had never left the room. A break wasn't worth it if someone's well-being became jeopardized.

She stared at the monitors. Before rushing to further IV medications to swing her patient's pressure one way or another, she needed to get to the bottom of the problem, to diagnose the original insult or cause.

Bonnie's pressure started to inch down and Viktoria cranked back the high amount of inhalation anesthetic Mick had instituted. She peered over the drapes, but nothing seemed amiss at the surgical site. Making sure, she said, "Dr. Pinto, are there any problems from your end? No nicks, punctures, or excessive bleeding while I was gone?"

"No. This is ticking along like clock work, or breast work." He chuckled and hung back his hand, waiting for her okay to start again.

She glanced up at a small empty bag next to the liter bag of normal IV fluids, and took it off the pole to read the label. "What? You gave her this class of antibiotics? She's allergic to Penicillin."

"Dr. Pinto ordered it given."

"But he probably didn't recall her drug allergy. That is your, or our, ultimate responsibility. Ms. Sandler did not mention a *possible* allergy in her preanesthetic evaluation. Her reaction was clear cut—she had to visit a medical facility for treatment because she experienced shortness of breath."

"Okay, my mistake. I don't remember you telling me though."

"I sure did tell you. I presume her blood pressure first bottomed out after the drug infusion began, and being hypotensive, you treated her with neosynephrine instead of stopping the IV drip. Then she went sky-high because you kept giving it to her." Viktoria shook her head. She rarely became angry enough to feel her blood boil, but it was simmering.

"You two stop arguing," Ernest said. "I'm hurrying and will be done here in a jiffy. After all, my next patient is waiting. And I haven't even met her yet." Thinking that funny, he laughed again.

Viktoria threw her head back in disgust. "All right, Mick, I'll take it from here. I think you should take a break yourself."

Her break provider pursed his lips over his dental implants and slunk out of the room.

After suturing up Bonnie's right breast, and both implants securely in place, Dr. Pinto snapped off his gloves and faced the door. Knowing that Rigoberto was letting him 'flip-flop' OR rooms for the bounty of surgical cases on his schedule for the day, he said, "Off to my next patient in another room. See you all back here for the patient after that."

Viktoria concentrated on her patient. After backing off on the anesthesia, she evaluated Bonnie off the ventilator, and she began breathing on her own. Although she didn't wake up, her breathing and vital signs were stable as they unhooked her from the monitors and the orderly slid a stretcher next to the table. On the count of three, they moved her over.

Viktoria helped steer from the top, her anesthetic paperwork tucked under the pillow, and the OR doors closed behind them. As they wheeled her to the recovery room, Bonnie suddenly clenched her fist. Her right arm went up and rubbed her left arm, and then it shot to the left side of her chest. A large moan came out of her mouth, and she opened her eyes.

Barely awake, she slightly lifted herself up on the gurney.

"Bonnie, what is it?" Viktoria asked.

Ms. Sandler wailed in apparent pain. She collapsed back down on the stretcher, and her eyes shut tight. Too tight.

"Hurry," Viktoria said, urging them through the recovery room doors. A nurse waved them over to an empty slot, but it was too far away for Viktoria's liking. She swung the stretcher to the first empty space with monitors.

In rapid succession, she applied a blood pressure cuff, while the recovery room nurse came over to help. The EKG machine was hooked up to the existing pads on Bonnie's skin, and the pulse oximeter was applied. Viktoria had her fingers pressed against her patient's carotid artery in her neck and found no pulse.

"Where's respiratory therapy?" she yelled. The EKG above confirmed her worst fear. No identifiable P waves, QRS complexes, or T waves pranced across the screen, and her patient's bizarre rhythm was erratic, up to five-hundred beats per minute.

"She's in ventricular fibrillation. Get the crash cart!"

Viktoria set herself up at the head of the bed and attended to Bonnie's airway, giving her the breaths she needed with an Ambu bag. With each succeeding second, she agonized over her patient knowing her ventricles were not contracting in a synchronized manner. Which mean she effectively had no cardiac output—no blood pumping to all her organs with life saving oxygen to support life. Right now, her heart inside her quivered like a dying mass of jellyfish.

Never before was Viktoria so happy to see an anesthesia tech. Lola jostled the red cart with needed supplies next to the stretcher. The pregnant woman panted and pushed her round glasses up over an expression of fear.

"Paddles!"

Viktoria grabbed the two paddles from Lola's hands and placed them on Bonnie's chest.

"Clear," Viktoria warned them as she delivered a dose of electric current to her patient. She held her breath, wanting the depolarized heart muscle to end the dysrhythmia, hoping the heart's sinoatrial node would reestablish a normal sinus rhythm. But the EKG showed otherwise.

"Clear!" Again, she applied a current, this time higher. Her own heart squeezed tight in her chest, adrenaline soaring in her bloodstream, panic-striken over her patient's fate.

The defibrillation of Bonnie's heart did nothing.

She remained unconscious and without a pulse.

CHAPTER 15

Never before did Viktoria work so hard at a code. Resorting to advanced cardiac life support drugs from the crash cart, she injected one medication after the other. Someone helped with Bonnie's airway, pumping oxygen into her lungs, but it was obvious that the staff at Amour Cosmetic Surgery rarely, if ever, dealt with such a problem. Worse than that, she believed, the personnel rarely did practice drills, or kept current with ACLS, and didn't know how to deal with botched up, bad-outcome cases—when a patient's heart flips into a deadly rhythm.

She put an empty epinephrine syringe on the top of the cart. An orderly and a recovery room nurse huddled against the wall, while Lola stood waiting to help in any way she could. The EKG tracing was now a flat line, and Viktoria sadly put her fingers on her patient's absent carotid pulse, and gently put her fingertips on Bonnie's eyelids, making sure they were fully closed.

Taking a big breath, Viktoria needed to replenish her own oxygen. She squeezed her eyes shut, now ready to 'call it.' How fatal, how final, how non-retractable. As she glanced at the wall clock, she hated every word she needed to say.

"I'm calling it. Time of death nine-fifty-three."

Viktoria relied on the recovery room nurse and Lola to gather up the papers she needed to immediately sign. Ernest Pinto, as well as Rigoberto Castillo, were in the OR and no other doctors or anesthesia personnel were around.

As she signed her signature on two forms, waves of disgust swept over her. Sadness, anger, and denial gripped her, and she fought with her brain, against her feelings, to keep going and now do the demanding task of informing family. Although knowledge of the commotion must have filtered back into the OR and up to the front desk, she nevertheless needed to tell Ernest Pinto and Lucy Murray herself.

Viktoria slipped behind the front desk and crouched down. Before she could say anything, Lucy said, "Yes, I know. Bonnie Sandler."

"Legally, she'll need an autopsy whether or not the family consents."

"I'm sure he will be the first one requesting it." She crunched up her face as she peered at the son in the waiting room, his brown boot impatiently swinging from his crossed leg. "I'll call the hospital right now."

"Leave word I want to meet the pathologist and be present when he or she does the autopsy."

With quick steps, she slipped up her OR mask, and pushed open the OR doors to Room 2. Dr. Pinto jerked his head up. "What on earth did you do? Something indefensible? Or did that woman just get up and have a heart attack on our watch?"

"Dr. Pinto, it is almost impossible to die in the presence of an anesthesiologist. And that includes patients under my care."

She scrutinized the plump implant bulging from his patient's half-sutured right breast. The tech waited for the surgeon to take the bovie cautery, and Ernest wiggled his head.

"Are you saying her death had something to do with me?"

"There is no room for a blame game, especially since an autopsy is needed. Please, at the moment, let's concentrate on her son in the waiting room. I will ask Andrew Sandler into the little room where patients pick out their implant size."

She waited for him to offer a suggestion. "I don't think he should wait for you to finish here," she said. "I will break him the news if you would like."

Without hesitation, Dr. Pinto nodded. "You were there, so better if you talk to him first. I will follow when I'm finished."

"By the way, Lucy is making the call. Your patient should be going to the morgue shortly."

She shifted towards the door. "I hate when this happens," she heard him mumble.

Seeing her next patient would have to wait. Dealing with deviations in a hectic OR schedule always posed a problem. Time for unforeseen problems was not entered into the planning for the day. They were disruptive for everyone, and delayed patients waiting for their cases to start and caused 'down' time and non-income earning operating room time, and a host of other troubles—particularly for this business called "Amour

Cosmetic Surgery."

Viktoria tossed her OR mask into the garbage behind the front desk. "Try not to take too long with him," Lucy said.

As usual, the waiting room was busy. Women glared at magazines with pictures of near perfect looking human beings who lived lifestyles which pampered their shape, skin and hair texture. She wondered if those models ever walked a grueling hike, or if they lived in a bubble.

As Viktoria stepped his way, and Andrew suspected his mother's surgery was over, he rose from the chair and moved forward.

"Come with me," she said softly.

The door to the tiny conference room was open, and she pointed inside.

"Isn't my mother's surgery finished?" he asked. "Can I see her in the recovery room?"

Viktoria swallowed so hard, she almost choked. "Please, sit."

The twenty-seven-year old sank into the leather love seat, but leaned his elbows on his knees. She took the chair forty-five degrees to him and sat on the edge.

"Andrew, the news I bear is the worst. Your mom did not make it through her surgery."

The young man stared at her with a blank expression. "What do you mean? Dr. Pinto had to stop? She didn't get her implants?"

"She passed away—after her case was finished."

His stillness was eerie, not a muscle moved in his body. In slow-motion, his eyelids rose, and his pupils dilated.

"No way. She's not sick. You're kidding. Right?"

"More than anything, I wish I were." She waited for him to digest what she said. Any information she gave him now would be useless unless he gripped the fact that his mother had died.

"No. You must mean someone else. My mom is Bonnie Sandler, and she's healthy. She had a forehead lift done here and is now following up with breast implants. Her surgeon is Ernest Pinto, and she requested you to do…"

He stopped. Dr. Thorsdottir was his mother's anesthesiologist because Bonnie had made sure of it. If anyone should know about her well-being, it should be the doctor sitting next to him.

Andrew inhaled a deep, quick breath as if it would stem the tide of the painful reality. His heart made a hard thump against his chest, and he squeezed his hands together.

"You mean it. My mother is dead?"

"Yes, Andrew. I am so sorry. We are all sorry. She became unstable on the way to the recovery room. We worked on reviving her for some time, but it was to no avail. I cannot tell you what caused her demise, because I am as shocked and befuddled as you are. An autopsy should tell us the cause of death."

She had seen it before. He was listening to her, but he would probably not remember a word. The news was too traumatic. If she were in his shoes, it would be no different.

Staring at the four silver-colored boxes on the table, Andrew lifted the lid of the closest one. A sample breast implant lay in the contoured bottom box, and he shook his head. "Because of this," he mumbled.

Leaving the cover off, he squared his shoulders. "I need to see her."

"Come, before EMS takes her away."

Viktoria rose and he mirrored her steps to the recovery room. She hoped Bonnie was exactly as she had left her. Simultaneously, the door to the waiting room opened and two EMS workers with a stretcher closed in.

"Fellas, hang back for a moment," she said when they arrived. With a light touch, she guided Andrew to the stretcher which had been moved against the back wall. Two patients stared with concern, and a nurse swung the drapes shut on both of their cubicles.

She stood beside Andrew and the stretcher, and folded the white sheet down to Bonnie's neck. Viktoria could think of no worse time ever in her career than to introduce a young man to his mother whom he'd been with a few short hours ago, never said good-bye to, and would never spend time with again in his entire life. Her upper chest felt so heavy, it was as if her heart was in her throat.

Andrew flinched. It was true. He placed his hand over his mother's forehead as if checking if she had a fever. Resting both elbows on the stretcher rail, he leaned in. First, his lips pressed her cheek, and then he dropped his head into the nook of her neck.

As ten seconds seemed like an eternity, he began to sob.

If Viktoria had learned anything, heartache was painful. Under normal situations of death, that was true, but what had happened this morning at Amour Cosmetic Surgery was beyond natural. If his sobbing turned into a tsunami of tears, she would understand. More than that, however, she was worried that soon enough, his anger would be far greater than his grief.

Bonnie's older son finally peeled himself away from his mother and Viktoria slid the sheet back up. The male and female paramedic stepped up, gave her eye contact, and Viktoria nodded.

"Andrew, they are going to take your mom over to the morgue." She gently placed her hand on his arm, and a paramedic handed him a form to sign.

"I'm bringing Mr. Sandler over to the consultation room," Viktoria told the paramedics. "Stop by there on your way out."

Andrew sat on one of the single chairs in the room and Viktoria went to fetch him something to drink. She poured a cup of coffee in the kitchen, and set it down in front of him with packets of sugar and creamers. "Andrew, I will leave you alone now. EMS will be by before they leave and Dr. Pinto will stop in as soon as he can. Is that okay?"

His eyes moist, and in a stupor, he nodded. Before her two steps to the door, he was pulling out his cell phone. He needed to place the worst phone call of his life.

Rick definitely had some stomach bug that was rolling around in his stomach, causing his discomfort, and GI symptoms which made him cringe. However, like he had discussed with Viktoria the day before, the cough which caused him to hack like an old man with a repugnant cigar between his lips, bothered him more. Now, not only did he rush to sit on the toilet a lot, but then he sat there trying to cough up material from his lungs which didn't exist. Or did it? He didn't know what was going on with him.

For once in his adult life, he wouldn't mind seeing a doctor. The walk-in fast-paced clinic was close by, and he had promised Viktoria. He poured a fresh cup of coffee into his favorite ceramic mug, grabbed his vaping products, and waved at Millie to follow him out the door.

Frequent rain had allowed the backyard grass to spring up, he thought, and it could use a mowing at the end of the season. He took a seat on the bench against the house, and readied his marijuana. Frowning, he remembered his therapy session booked for today on the calendar. Perhaps he could skip. After all, he was sick.

Millie whisked her tail stump as she raced forward and studied the corners of the yard for a fresh place to pee. After that, she found her hollow rubber ball with holes in it, trotted to Rick, and shoved it into his lap. She backed up and barked.

"Damn it," Millie. "I don't have all day to play with you. Knock it off."

Twisting his mouth with contempt that Viktoria had brought the dog home to live with them, he threw the ball to get rid of her, and focused on the weed ready for his 'consumption.'

Which was the word he used in his thoughts. A day was not full or whole if he didn't consume the psychoactive substance. As sure as sitting on the bench and being alive, his dependence on hemp was complete, and no one could convince him that he could 'give up' his addiction.

Lucky for him, his brain buzzed with pleasure by the time he jerked up and rushed inside to go to the bathroom. His mug and paraphernalia still on the bench, he slammed the door closed behind him.

Rick finished his emergent need. Rain was predicted during the day, so he grabbed a thin nylon jacket, went to the garage, and started his Mazda. The doc-in-a-box was located between the house and Harbour Village, and he soon pulled into the parking lot. He should have stopped for a late breakfast, he thought, wanting to satisfy the 'munchies,' he now desired. Better yet, he decided to go to "Captain's on the Water" after seeing the doctor, and eat crab cakes like he and Viktoria had done when they first met. There were still good memories there.

He walked in and found only one middle-aged woman sitting in the miniature waiting room. At the desk, he signed in on a sheet, as if the long paper would be full of names by the end of the day.

The sliding glass window opened. "You want to see a medical person?" a woman with thick glasses and thin lips asked.

"I think that's why I'm here."

"I need to see your insurance cards," she snapped back at the wise-cracker of a man.

Rick produced his card and soon a young woman tightened a blood pressure cuff around his right arm and left him to sit on a paper covered exam table.

The door squeaked open and a Doogie Howser looking fellow walked in. If Rick had kids, he imagined them to be the same age as the youngster in front of him.

"I'm Tim Stone" he said. "What brought you in today, Mr. Richter?"

"Are you a doctor?"

"Physician's assistant."

Rick didn't care who saw him. All he wanted was to leave with an antibiotic. "I'm here for two different problems."

"And what may they be?"

"My GI tract is in an uproar and my chest is in an upheaval."

Ready to hear more, the young man sat on the stool. "Maybe the two problems stem from the same thing. Tell me what's been going on."

CHAPTER 16

The P.A., Tim Stone, washed his hands over the sink after examining Rick.

"We have the ability to run minor X-rays here," he said, "but I'm afraid our tech called in sick today. I'm sending you over to the hospital with an order for a chest X-ray."

· Rick leaned back on the palms of his hands. "Is that really necessary?"

"Mr. Richter, you are here for answers, aren't you?"

"No, I'm here for treatment."

"Treatment comes after a clear understanding of the problem."

"You sound like my wife."

"Smart lady."

"She's a doctor, which leaves a big divide between us."

Tim had no desire to listen to the man's personal problems, so wrote out an order, and handed it to him.

"Come back. I will call the radiologist for the results. He treats me well when my tech is out."

Tim left and Rick grabbed his T-shirt and slipped it on. Sounded to him like the clinic ran on a shoestring. His gut rumbled and both sides of his chest felt full. He took his cell phone out of his pocket, slipped on his trousers, and stilled where he stood. A strong sense of foreboding crept through his body.

In his mind, there was no explanation for it. He punched contacts on his phone and placed a call to his psychologist, Paula Spinner.

"Hello," her soft voice said.

"Dr. Spinner, this is Rick Richter."

"I am between patients, Mr. Richter. What can I do for you? Will you be making our appointment later in the day?"

"No. I don't think so. I am quitting my visits with you as well as the group discussions. Nothing personal."

Silence crowded the few miles between them. "Why? Your decision is disconcerting to me."

"I don't need therapy. Plus, medically, I don't feel great."

The slender woman stood from her desk and peeked between the blinds. "I'm sorry to hear that. If you change your mind, you know where to find me." She hung up. During her career, she always wondered what was worse—the people who never sought help, or the ones who did, and then sank back into muddy waters thinking they could overcome their problems by themselves.

Rick cinched his belt, stuffed the piece of paper in his pocket, and shortly arrived at the entrance to the hospital. He bought a water bottle from a machine and was told to wait in the lobby, which he considered a ridiculous thing to do—to register in the hospital for an outpatient procedure in the X-ray department. Being asked to do that seemed like some kind of scam. Somehow, the system must make money by doing it that way, but he couldn't figure it out. His brain could stand to be a lot clearer.

Although he finished drinking the twelve ounces of water, Rick felt dry and wobbly like a fish out of water. After forty-five minutes of waiting, he registered, and a woman put a paper bracelet with his name on it on his wrist. After that twenty minutes, he was sent back to the X-ray department where he signed in again and sat for another half hour. A sullen looking, chunky lady finally escorted him to a darkened room where eventually she took films of his chest."

"You're free to go," she said, pleased with the X-rays she took.

Rick ambled out, slowing down by the minute, and bought another twelve ounce bottle of water. He drove the couple of miles back to the clinic, most of the time with a tailgater on his back bumper, but gave the guy the benefit of the doubt. He did suspect he was driving too slow.

The woman at the walk-in clinic popped her head up from the magazine she was reading. "Oh, you again."

"The P.A. will be expecting me."

"He stepped out for lunch. Have a seat."

"This is a no-appointment, walk-in medical care place where the provider leaves to eat lunch in a restaurant?"

She shrugged. "It seemed like a good idea to him. There was nobody here."

"There is now."

She wiggled her shoulders again and went back to her magazine.

Rick sunk into a plastic chair with no frill armrests, leaned forward, and put his head in his hands.

Andrew was just about to call his brother, Jack, when the door pushed open and Dr. Pinto lowered himself into the solo leather chair. He chose his words carefully and tried not to blurt out his defense.

"I am as shocked as you are about your mother. I was operating on my next patient when your mom coded in the hallway. If anybody doesn't understand what happened, it's me. Her surgery was easy and uneventful." He took a quick sigh.

"I would hardly call this uneventful," Andrew shot back, letting the anger which he'd been harboring begin to surface.

"My surgery on your mother was uneventful. Any medical problem, and obviously she suffered some medical problem, had nothing to do with me." He quickly remembered the words he was supposed to say. "I'm sorry, Mr. Sandler."

"I bet." Andrew balled up his fist, but then let the pressure relax. "I wish she'd never come here. I wish we'd had a fender bender leaving the house this morning, and never made it here. I wish you fouled up her forehead lift, and she never considered cosmetic surgery again. Anything but this."

Ernest listened and thought Andrew's outrage was calming down. In front of him were the lined up boxes of sample breast implants. He wondered if they were in the order he liked them—from small to large going from left to right. Sometimes the boxes got mixed up.

"You can't even imagine how much trouble my brother and I went through to arrange for her surgery today. I am going to wake up tomorrow morning and believe that this is all a dream—that my mother is still alive and smiling in front of the mirror, her red freckles catching the light, and that she is breathing life to the fullest, still overseeing, in her own motherly way, her two grown sons.

"She safeguarded Jack and I all these years, and now we failed her. This place cheated her too."

Ernest let a silence linger, and then tweaked his words with as much empathy as he could muster. "Mr. Sandler, if you need to talk to me again today, I will be in and out of the operating room."

Andrew nodded, but if he wanted to say another thing, he was not afforded the opportunity. Ernest slipped out the door.

Alone again, Andrew needed to call Jack. He punched his number. When his brother answered, he realized he had not prepared the critical words in his mind. Yet, he thought, no one could groom a speech to tell another family member that their parent has died, especially if it was unforeseen and precipitous.

His enthusiastic twenty-four-year-old brother answered. "Andrew, how'd it go? I bet Mom is happy as a clam at high tide!"

"Oh no," Andrew stammered, his voice chock-full of emotion. "Maybe you should leave work and get over here, or we should meet somewhere."

"Why?" Jack tapered his spirit. Andrew left out the part about their mother. "What's going on?"

"This is bad, Jack, and I hate to be the one to tell you this. Mom died after the surgery. They can't figure out what happened, but she's at the morgue for an autopsy."

Jack hunched over a table with a work colleague, going over a deck design. He dropped his pencil and waved his buddy out of the room. "Oh my God," he mumbled into the phone.

"Let's meet at mom's. Leave work. Don't have an accident."

Jack nodded to himself. His older brother always called the shots.

"Okay," he said, wanting to hear every minute detail of what his brother was told. They needed each other at this time.

Excusing himself from his co-worker, and not sharing any details, he hopped in his car and headed out. But if this news was true, the entire incident was intolerable, and he would never be able to live with himself for it. His brother was the one who had twisted his arm to choke up the money—for them to pay for their mother's non-needed, non-medical, cosmetic surgery. A surgery which had killed her.

The door flung open and Tim Stone strutted through the lobby, clinging to his cell phone. He almost tripped over Rick's legs sticking out in front of him.

"You're back," he said, glancing up. "I'll be with you in a minute after I call about your chest film."

More miserable by the minute, Rick closed his eyes as the seconds ticked away into minutes. These people working in health care had it made, he thought. From nurses, to doctors, they owned their own monopoly because of supply and demand. The public couldn't do without them. And as older physicians retire, and younger ones won't work the long hours that used to be routine, the shortage would only get worse. Meanwhile, he figured, increasing numbers of older Americans would need more complex medical care.

His wife worked in the system, but he could exonerate her for any part she played in ineptness because her salary primarily paid their bills. The money he made was sporadic and didn't alone cover any major expenditure they had between them. Actually, he never realized it before but, in a way, she subsidized his euphoric habit. A wry smile crossed his lips.

The woman at the desk tapped his upper arm. "Mr. Richter, I said you could go talk to our P.A."

Rick rubbed his eyes and glanced at the clock as he walked back. "The day is shot to hell," he said out loud.

Tim waved him into the exam room and kept standing. "When you are sick, that's the way it goes. Your chest x-ray, your GI symptoms, and the blood work panel I did make me too suspicious to treat you from ..."

"What's so bad about my blood work?" Rick interrupted.

"You are dehydrated. I'm sending you over to the emergency room."

"Crap," he blurted out, but failed to say it forcefully. "I could'a gone there to start with but, no, I didn't. You are telling me I have to start all over. Why do you people even exist?"

Tim ignored the sarcasm. "Here's a copy of the chest X-ray report they faxed over. Good luck, Mr. Richter. I tell you what, I'll call and let them know you're coming."

Rick grabbed the sheet and swung open the door. The P.A.s words were meant to appease him, shut him up, and get him on his way. He looked back at the woman at the front desk. "I won't be seeing you again. Good riddance!"

In the continuing rain, he scrambled behind the wheel of his Mazda and had the utmost desire to vape before becoming a patient again. After shutting off his engine in the ER's parking lot, he did just that, and listened to the rain as it pinged off the roof of his car.

Viktoria dropped her next patient off in the recovery room. There was a gap between cases, so she whisked into the kitchen. No one had given her a lunch break, and food was on her mind. She figured going to the sandwich place next door was a useless wish, and found a stock of yogurt containers and drink supplements in the refrigerator. Taking one of each, she also found the stash of cracker packets that the recovery room nurses used to feed patients while they were waiting to go home.

She sat down with all three items and ripped open the yogurt. After finishing it, she scrolled in her phone for the local hospital's number and called.

"Please put me through to the morgue," she asked the operator.

The phone rang so long, she thought about hanging up. But a curt male voice came on. She imagined he must have pulled his hands out of a chest cavity and needed to wipe his hands before answering.

"Hello. Dawton here."

"This is Dr. Thorsdottir, working temporarily at Amour Cosmetic Surgery."

"I got a body from y'all today."

"Yes, unfortunately. Are you the one I should speak to about her?"
"I'm the M.D. here. Mack Dawton. I see dead bodies. No, just kidding. That is a joke I can't stand. I put it out there so it's out of the way before someone needs to tell me that cryptic movie line." He spoke fast, like the dead bodies were waiting on him.

"What can I do for you?"

"Dr. Dawton, I am the anesthesiologist who was involved with Bonnie Sandler's case and advanced cardiac life support. Sadly enough, I failed."

"Fellow doctor, don't say that. We both know that you did not 'fail.'"

"I appreciate your words. Is it possible for me to be present while you do her autopsy?"

"Certainly. I love to have living human beings visit my lab."

"Wonderful." She wanted to chuckle at his view on life—to specifically differentiate bodies as alive versus dead.

"However, I work on Saturdays, and I'll be doing hers tomorrow. Are you going to waste a living day off by visiting me?"

"Yes, Mack, if I may call you Mack."

"Viktoria, I have your caller ID number. I will text or call you when I begin."

"Appreciate that. See you tomorrow."

She tore open the cracker package and poured the nutrition drink as Ernest Pinto rounded the corner. He went straight for coffee.

"We need to talk," he said. "Get our story straight for the rest of the day, in case more family members ask more questions. I expect more, more, more."

"The way you put it, makes me think of a cover up. Please, we can mash through the facts together, but don't put it that way."

"If you prefer." He raised his eyes over the mug hiding half his face. "Sensitive, aren't you?"

"I have wanted to ask you something, and now's the time. Where did you train in plastic surgery, Dr. Pinto, and are you board certified?"

CHAPTER 17

Ernest Pinto was a soft-spoken man, and Viktoria hated to sound harsh with him. She did not believe the breast implant surgery he performed on Bonnie Sandler had directly caused her death, but the possibility still existed. And she did not believe him to be an inherently bad person. Her opinion of him was more tapered to his nonchalant attitude of turning plastic surgery into what seemed like a scam—line 'em up and crank out boobs, and lips, and buttocks like women were slabs of meat. Rake the money into Swiss bank accounts, she thought. That's how sleazy it felt to her.

She waited for his answer, her fingers paused on the cream cheese and chive cracker in her hand. "It's a simple question, Dr. Pinto. I am a physician delivering anesthesia for some of your cases, and I have the right to know who I'm working with. We are both medically culpable for what happens to any person under our care."

A sigh escaped his lips. "No, I'm not board certified. There are physicians actively practicing who are not board certified, you know."

"That is true. However, most excellent physician groups hire only doctors who are certified in their specialty. What, then, are your qualifications to do plastic surgery? Where did you train?"

"After my first year internship, I stayed with a plastic surgeon for a while." He turned around, faced the sink, and dumped the rest of his coffee.

She understood what that all meant, and wanted to fire off another question as he moved towards the door. "Where'd you go to medical school?"

"You wouldn't know it."

"Outside the U.S.?"

She barely saw his nod as he scooted out the doorway.

Rick loaded his paraphernalia back into the generic-looking, secret bag he kept for marijuana products, and let it slip to the right-sided floor of his

Mazda. He tried taking a deep breath to get more air into his lungs, but only spluttered out with a cough. The rain still pinged on the top of his vehicle as he stared at the entrance to the E.R.

He swung open the door and swiveled his feet onto the asphalt. Locking the door with his key fob, he ducked his head down as if he wouldn't get rained on, and went inside.

"I've been here already today," he said to a hefty woman. She sat behind the glass window with a little hole. The weed rumbled around his head—he'd had a good hit in the car.

Rick leaned into the glass and talked through the round hole. "Lady dressed all in black, are you going to your own funeral?"

"Very funny. Be careful what you say or you may not be as sick as you think you are to see a doctor."

"Like I said, I was just here, so I'm all registered and everything. I visited the X-ray department and had a picture taken. See? I'm still wearing a bracelet." He pulled his head away and thrust his hand through the opening.

"Doesn't matter," she said. "We're starting all over. What's you name, date of birth, insurance information, and the name of your great-great grandfather on your mother's side of the family?" A snicker wrinkled up the right side of her lips.

"Wise-cracker. Watch it, or I'll go somewhere else."

"Be my guest."

Rick rolled his eyes. "My name is Rick Richter, and by the way, I am married to a doctor."

"So what. I'll pull up your information. Go take a seat."

When Rick turned around, he eyed an isolated chair away from the sick, coughing people. Although he counted as one of them, he did not smoke cigarettes, so those folks deserved whatever damage they'd done to their lungs. Plus, he used to be a personal trainer. These people need to emulate his life style, he thought.

The bulk of magazines lying on the tables were geared for women. Their overt message was how to look beautiful for men. Why hadn't these magazine companies kept up with the fact that their lives were more meaningful than that. At least his wife didn't follow all that crap. He searched through a pile, and finally found a guy's magazine geared for hunting. Knowing nothing about the subject, he stared at a page as if he did.

Before he started talking to some doctor, Rick wanted to clear his head. When he felt this great, he had learned that he could not trust his mind to say or do things like when he was straight. Which was always the trick doing weed at the house—to allow enough time before Viktoria showed up and interacted with him. Living a lie created a lot of work, but it was worth it.

Only an hour passed, when a young man called his name. Rick followed the young male wearing blue scrubs and was directed to a small room. After the routine of taking vital signs, the man left and another one replaced him.

"I'm Dr. Kingston," he said, and dived into asking him questions. Rick was impressed. The questions were delivered fast and pointedly, and he decided to use this ER as his future health care clinic.

"What about your social history?" Dr. Kingston asked. "Do you smoke?"

Rick shook his head proudly. "Never did."

"Alcohol use?"

"Once in a while, like a few beers a week."

"Recreational drugs?"

Rick's eyes darted downward to the white paper on the black table.

Dr. Kingston knew the answer. "Marijuana, cocaine, meth, street mixtures, or a combination of all of them?"

Rick's mind swirled around, fishing for a plausible lie. Or should he tell the truth? Did doctors report illegal drug use to law enforcement? He never heard Viktoria talk about such a thing, so he decided to come clean.

He put his hand over his forehead. "Yeah, yeah. I use marijuana."

"How much?"

"I quit seeing the psychologist. Apparently I'm addicted."

"Mr. Richter, do you vape?"

Rick nodded.

The man listened to Rick's heart and lungs, and checked his neck for swollen lymph nodes. The doctor palpated his abdomen as if looking for his last meal.

It became difficult for Rick to cooperate and sit there like a good patient. He wanted to bed down and go to sleep, but in just a few more minutes, he would have the antibiotic prescription he needed in his hands, and be able to go home.

Dr. Kingston leaned against the counter, clipboard in hand. "I'm admitting you to the hospital."

Viktoria darted out the front door of Amour Cosmetic Surgery at the end of the day wanting to put her day at work behind her. It had been the worst Friday in a while that she could think of. One week down at this place, she thought, and three more to go. She always fulfilled her assignments but, if she could, she would step away from this shady place if it were easy.

The rain still showered down like it had in the early morning, and she clasped the neckline of the light waterproof jacket she wore as she jogged to her car. Getting in, she turned on the ignition and clasped the steering wheel. It was too difficult to get out of her mind—tonight the Sandler boys lived with the fact that their mother was gone. For her own good, she needed to separate her personal feelings regarding patients from her professional job working with them. That was the way it should be as a physician, otherwise a doctor could lose their objectivity.

But it was easy to be emotionally attached to Bonnie Sandler, her sons, and the situation which unfolded today. She was only human, and if she lost any significant compassion or empathy for her patients, then she counted as nothing more than an inanimate object.

She put the car in drive. Tomorrow's autopsy would give her more answers and closure to Bonnie's death. For the rest of the day, she needed to refocus on the things that made her happy. She pulled out to the main street, and couldn't wait to see Millie.

When she pulled into the empty garage, she hoped Rick was visiting a walk-in clinic. Whatever was wrong with that man, he needed to sort it out. Sometimes he became annoyed at her because she wouldn't 'treat' him, but that was another unwritten law—it was unwise as a physician to treat friends and family members because all objectivity goes out the window.

Viktoria unlocked the door to the disappointing realization that Millie did not greet her. She put her things on the counter, checked the dog bed, and searched the rest of the first floor.

Maybe Rick had taken her with him, but that would have been unfair to the dog to have to wait. Medical appointments can take forever.

She crossed to the back door and glanced out. The poor little dog was drenched and dirty, and sat leaning against the house. She slid open the door and Millie scurried straight in.

"You're not an outside dog, Millie. Look at you. You're a mess." She crouched down, the dog pushed against her legs, and Viktoria gave her a big squeeze. When she let go, the dog bolted for the water bowl and gulped quickly.

Viktoria stood over her. "It appears you spent your entire day out there." She chewed her lip. What was it going to take to ensure the dog's welfare while she provided anesthesia services? The man she had married, although doing weed at that time, was more stable then compared to the behavior he exhibited these days. There was no more dependability, rational thinking, or even honesty left in him.

Millie quenched her thirst and Viktoria guided the energetic dog into the bathroom. She picked up the bundle of love, placed her in the tub, and rinsed off the muddy residue on her long, fluffy leg hair, and underneath her belly. Talking to her the entire time, the dog enjoyed the manhandling, her round blue eyes sparkling with enthusiasm over the rubbing and attention.

"Millie, I just love you. I have come to believe that a heart's best friend may be dog ownership."

She hoisted her up, set her on the bathroom rug, and grabbed a towel off the rack. On her knees, she dried her in the small space. After opening the door, Millie shook and smoothly exited the bathroom.

Viktoria inhaled a big, calming breath, and fetched her cell phone. She pressed Rick's number.

"Hey, Viktoria," he said. "I'm kind of tied up at the moment—they're taking more blood from me. I think they're all vampires in disguise." He held the phone in his right hand, his left arm extended. With a tourniquet on his upper arm, a needle sucked venous blood into a colored vial.

"Where are you?"

"In the hospital."

"The ER?"

"No. Our local hospital. In my own bed, in my own room. Like I checked into a hotel." He finished with a chuckle, and added, "This won't take long. I just need a tune-up."

She didn't find it funny, but if it were true, at least he wasn't being a wimp about it. However, he had that ridiculous edge to his voice. Was he high on dope? Asking him why they admitted him was pointless, she needed to ask the staff herself.

"I'm leaving in a few minutes. Be there shortly."

"Hmm," she mumbled after hanging up. What now? An early-season flu? A respiratory infection? Were they worried about his mental status, like he'd had a TIA at his age? If he did not tell them the truth about his drug history, they could be thinking anything.

She scooped out Millie's kibbles from the plastic container, and placed her dinner bowl on the floor.

"Mom's leaving again, girl. Mind the house."

The rain let up as Viktoria made her way into the local hospital in Harbour Village. The inviting small entrance was a lot nicer than entering via the ER. Three tall plants grew from large ceramic pots and the landscape pictures on the wall were all painted by local artists. For sure, the community always supported their own.

The man stationed at the front desk told her Rick's room number, and she took the elevator up to the fourth floor. She passed the nurse's station, rapped on the door, and entered.

"Hey," Rick said, his hands grasping the white blanket up around his neck.

"Hey, yourself. You went from a doc-in-the-box to the hospital? What's going on?" She ended up beside the bed. He still shivered despite a sheet and two spreads covering him up.

"You'll have to ask them."

"I figured that, but how are you feeling?"

"The usual today." He looked at the ceiling, coughed for a spell, and then managed to sigh. "All that embarrassing GI stuff hasn't gone away, and they said I have a fever."

"You're shaking like a leaf about to fall."

"And someone said I'm dehydrated."

She studied him, realizing he had also lost weight in the last week, and his breathing was labored.

"You might as well sit down," he said. "I've seen so many people today, I can't keep them straight, but the doctor is coming back when he does his evening rounds."

Viktoria nestled into the uncomfortable couch against the window wall. She tried to guess what Rick's diagnosis was, but without seeing his labs and x-rays, she stayed in the dark. His eyes were shut tight, and she didn't mention his neglect of leaving Millie out all day. Friday night was turning out to be an extension of one long, lousy day.

CHAPTER 18

Viktoria snapped her head upright after her chin practically touched the bottom of her neck. It was the second time she'd nodded off on the couch, while Rick slept in the bed, his chest rising with a labored breathing pattern.

The overhead light flicked on and an overweight, middle-aged man hustled in. He wore a white, long-coat and, after placing a chart on the nightstand, he ended up between the bed and Viktoria.

"I'm Dr. Blair," he said with a hoarse voice.

Viktoria stood, blinked away her tiredness, and was glad she didn't wear bags under her eyes like her husband's doctor. "I'm Viktoria Thorsdottir, Rick's wife. I'm also an anesthesiologist."

"Nice to meet you. Then you will better understand your husband's condition."

Rick opened his eyes, scooted up in the bed, and coughed. "Dr. Blair, you've met my wife."

"Yes. I am glad both of you are here. Technically, we won't have a definitive diagnosis until your lung fluid sample is sent to the CDC and tested."

The potential diagnosis crept into Viktoria's head. Maybe it had been lingering there all along, she thought, as the doctor continued.

"Mr. Richter, I believe you have E-cigarette or vaping associated lung injury. For short, we call it 'EVALI.'"

Rick stared blankly at the physician and Viktoria frowned.

The physician in front of them believed in a patient's accountability and spoke directly about diagnoses if they had been preventable in the first place. "Weren't you aware of the outbreak, Mr. Richter, and the need for individuals to stop their vaping habit?"

"I suppose I heard some rumors about that, but I don't work in the health care field. I wouldn't know what the medical truth is to all of that anyway."

"Poor excuse." He shot a glance at Viktoria, and she lightly shook her head. "The major role in the outbreak comes from THC or tetrahydocannabinol-containing e-cigarettes, or vaping products. I don't know where you get your illicit source from, but most users get their stash from friends or family, or in-person or online dealers."

Rick stole a glance at his wife. In no way was he going to follow up with the physician's comment about the source of his weed.

"What's the current update from research?" Viktoria asked. "Is the lung injury believed to come from contaminants?"

"The national and state data we have right now is that Vitamin E acetate is the culprit. It is an additive to the THC-containing cigarette, or vaping products, and is strongly linked to the EVALI outbreak. Or as the CDC likes to say, Vitamin E acetate has not been found in the lung fluid of people that *do not* have EVALI.

"However, other chemicals in these products may contribute to the problem. We need more evidence to determine what kind of role they may or may not play."

"I have not heard of anyone in the region with EVALI," Viktoria said. "Is Rick the first?"

"No, we've had a few, but nationwide, we're up to three thousand hospitalizations and seventy deaths."

"Deaths?" Rick's eyebrows shot up. He took a labored breath and sagged into his sheets as Dr. Blair nodded.

"When will the lung fluid results be back?" Viktoria asked.

"Next week. In the meantime, as you would suspect, Dr. Thorsdottir, care for your husband will be supportive. I am a specialist in pulmonary medicine, so he's in good hands."

"Thank you. We both thank you."

Viktoria stayed with Rick for two more hours and realized that for her to stay overnight in a make-shift cot made no sense. He was dead asleep and her own fatigue told her to go home and sleep in her own bed.

After the short drive home, she opened the house door to find Millie lying flat on the runner rug, her blue eyes glued on her master with nothing but joy.

"That's my girl. I am home to crash, but first we'll go for a spin." Viktoria hooked the young dog to her leash, and they stepped outside. She glanced over the night sky, disappointment registering on her face because of the absence of stars. They were there, of course, but the population on Long Island, and all the city lights or light pollution, prevented her from seeing them. As Millie squatted, she thought of her own place of origin. She could still gaze at the stars in Iceland, even in Reykjavik, the capital of the country where sixty percent of the country's inhabitants lived, and she hoped that the beauty of that northern night sky would never change.

Millie gave a slight tug, wanting to venture further along on the lawn, and Viktoria obliged. It was heartwarming to walk along the sidewalk and let the cooped up dog experience the fresh air, and to forget the day's struggles and her husband's condition.

Although tired, the stroll was just what she needed, and after fifteen minutes, they were back inside at midnight and ready to sleep. Viktoria changed into pajamas and, after she found the perfect position in bed, Millie jumped up, slunk alongside her, and rested her head beside her chest.

"Good night, girl."

Millie stretched her hindquarters and closed her eyes before Viktoria.

The abrupt ringing of her cell phone startled Viktoria awake. Millie jumped off the bed as she scrambled to free loose of the covers and figure out where she'd put her phone and where the sound came from. She found it outside the bedroom door on a display table with a vase of artificial flowers. The caller id displayed the hospital's number, and she answered swiftly.

"Dr. Thorsdottir, good morning. Your husband had a turn of events this morning."

Dr. Blair's voice was undeniable. "Oh?"

"Yes, he's been transferred to the ICU and is on a ventilator. I intubated him two hours ago after I made rounds. After waking up around five, his work of breathing began tiring him out so much, he sent away the early breakfast the dietitian brought to his room. Then, his oxygen saturation slipped from the mid nineties and his blood gases came back poor."

"Oh no. Do you have him sedated?"

"Yes, and as you must realize, sedation will make it easier for him to tolerate the endotracheal tube down his trachea."

"I'll be there as soon as I can."

"I'll be leaving soon. There is another doctor on call. No hurry. Your husband isn't going anywhere."

"Thank you for the call."

Hanging up, she glanced at the time and exclaimed in her Icelandic language, "Rusinan i pylsuendanum!" The old native saying meant she was as surprised to see the time of ten o'clock as seeing a raisin at the end of a hot dog. She looked down at Millie, who waited for not only a walk, but her breakfast as well.

"Let's get this day going, girl, so I can take care of you and visit Rick as well. In layman's terms, he's not doing so hot."

She went to the door, acknowledging the dog's need for a walk, "I'll let you out in the back yard instead."

Viktoria walked to the bedroom to change and realized another important matter scheduled for Saturday morning—Bonnie Sandler's autopsy!

Viktoria changed into comfortable pants and an attractive sweat shirt. She felt less rushed once she realized Mack Dawton, the MD pathologist, had told her he would call or text before starting Bonnie's autopsy. She brewed a small pot of coffee, let Millie back in, and put down the dog's food. Her text alert sounded on her phone with a message from the pathologist that the woman's autopsy was imminent.

She placed down fresh water and held Millie's face in her hands. "I'll see you later girl. I'll swing back by no matter what."

It had been a long time since Viktoria had been in a morgue for an autopsy. Not all medical students shadow a forensic medical examiner in an elective course, but she had. As far as pathology as a specialty, she thought of it as the most 'hands on' and challenging, and not for the weak of heart. Not only was it a physical and gruesome job, but it could be gut-wrenching to realize the manner in which some people die—such as when a person had been abused or tortured.

The day was picture perfect with clear skies like overnight, and the temperature catalyzed her desire to avoid the medical situations ahead of her, and go for a hike with Millie. But she went in the building and, standing before the coroner's lab door, she made a promise to herself—when the dust settled, she would take her Miniature American Shepherd to Jones Beach. They would walk the boardwalk with the ocean breeze in their faces until they tired. With that firm promise, she clenched her teeth to step into the place of dead bodies.

Mack Dawton stood over his dissection table, his working white coat faded with apparent years of use, and grinned at Viktoria. "Perfect timing. The toxicology screen and other labs are pending. Mrs. Sandler's been cleaned, weighed, and measured, and I'm ready for the internal examination."

"Thank you for contacting me."

"I take it there must be a reason for your interest in this case. Her recent surgery history is unusual for me to encounter here, although, whenever I think I've seen it all…"

How true, Viktoria thought, staring at her previous patient. Bonnie Sandler had the fresh surgical cuts, sutures, and bruising of both a forehead lift and breast implants, and looked like a battered corpse.

She had wanted to look like a movie star by having plastic surgery and here she was disfigured and dead.

Dr. Dawton adjusted his big round glasses on his nose, picked up a microphone, and began recording. "Bonnie Sandler is a forty-eight-year-old white Caucasian female." He proceeded to describe the obvious about her condition, and skipped most of what the woman would have focused on herself. The silky red highlights in her hair, which matched the red freckles on her cheeks, now didn't mean a thing.

In a short time, Bonnie's chest was open, and the left and right sides of her chest were off to the side. "Hmm," Dr. Dawton hummed, "see this?" He pointed at a perforation, clear through the front of her left chest and out the other side. "The surgeon came clear through the chest wall and straight down near to the heart."

He straightened his posture and continued. "Although the damage is damn close, it doesn't appear he daggered her heart, however. Damn close, though. Nothing like getting stabbed while you're asleep."

"Especially when it's not planned or has anything to do with the procedure."

"Were you the anesthesiologist in the room the whole time?"

"Unfortunately, I went out for a short time on a belated break."

He nodded. "Just like everything else, there's only so much a person can control. Don't beat yourself up about it." He drew in a big breath like he tried to practice his own advice. "Want to give me more insight?"

"She had a penicillin allergy and received an IV derivative while I was gone. The record shows her vital signs sagged, and she needed vasoconstrictors to raise her blood pressure back up."

He nodded. "All right. Let's keep going then." His sharp, hand-held instruments went back to work and soon Bonnie's heart was in his hands for a closer examination.

"I am never happy about the limitations of autopsy in the diagnosis of death due to ischemic heart disease," he said, and sighed. "In the living, doctors have the benefit of using the reliable biochemical assay of cardiac troponins for the diagnosis of a heart attack."

He turned to her as a drop of blood dripped off the organ. "Did you get bloodwork?"

"Yes and, as we know, when a heart is damaged it releases troponin into the bloodstream. I most certainly ordered it. The results should be back today, maybe tomorrow. But did I tell you that her father died at thirty-nine-years-old from a heart attack?"

"No." He raised an eyebrow and placed down the heart. "Hmm. Alright then, let's take a look, but realize that the histologic examination of the myocardium, valves, and cardiac blood vessels is often as important as the gross examination."

Viktoria stayed through thick and thin, the fresh cadaver dissection so different and telling than the older, stale bodies that first-year medical students dissect during their first-semester anatomy class. And as before when she took her elective pathology course, the smells of working alongside a pathologist in the morgue came back to her.

Mack subsequently spared his words like keeping a minimum word count in a short story, but there was no doubt he enjoyed his work, especially when he summarized his findings of an organ into his recorder.

When he finished, Mack Dawton sewed Bonnie back up. But it was nothing like a surgeon's finishing touches. He pulled the thick needle through her abdominal and chest wall with large, spacious movements until the incisions were closed.

"There we go, Dr. Thorsdottir. I will give you a call when the blood work is ready. Between the both of us, we'll be sure of the cause of death. In all likelihood, we are dealing with a heart attack. Her left anterior descending coronary artery was as narrow as a seventy-year-old with coronary artery stenosis."

He stepped back from the table. "I appreciated your company today. It's not every day people talk to me in here."

"I can understand why." She thanked him, and adamantly scrubbed her hands at the sink. Above all, she wished she could wash the smell off her clothes and replace it with lavender before going to the hospital's ICU or back home to Millie.

As she turned to leave, her cell phone rang. The caller ID name showed Jeffrey Appleton.

CHAPTER 19

Viktoria made it to the outside of the building and answered the call on the fourth ring.

"Jeffrey, hello. Not that I'm complaining, but it seems like we just texted. This time, it is nice to hear your voice."

"Is it a bad time?"

"No. A few minutes ago I was hovering over a corpse and watching an autopsy, but talking right now is fine."

"I had no idea that time in the morgue falls under an anesthesiologist's job description."

"It doesn't, but an extenuating circumstance arose. Call it an extracurricular interest in a patient."

"Coming from you, I'm not surprised. I was wondering…" He stopped, not sure how to go on.

"Yes?"

"The business trip I mentioned to you… Because of scheduling problems with the other party, my trip has been moved up. I'm leaving tomorrow, and will meet with the hospital's Director of Surgical Services on Monday morning. Our two hospitals, as well as others, are merging together. You know, the bigger the parent health care company, the better the care and revenue. So they say." He lowered his voice. "Can we meet?"

Viktoria's heart fluttered. The timing was against her due to the havoc going on in her personal and professional life, yet meeting him for even a short time would destress her and lift her spirits. When taking care of others, as professionals always said, a person needs to take care of themself first. She argued with herself quickly. They had been lovers for a short time before she left Pennsylvania. Could she justify meeting with him?

"So much is going on right now, Jeff." She shook her head. "But that's the new 'normal' lately. Yes, if I can break away from what I'm dealing with."

"I hope so," he said, continuing in a low tone. "I admit I've been thinking about you."

"I'm flattered. What airport are you flying into and where will you be staying?"

"MacArthur airport, much easier than LaGuardia, and staying at a Hilton about fifteen minutes away. Will that be in the ballpark of us meeting somewhere?"

"Sounds perfect. I may be tied up at the hospital tomorrow, but that should still work."

"I thought you were working at a plastic surgery center and had the weekend off."

"Yes, I am, but my husband is a patient in the hospital since yesterday. It comes down to what I was telling you about him. I am saddened, but his behavior has landed him in trouble."

"I'm sorry, Viktoria. If there's anything I can do…"

"What hospital did you say you have business with?"

"The one north of the main drag from MacArthur Airport and the Hilton—on the North Shore."

"That's where he is, and he's been transferred to the ICU."

"His condition sounds serious."

"His symptoms are all pulmonary. You may or may not have heard about EVALI?"

"Yes, the doctors here at Masonville General have taken care of several patients. For vapers, it must be impossible to find weed that is not spiked with dangerous compounds."

Viktoria silenced. There was no point in discussing her husband's addiction or medical problem. Soon, she'd be in his ICU room and have to deal with it. No doubt, it would be difficult to see the person she once loved hooked up to a ventilator.

"Jeff?"

"Yes?"

"I look forward to seeing you. Text me tomorrow after your travels."

"Will do."

In the ICU, Dr. Blair's order for Rick's sedation had taken full effect, allowing him to better tolerate the ventilator and his pulmonary symptoms. His eyes were closed and the endotracheal tube jutted from his mouth and was taped to the right side. The nursing staff had tucked him into the sheet and white hospital blanket like he was in a comparable five-star hotel room.

One thing Viktoria always liked about Rick was his frequent smiling. Her husband was not smiling now, she thought, as she pulled over a chair and sat down. She slipped her hand under the handrail and blanket, and clasped his limp hand.

She had not noticed before but, during the recent uptick of his "habit," he had let his hair grow longer than normal, especially in the back. Wisps of hair were settled to the side of his neck on the pillow, and his well-developed shoulders seemed to have lost some of their developed muscle. The monitors above the bed streamed the familiar traces she worked with every day, and she scrutinized the numbers as if he were her own patient.

He was stable as far as she could tell, especially since there were no infusions going into his IV, such as vasopressors or inotropes, which were meant to support a sagging blood pressure or a tired heart muscle. IV fluids dripped at a maintenance rate, and an empty antibiotic bag hung from the pole.

Wearing latex gloves, a slender nurse rounded the corner. "Hi. I didn't know Mr. Richter had a visitor."

"I'm his wife, Viktoria Thorsdottir. How's he doing?"

"Dr. Blair told me he called you. You're a physician, correct?"

"Yes."

"I'm Joanie. We'll take fine care of him." She bent over the Foley catheter bag hanging off the side of the bed and wrote on the clipboard.

"Is his urine output okay?"

"Seems to be."

"How about his labs?"

"Blood gases are pending again. I think the respiratory therapist made a ventilator change earlier after Dr. Blair made a tidal volume correction."

Viktoria glanced over at the ventilator, nodded, and looked back. "I envy your gorgeous braid half-way down your back."

"Thanks. I'm proud of it too." She smiled and narrowed her eyes. "Your husband does have a temperature, but it hasn't gotten any higher since he's been here."

"I'll cross my fingers about that. Listen, don't mind me, I'll probably sit right here until I try your standard food fare in the cafeteria, and check on something else in the hospital's lab—to do with another patient."

"No problem. I'm sure your husband would be thrilled to see you if he were awake.""

Joanie left and Viktoria leaned back. With her legs crossed, she closed her eyes, and tried to relax along with the in and out cycle of the ventilator. She hoped Rick's lungs could fight off the peril they were in, and that he would kick his vaping once and for all after Dr. Blair made him better.

For forty-five minutes, Viktoria's tiredness overtook her, and she nodded off in a slumber. She pulled her hand back into her lap, and her head occasionally bobbed. Under the circumstances, the drone of the ventilator and monitors was appeasing, and fleeting thoughts formed in her mind about Millie.

But a lot different scenario was going on in Rick's mind. First, the tube in his throat and the ventilator blowing his lungs up and down were the strangest phenomena he'd ever been subjected to. Then, even if he wanted to, he couldn't move.

He attributed that to what he remembered—something his wife had told him about her profession and people on ventilators—that doctors gave patients drugs which paralyzed them, to allow them to tolerate the breathing machine and surgery much better. For a short time, he felt the touch of a hand, fingers wrapped around his left hand. Trying to make sense of his situation, he figured it must be Viktoria, but his lack of motion did not allow him to give her hand a return squeeze.

Earlier in the morning, nonsensical dreams had filtered through his brain, but now he grasped onto thoughts about his wife and the choices he had made. This was all his fault. She had told him so, and the therapist had told him so, but he had continued to smoke his pot. And in doing so, it had led to one thing after another. He even had his own 'drug' dealer!

He was lucky she had stayed married to him. After all, from the beginning, he had deceived her. Although he carried fond memories of how and when they had met, what shamefully stuck in his brain now was the first time she had discovered him smoking pot.

That accidental first time was because of an out-of-state assignment she had been working. They had relieved her of her duties in a New Jersey hospital at noon on a Friday. There had been some kind of gas leak, and the ORs were shut down until they determined the source of the problem.

She drove home to Long Island for the weekend much earlier than anticipated and decided not to call Rick ahead of time. She would surprise him with her early arrival—in time for a romantic dinner at their favorite spot.

Rick remembered the day, slouching off from work on his computer, and peeling into the backyard to take on a buzz. One reason he had ramped up his use was that he transitioned from a workplace environment at a gym, to work which mostly entailed working from home. It became that much easier to smoke a joint, or two, or half a dozen.

He sat on the bench against the house and pulled out the plastic baggie filled with his goodies. After rolling the perfect joint, he finished it, and sculpted another. He smoked until his thinking was impaired, but at that point, he knew to stop. Later in the evening his wife would be home, so he needed to clear his head of the cannabis plant before then.

But he had no idea that the garage door had just opened, she had rolled into the garage, and had entered the house. She scanned around and, not finding him, she opened the back door.

Viktoria sidled next to the bench and peered at the paraphernalia on the bench. After letting out a gasp, she stared at his face. He tried to talk, but nothing came out, at least nothing sensible at first that he could remember.

Each of the three worded syllables that came out of her mouth were slow and emphatic. "What the hell?!"

He was more than shocked to find her there. "You're home early! It's not every day that I grab a joint while taking a short work break." He was sure it didn't come out of his mouth that way, but it was what he wanted to say. He forged ahead, "Would you like to try it before my one and only is gone?"

"You're potted or stoned, whatever you want to call it. Since when do you smoke marijuana?"

He shrugged his shoulders and frowned. "For awhile."

Viktoria did not have high blood pressure, but she was sure her numbers were going up. "Awhile?" she said, the volume of her voice raised, and the tone incriminating.

"Let's not fight outside."

"You bet'cha. Let's take this inside. Last time I checked, marijuana was illegal. Secondly, did I marry some kind of addict for you to be sneaking this while I'm away?"

The ramifications to her were troubling, but to Rick, none of that really mattered. Feeling good was far superior to what society, or his wife, thought about cannabis. They took their argument inside where a romantic dinner was the last thing on Viktoria's mind.

Rick reflected upon that day. Hindsight was easy, but he wished he'd turned the corner at that point. If he had, he wouldn't be lying in the present hospital bed attached to artificial breathing. He should have heeded his wife's advice. But more than anything, he hoped he'd be out of the ICU soon so that he could apologize to her and make things right.

He hoped she would give him a second chance. They could start all over again. And as soon as the muscle relaxant wore away, he would be able to squeeze her hand.

Viktoria yawned, rubbed her eyes, and rose. After noting Rick's vital signs one more time, she rubbed his shoulder through the blanket.

It was time to step away, and she needed to check in the hospital's laboratory if Bonnie Sandler's lab results were available yet. The hospital's lab ran analyses for Amour Cosmetic Surgery, and Viktoria had ordered Bonnie's because of her code.

She rode the elevator several floors up and entered a brightly lit front room where a woman with braces gave her a half smile.

"I'm Dr. Thorsdottir. Are Bonnie Sandler's lab results ready yet? I sent them over from Amour Cosmetic Surgery yesterday."

The woman pointed to her teeth. "Instead of getting a forehead lift over there, I got braces instead. I could only afford one or the other, so I hope I made the right decision."

"I think you did," Viktoria said, knowing she wouldn't pay two cents to be a patient at Amour.

The lady nodded and placed her fingers on the computer's keyboard in front of her, and soon printed out the blood chemistry and special labs which Viktoria had ordered.

With the two sheets in her hand, Viktoria thanked her, and sat on one of the chairs against the wall. She scanned up and down the first page and noted the labs which were slightly above or below normal. But it was the second page which told her what she really wanted to know—the values of the cardiac troponins.

Viktoria, as well as Mack Dawton, knew of the limited value of postmortem troponin T in establishing a cardiac-related cause of death. But in the living, the biochemical assay for cardiac troponins was reliable and used in the diagnoses of acute myocardial ischemia.

She gazed at the numbers, marked 'above normal' on the lab sheet, and nodded to herself. The anaphylactic reaction that Bonnie had to the antibiotic when she was out of the room, the ensuing hypotension, and subsequent high rebound after being given a vasopressor, taxed her heart. The big middle piece of the puzzle was that, genetically, she probably carried her father's predisposition to early heart disease.

Viktoria pushed back against the chair and bit the side of her lip. She adamantly hated that Bonnie had passed away—at least now there was an explanation. She stayed put and called Dr. Dawton.

"Mack, it's Viktoria again. Along with your suspicion of heart disease during autopsy, Bonnie Sandler's lab work came back with higher than normal cardiac troponins before death."

"There we have it, Dr. Thorsdottir. Sorry to say, at least now you have an explanation for the family."

"No matter what the reason for their mother's death, they are rightfully grief striken. I'm saddened myself, and it'll be tough to talk to them again."

CHAPTER 20

With the red plaid leash in her hand, Viktoria took Millie for a long walk, as much for herself as the dog. It was late afternoon, and since she'd missed lunch, she was hungry. But she wanted and needed the fresh air and exercise, so she kept walking at a brisk pace. She held a plastic bag in case Millie did her business on someone's lawn, and occasionally praised the dog for walking so politely.

She realized she needed to call Dr. Pinto. What if he had found out the causes of Bonnie Sandler's death just like her, and had already called her two sons? Her instinct told her probably not.

Viktoria and Millie passed a half mile of neighborhood homes, some with picket fences, some with too many cars in their driveways, and some with youngsters making noise from the backyards. They arrived at a main street with businesses and a four lane road. The restaurants and stores were not as charming as the downtown historic area, but they were her local go-to places. They walked another block where she stopped at a pizza place, and stepped to the side of the building to the take-out window.

"I didn't call ahead, and I'm walking my dog. How about a small Brooklyn style pizza with extra cheese?"

"Sure thing. We have a few tables inside and no customers right now. We do more take out and delivery, especially this time of day. If you'd like, come on in and tether her to your table while you eat."

"That would be splendid." Viktoria slipped in, ordered a drink, and put Millie in a stay next to the round table in the front corner. She pulled up Ernest Pinto on her cell phone, grateful that they'd exchanged numbers.

His voice came on the line. "Dr. Thorsdottir, I imagine you attended our patient's autopsy, which is one reason I didn't go myself. Did you find out anything?"

"Yes. The postmortem examination, as well as the blood work I sent off during and after the code, point to a cardiac factor. The Penicillin derivative you ordered, her allergic reaction, and the poor management of her hypotension, was the be-all and end-all. Like her father, she had an early MI."

"Genetic backgrounds are important. Maybe I should stop operating on

134

patients who have early death in their genetic family history."

Maybe you should stop operating on anyone, she thought, but kept her words to herself. "Will you call Mrs. Sandler's sons to tell them the definitive cause?"

"Someone needs to. Instead of me, would you mind calling? You bring a woman's touch to the equation."

Her lips tensed. "A woman's touch" was a poor excuse not to do it himself, but she didn't mind.

"I would be happy to."

"Thanks." He ended the call and, as she sat watching the young man back by the ovens toss pizza dough, she grimaced. Overall, however, she thought it better that she talk to one of Bonnie's sons herself.

The likely man to call was the older brother, Andrew. He'd been there for his mother's augmentation and news of her death. She glanced down at Millie. Stretched out on the floor, her blue eyes were keyed on Viktoria or the front counter, and her nose twitched from the potent smell of tomato sauce and melting cheese.

"You keep being a good girl while I make an important phone call." Viktoria scrolled to Andrew Sandler's phone number and dialed.

"Andrew?"

"Yes?" he answered, his voice weighty, full of sadness.

"This is Dr. Thorsdottir. The cause of your mom's death is definitive today. The coroner finished his examination and the lab work came back." She finished with an explanation which he would understand, but hid nothing.

"She would have never died if she hadn't of had that stupid surgery. A surgery which Jack and I made possible for her. I will never forgive myself. But in the meantime, Jack is hoping to hire an attorney and you might as well know, we are suing everyone involved."

"I understand. My thoughts are truly with you and your brother. I hope someday you can get past the hurt and guilt."

"Me too," he said, his voice softer.

"I'm sure the attorney you've hired will be able to get a hold of me if needed. Please take care of yourself."

"Dr. Thorsdottir?"

"Yes?"

"Thanks for calling and letting me know."

"You're welcome." She put the phone on the table, and sighed softly.

A woman came from behind the counter and placed the pizza, silverware, and a plate on the table.

"Thanks," Viktoria said. Millie stood and nuzzled her snout to the edge of the table. The aroma was too much for her, and Viktoria laughed.

"I bet your dog won't get out of here without you giving her a sample," the woman said.

"I'll see that she tries pizza for the first time," Viktoria agreed. She tugged a piece out of the small pie, the stringy cheese making a mess, and folded it. A drop of oil dripped off the side, and she took a bite.

"I'm in heaven, Millie."

Viktoria cut out a corner and, after letting it cool, gave it to Millie. The dog gulped it down in a flash, sat, and pleaded with her eyes. One piece was not enough. It was the best food she'd ever gulped down so far in her entire short life.

Viktoria's chores-to-do at the house had grown like a stockpile of old books. It was seven o'clock, and she neither had the energy or motivation to go back to the ICU and sit at Rick's bedside. She needed to get through a stack of mail, at least the layer of bills that her husband had neglected to keep current with. Even his car registration had almost expired, a fault, no doubt, because of his preoccupation of being high at the house.

She sat at her desk with Millie beside her and wrote checks. When she was out of town on her assignments, she left those errands to him, but she soon found out by looking through the records, that their credit card bill was usually paid late.

Great, she thought. It was mostly her bringing in the income while he squandered away money on late fees. After a big sigh, she scooped Millie into her arms, and carried her to the bedroom.

Nestled in bed, Millie conformed her furry body into Viktoria's, and they closed their eyes. So peaceful and comfortable with her dog, and the sheet and light comforter up around her shoulders, her thoughts turned to Jeffrey. Every time he had entered her thoughts during the day, she had tried hard to push them aside.

Now she could devote her thoughts entirely to him—the considerate, handsome, smart man who had popped into her life out of the blue. Neither of them had planned, nor contrived, their attraction towards each other during those chance encounters at the Pennsylvania hospital. Sometimes things like that just happen, she thought, and she gave herself slack for going to bed with him. After all, her marriage was broken. Actually, she realized, a court would consider her marriage irretrievably broken because she had committed adultery. But, hell, wasn't Rick's use of illegal drugs and being in an altered state of mind most of the time, grounds for a broken marriage more than cheating?

It didn't matter. The more things change, the more they stay the same. Would they continue playing their games—his game of marijuana and trying to hide using it, and now her rare encounter with Jeffrey Appleton? Of course, it was the fact that marijuana and the crap it was laced with, the black market products laced into the weed, had turned Rick into a different, unstable person and that was the problem.

And she was still dead set against a divorce. She knew how that would go for her, and she did not want to pay a deadhead alimony or half, no, more than half, of what she'd earned. Besides, she worked almost exclusively away from home and now Millie would accompany her. God forbid if she left her new dog at home with him.

Tomorrow she would relish seeing Jeff. It would fill her heart to talk to him, kiss him, and feel his embrace, but she pushed away the thought of going to bed with him. The timing or the circumstances didn't seem right.

Visiting Rick would be reassuring as well because she believed his doctor was managing him well. For the time being, the mechanical ventilation was the correct treatment for his EVALI as well as the sedation and antibiotics. Perhaps her husband would turn the corner after this illness, go back to his therapist, and kick his habit. But she doubted that. Every time he'd addressed quitting, it never worked. Once an addict, always an addict?

She bordered on falling asleep while her imagination conjured up Jeff Appleton—his smiling eyes, his easy manner, and his attentiveness while listening to her. His body throbbed her with desire as well, and as Millie drifted off into a REM, physically active sleep, she also succumbed into overdue sleep.

The three nurses on the night shift took care of three patients each. Their station was much quieter than during the day when doctors, lab techs, and X-ray technicians were abuzz, and visitors routinely came and went. Rick Richter's RN, Tonya, rounded on her patients and shook her head. Each one of them was sicker than a dying horse was the way she viewed their situations. She'd grown up on a farm and horses would often croak before a vet could make it to their rural site far from town.

Tonya's renal failure patient was taking up most of her time since she arrived at eleven o'clock. The old man on a ventilator was on so many IV drips, that all she kept doing was changing bags, checking orders, and calling the pharmacy. She stepped out of his room at two a.m., overdue for a cup of coffee. With only a sidewards glance, she passed Rick's room, and slid into the little spot where the nurses made coffee.

As the coffee brewed, she thought about what Joanie had told her during their shift change. Dr. Blair had educated her that Rick's deadly illness hospitalizes nearly all of its patients, and that males died more frequently from it than females. Tonya couldn't understand why people let drugs overturn their lives, and she didn't have as much empathy for him as she had for her dying renal patient.

One of her colleagues waved her hand from the desk, letting Tonya know she was heading to a cafeteria machine to buy a prepared sandwich. The coffee stopped dripping, and she peppered a cup with cream and sugar. The monitors at the nurse's station began to beep, and her head bobbed out the door. Although she quickly surmised an irregularity on two monitors, one of them was her end-stage renal patient, and she half-ran into his room.

The old diabetic's heartbeat had slumped into a bradycardia. It may be his time, she thought. After all, his urine output, despite massive doses of diuretics, was down to such a trickle as to be almost nonexistent. She jumped over to his bedside. A physician's standing order gave her leeway to increase the heart medications going into his central line, and she hurriedly stepped up the dose.

Behind her, the third nurse in the unit arrived. "You need help?"

"No, let's see if he responds. Otherwise, we'll need to call a code in a minute."

"There are two other monitors making a racket out there."

"Damn, when it rains, it pours."

"One of them is my trauma patient. I'll try to be back in a minute."

Tonya was an excellent nurse, so she waited for her patient's heart rate to respond to what she did. Since his circulation was so slow, she knew not to keep adjusting the rate upwards, but to wait to see if he responded. His heart rate finally went above fifty, then sixty, and the monitor inside and outside his room stopped alarming.

She popped off her disposable gloves and honed in on the other beeping alarm. Assured that it came from her EVALI patient next door, she rounded the corner and went into Rick's room. For a split-second, she witnessed a ventricular fibrillation, and then the EKG went flatline.

Codes in the sleepy middle of the night never brought the unending stream of doctors, health care providers, and gawkers that they do during the day. Quite aware of this fact, Tonya tried as diligently as the few helpers who arrived to resuscitate her patient. The ER doctor who took the elevator instead of running up six flights of stairs, took charge, but his valid attempts to save Rick were futile. The EVALI patient's lungs were toast and the doctor knew it. Even a breathing machine or an inflating Ambu bag couldn't make his lungs deliver the oxygen he needed to all the cells in his body.

Rick never fooled himself again into thinking he could quit his addiction or to start over in his marriage.

CHAPTER 21

Awakening her, Viktoria's cell phone rang like a siren in the night, making her cringe and recoil from the sound. Millie jumped off the bed, and Viktoria glanced toward the nightstand. It was a little after three a.m. She did not take call doing her locum tenens assignments, that was part of the allure of working that way, so she could not make sense of a phone call in the middle of the night. *Unless it was the hospital …*

She plucked her phone off the table, and immediately viewed the caller ID. Rick was safely on a ventilator, so what would be so dire for Dr. Blair to call now? Plus, he was not the physician on call. Perhaps medical staff needed permission to do a medical procedure on her husband. Yes, that must be it, she thought.

Dr. Blair's hoarse voice came on the line. "Dr. Thorsdottir, are you there?"

"Yes," she said, her voice wakening up.

"I'm afraid I have bad news to tell you." She waited, not liking what he said. "Your husband's lungs became worse and worse. He passed away a short time ago."

The words rumbled around in her brain like shaking dice in a cup. On one hand, she grasped what he said, on the other, his words were not believable. The good doctor on the other end let her maintain silence.

"That's crazy. I never expected …"

"Neither did I. Death often doesn't forewarn us, does it?"

"No. Are you at the hospital?"

"No. The ER physician who ran the code just called me. They tried their best, Viktoria, but your husband's lungs were exchanging less and less oxygen and carbon dioxide since his admission to the ICU. His arterial blood gases were deplorable and his pulmonary failure was complete."

Viktoria stared at Millie, stretched out on the carpet, wearing a forlorn expression. The moonlight streamed through the blinds, with enough light to make out the furniture and the dog. She sighed and filled her lungs to capacity, as if breathing life back into her dead husband.

"This is the first time, since years ago, that I am in this position with a loved one," she stammered. "I don't know what to do first."

"I understand. For now, I don't think your husband needs an autopsy, unless you want one."

"No, I agree with you. Let's forego that."

"The rest can wait until the morning. Go back to sleep if you can."

"Thank you, Dr. Blair."

The phone went dead. She remained motionless, but now wide awake, her eyes alert and her heart like a pendulum inside her chest. The situation was too surreal. Her husband had committed a type of drastic behavior that jeopardized his own living, yet he did it to experience thrills and the time of his life. How ironic.

He would never come home again. At least the problems he brought to their relationship were now in the past, but this certainly was not the way for them to go away.

Life would go on differently for her at some level, she figured. But first, she bet there were too many details to take care of with the death of a spouse. In grief, they can't be easy to deal with. The only way to get through was with one step at a time.

"Millie, come back." She patted the mattress, the young dog sprang up beside her, and she slipped the cell phone under her pillow. Closing her eyes, sleep came an hour later. By five a.m., however, her feet dropped to the floor, she showered, and brainstormed what needed to be done.

As the morning hours ticked away, Viktoria did the most important tasks first. Fortunately, she knew Mack Dawton, but unfortunately, she paid him another visit.

The hospital's morgue room door was ajar, and she entered without knocking. Dr. Dawton's head was bent over a jar on a counter.

"Unbelievable dedication," Viktoria said. "You work on Sundays too?"

His head bobbed up from a brain specimen stuffed in a jar with a liquid solution all around it. "I should ask the same thing of you. For me, people who die don't care what day of the week it is. My partner and I work seven days on, seven days off. What's your excuse?"

Viktoria bit her lip. "I understand that you have a hospital patient that died a few hours ago—a Rick Richter."

"Another one of your former anesthesia patients?" Mack adjusted his round glasses on his nose. He wasn't wearing his lab coat, and wore a weathered sweat shirt.

"No. He was my husband."

Mack stared blankly at her and was at a loss for words.

"Yes, people who die," she said, "not only don't care what day of the week it is, but they can care less about how old they are, or how they abused their bodies."

"Dr. Thorsdottir, I am so sorry."

"It's okay. I'm in somewhat of a shock, but I do need to see his body. He and I never talked about death, so I am guessing what his wishes would have been. The North Shore Crematorium will be picking him up."

Mack nodded, and turned. They walked to the back wall, and he slid Rick's body out from his enclosure. Viktoria took a deep breath as Mack turned down the white sheet. The true reality of his death sunk in as she fixated on his dead still body. This was not the man she had married and fell in love with. How time can change anything.

She gave Mack a slow nod.

"Do you want a minute?" he asked, stepping back at the same time.

Viktoria placed the palm of her hand over the area of his heart. "I hope you find peace and solace in death, Rick." She kissed two fingers, pressed them on his lips, and turned.

"I have paperwork for you to sign," Mack said. He slid Rick back in and steered Viktoria to an office in the corner. She sat in his visitor's chair, and penned her name in several places.

"I can't say it's been a fun weekend with you," she said, handing him the clipboard, and trying to crack a smile.

"Listen, if you need anything else from me, you just holler. You'll get through this. It will take time."

"Thanks. There's nothing like support from colleagues when we become overwhelmed in our medical field or personal lives."

Mack grasped her hand and softly shook it. "Come on, I'll walk you out."

Trying to enjoy the few minutes outdoors, Viktoria brought Millie outside for a walk. So far, it seemed like she'd spent her whole weekend in the morgue, and she wanted to clear her head and focus. The death of a family member was a rare event, and more details needed to be figured out.

Millie finished squatting and nibbled at the greener grass next to the sidewalk while a woman around Viktoria's age approached with her own dog, a Golden Retriever, and slowed.

"Hi there J.D.," she said. She petted Millie while her dog wagged her tail.

Viktoria raised her eyebrows. "J.D.? My dog's name is Millie."

"Oh. I'm sure this is the same dog, same plaid leash and all, that a guy was walking a few days ago. We talked a bit, and he said her name was J.D. I asked him what J.D. stood for, and he said 'Just Dog.'"

"Really?" Viktoria shook her head. No doubt, she thought, Rick must have been high as a kite, and didn't even remember Millie's name.

"Anyway, Millie is much more personal than J.D. This is Roxanne. She's my sweet Golden. If you ever need a dog sitter for your Mini American Shepherd, I work from home."

Viktoria patted Roxanne on the head. "Thanks. I'll remember that."

"I live on the corner." She pointed to the last house.

Viktoria nodded and gave Millie a tug. When they walked back into the house, she dreaded making a terrible phone call. Rick's mother had died a few years back from cancer, but his father was a healthy man, an engineer, who had only retired two years ago at seventy years old. The call to him needed to be made but, in her opinion, she felt a burden lifted from her shoulders. To call a mother that her son had died would have been far worse.

She placed fresh water down for Millie, sat at the kitchen counter, and pulled up the number for Rick's dad, Pete. Realizing a big mistake she'd made, she tightened her hand into a fist. She should have called him when Rick was admitted to the hospital or the ICU on Saturday. Then the total news of his hospitalization *and* death wouldn't come straight out of the blue. She could kick herself. Hindsight is 20/20, she thought.

"Pete, this is Viktoria."

"It's always wonderful hearing from my son and daughter-in-law." The man's voice was vibrant, like the life he lived. He did better than anyone she knew of to not allow his age to slow him down. Rick, however, had not been a chip off the old block.

"It is good to hear your voice too, but I have terrible news. This will come as a shock. Your son was admitted to the hospital late on Friday. He had a lung issue, and they put him on a ventilator yesterday." She gulped. Leading up to the news of his son's fatal outcome was the correct manner to tell him.

"That sounds serious." Pete's tone scaled down from chipper to concerned. He'd pulled his vehicle into the garage, and held off unloading the hardware it carried.

"What lung issue? Rick's never had any problems with his lungs. He's never even smoked."

"That's true, I believe. Rick never smoked cigarettes, but he smoked marijuana."

Pete considered her words. Marijuana? His own son would do something so stupid? That was hard to believe. Worse than that, however, was Viktoria talking about him in the past tense?

And then it dawned on him—Viktoria's brittle voice. She *did* have worse news, and she was about to drop it on him.

"Rick passed away, Mr. Richter, early this morning."

A pain shot through his heart, like a sudden zap, and he grasped the back door of the hatchback.

"No," he gasped. "How?"

"It was from a new illness associated with tainted marijuana and vaping. He'd been vaping for some time, and occasionally saw a therapist to help him stop, but that wasn't working. He died of pulmonary failure."

Pete was of the age to have experienced the seventies hippie culture, but he never partook in their behavior with drugs. He knew drugs were an ongoing social problem these days, but he had no idea of what really went on. His son's death was a shock, but so was his behavior.

"I don't think his mother could have withstood this news."

Just like Pete, Viktoria thought, thinking about someone else. "I'm so sorry," she said. "And I'm sorry I didn't call you earlier today. There were several issues, like going to the morgue, I needed to attend to. Also, to no avail, please know that I tried my best to make him stop his addiction."

"His addiction," he echoed flatly. "I had no idea my son was an addict. You think you know somebody, even your own kid, but apparently that wasn't the case. My heart is broken."

Viktoria felt paralyzed. She always liked Rick's father and hated this for him. "I can understand. I hope you will agree with the arrangements I've made for his cremation. And I'm thinking of a celebration of his life, a memorial service, for next weekend. Is that okay with you?"

"Absolutely. Here I am not thinking of you, now a widow. What can I do to help?"

"Be well, Mr. Richter. Please be well. Let's get through this."

This would be short notice to pull on Amour Cosmetic Surgery, Viktoria realized, but she could do nothing else about it. Although it was Sunday, she called Regina, the woman in charge of the locum tenens agency that she used.

"Sorry to disturb you on the weekend," Viktoria started, "but we need to make an adjustment to my schedule."

"Dr. Thorsdottir, you're one of my most dependable doctors. What do you need?"

"I had a death in the family today. Even though my head still isn't wrapped around this fact, my husband passed away."

"Viktoria! An accident?"

"No. He ended up with a potent side effect of his drug addiction to marijuana. Basically, his lungs were dealt a severe blow. He died of pulmonary failure while hooked up to an ICU ventilator."

"Oh, I'm so sorry. Is there anything I can do for you? Obviously, you need time off."

"Thanks. He's being cremated tomorrow. After Monday and Tuesday off, I'd like to return to Amour on Wednesday."

"You're not giving yourself enough time. Take the week."

"I plan on his 'funeral' service next weekend. Honestly, going back to work on Wednesday will keep my mind busy. As it is, the plastic surgery center will be short on anesthesia help due to my absence."

"But they'll survive. Are you sure you want it this way?"

"Yes, ma'am. Be sure you tell Rigoberto Castillo, the main doctor in charge. Otherwise, the message may not fall into the correct hands."

"I have his private number. I'll get a hold of him as soon as we hang up." Regina directed her wheel chair over to the spare Rolodex she kept with business numbers. "Listen, if you change your mind, let me know.

You take care of yourself, and send me pertinent information, so I can send some flowers."

"Thank you, Regina."

Viktoria glanced down after hanging up. Millie was attentive, wearing a gleam of hope that her master would feed her an overdue dinner.

"Yes, I've forgotten all about you. Myself as well. I'll scoop out your kibbles, but I'm not holding my breath for dinner tonight."

Millie gobbled her food and pranced to the door, wanting a last walk. Viktoria obliged and, back in the house, skipped dinner. It was early for bed, but she was mentally exhausted and changed into pajamas. Climbing into bed, her cell phone dinged with a text message.

Through the haze of the day, she'd forgotten about Jeffrey Appleton. She closed her eyes for a moment, and thought that the timing couldn't be more ironic.

CHAPTER 22

Viktoria read Jeff's text message.

"My flight into MacArthur was cancelled, and I had to be rebooked. Only now checked into the hotel. Sorry it's late. Can we work around our schedules tomorrow to meet?"

She nodded to herself, but there was no reason to text since her husband was no longer around. They could just as well talk on the phone, so she placed the call.

His voice, subdued and inquisitive, came on. "Is it okay to talk?"

"Yes," she sighed.

"Is something the matter?"

"Yes. In the early morning hours today, my husband passed away."

The phone went silent.

"Viktoria, I'm stunned. What on earth happened?"

"It was the vaping, Jeff. It only took two days of more severe symptoms than he'd been experiencing. He was admitted to the ICU, intubated, and yet his lungs still went into a full-blown pulmonary disaster. This happened so fast, I'm still reeling."

"Yes, death can do that, and many of those EVALI cases are unprecedented. Is there anything I can do for you?"

"At this time, I'm not sure. I think I'll be fumbling along this week and, later on, I'll think back and it will be one big blur. Tomorrow Rick gets cremated."

"Have you made arrangements to be off for a while?"

"Two days is all I'm taking."

"Most physicians are Type A personalities, but now is not the time to prove it."

"No, really. This is what I want."

"Listen, my primary meeting is in the morning. It'll most likely last into the early afternoon. Why don't I take you for an early dinner tomorrow? You still need to eat, and we need not consider it a date. I'm helpful when it comes to rendering emotional support."

His words were reassuring. She could hear the sincerity behind each one, and he warmed her heart.

"Sure. Why not?"

"I'll call you when I'm finished. We can make a plan based on you."

"Jeff, thanks. Good night."

"You're welcome. Get some sleep and give that dog of yours a hug."

"I'll take one too." She lightened up and cracked a smile.

"Certainly. Sweet dreams."

Monday morning rolled around too fast and, in her pajamas, Viktoria opened the back door for Millie to go in the yard. As the minutes ticked by, a guilty feeling started to take hold. If she were to be truthful to herself, her marriage had been bad enough for her to revisit the idea of divorcing Rick every so often. This was a hell of a way for the marriage to end, but she shouldn't blame herself in any way.

She must have needed a fresh start in a relationship to have gotten involved with Jeffrey and, come to think of it, she had probably swapped out her husband for Buddy, the dog she found in Pennsylvania, and then Millie. Yes, who was she kidding. The man being cremated today was recently less of a husband than he was a former lover and friend.

She would see that all details after Rick's death, however, would be done with sincerity and professionalism. There would be the decision about what to do with his ashes as well. Maybe his dad would have some suggestions. Asking Pete would be the correct thing to do.

It was strange not going into work, and she sat all morning in her pajamas and sipping from a coffee mug. Through internet websites and phone calls, she advised multiple companies of Rick's demise. Utility bills, banking, etc. would now be under her name only. Certain companies needed a copy of the death certificate, so she made a note for when she picked it up later in the day.

More importantly, she'd need to dismantle his art auction site, "A Queen's Art," and check with the insurance company where he'd been an adjuster. Those were more complicated issues, so she put them on the back burner to consult a certified public accountant about how to do it correctly.

She felt uncomfortable to be near her husband's cremation, so Viktoria stayed at home. In the early afternoon, her phone rang, and the crematorium's operator was on the line.

"Mrs. Thorsdottir," he said, "Everything went well. Your husband's ashes are ready, and I've placed them in a temporary container. You may bring your own urn when you come, and we can transfer the ashes or, if you'd like, we have an assortment of urns for purchase here."

"I'll be right over."

Millie cocked her head when Viktoria got up. "It's about time I get dressed," she said, "and then I'll take you for a ride. You'll like that."

With Millie in the back seat of her Honda, Viktoria drove to the crematorium. An older man met her inside the lobby, and pointed to a room. It was two brothers that ran the place, and she figured he was the 'meet and greeter,' and the other brother did the cremation process.

"Sorry about your loss," he said. He wore a dark shirt, and black pants, and stopped in front of a long wall shelf filled with a variety of containers for ashes. Some were simple, but most were colorful ceramic pieces with lids. There were urns for every type of person and their hobby or passion in life, from colorful pieces with fish, birds, or flowers, to artistic expressions of still lifes and rainbow blocks of color.

"Can we separate his ashes and put them into three urns? I'd like to give one to his dad as well as his brother."

"Yes, ma'am. That gets done all the time."

Viktoria selected three of the same—a muted orange sunset which wrapped around the mini urns. It made her think of the day she had met him by the water.

"If you would like to wait awhile in the lobby, I can take care of this for you. Or come back tomorrow."

"My dog is in the car. I will walk her and come back."

"Perfect. Give me thirty minutes."

Viktoria nodded and went outside. The clouds threatened to rain, and a snappy breeze popped up, but it didn't stop her and Millie from taking a brisk half-hour walk. The blue Merle shepherd garnered attention along the sidewalk, even from drivers in their cars.

She bypassed the fast food places, bakery, and hardware store, and ambled back to the car. Millie settled again on the back seat, Viktoria went back in, and picked up Rick in his terminal resting places. At home, she placed the urns on the knickknack shelf in the kitchen alongside the window.

Viktoria's phone rang, and she scrambled to find it on the top of her desk.

"How are you today?" Jeff queried.

"I'm pacing myself. Taking care of death details is no fun."

"I bet. Are you up to going out for something to eat?"

"Yes, I would appreciate that."

"You're the expert around here, so you pick where you'd like to go. No-frills simple or something to preoccupy your taste buds—either way is fine with me."

"Let's go to the downtown area of Harbour Village. It's quaint and there's a host of eateries. We can sit undisturbed with a fine sandwich and salad."

"How about I do the driving?"

She rattled off her address, and added, "I'll meet you out front. Having you come in would feel too strange."

"No problem. Be there in a half hour?"

"Sure."

Viktoria went to the bathroom mirror and slid off her elastic hair tie and, for a change, brushed out her shiny black hair and let it fall on her shoulders. She slid on lipstick, but didn't see the need to switch her outfit.

Wanting to stay busy, she went to the laundry room, pulled out clothes from the dryer which had sat there for two days, and began folding them. Some of them were Rick's. She took a big sigh, folded them neatly, and set them in the corner of the counter.

Viktoria gave Millie a pat on the head, grabbed a purse, and slipped the strap on her shoulder. She waited on the porch, a red sedan crept down the street, and stopped. Jeff popped out from the driver's side, and opened the front seat passenger's door.

They exchanged a small hug and the barest of smiles.

"These are poor circumstances," he said in the car, "but I am nevertheless glad to see you."

"Likewise," she nodded. "What about you? How did the hospital meeting go?"

"Fine. I'm finding them a pleasure to work with on our merger. The goal is to make them follow our proven protocols, which are better than what they have in place now."

"You are good at what you do, Jeff. O.R.s can only run effectively with people who provide decent rules and procedures."

He turned the key and peered over at her. "Which way?"

Viktoria guided him to downtown Harbour Village. After they parked and walked one of the busy sidewalks, she shunned away from suggesting any restaurant that Rick and she had frequented.

They paused at a menu posted to a door. "This one?" he asked.

"Sure. I've never been, but there is no bad place to eat around here."

Inside, they chose their own table, and a server with a dark ponytail and bangs brought them water. "I'm Linda, your own dedicated waitress today. May I rattle off our special, which is always a soup and sandwich?"

"Go for it," Viktoria said.

"Our chef made tomato pesto soup today, and he's whipping up Reubens on rye."

Their eyes met. "We'll take them," Viktoria said.

"Bowl or cup of soup?"

"Two cups?" she asked Jeff.

Jeff nodded. "And I'll take coffee."

The woman left, still holding the unused menus, and Viktoria and Jeff leaned forward.

"You must be making a lot of phone calls," Jeff said, "advising people about your husband's death."

"I've gotten around to Rick's father, and he called his other son, and some cousins. But I have yet to tell my mother, and my two brothers. My mom's in a step-up assisted living home but, yes, I need to go tell her. Better in person than the phone. And my brothers in Iceland, well, I am hesitant to tell them because I don't want them jumping on a plane and traveling all the way here."

"Isn't that for them to decide?" he asked hesitantly. "They may want to support their only sister in a time of need."

Viktoria frowned. "You're right, of course. I suppose I should leave it up to them."

"Where is your mom's nursing home?"

151

"Not too far away."

"What about your dad? Did you tell me he's deceased?"

"Yes, he passed. He stayed with my brothers in Iceland, and I wished I had seen him more often after my mom and I moved here."

The waitress put down Jeff's black coffee and creamers, moved the bowl of sugar packets in front of him, and left.

"Did your mom and dad have a good marriage?"

"Surprisingly so, although you wouldn't think it since they ended up on two different continents. They were tough cookies, and the kids came first. In a way, my mom sacrificed her own relationship to take me where she thought I would have a better life and, eventually a more lucrative career." She shook her head. "What devotion to her daughter. After I married Rick, I never burdened her with stories of his addiction. I wanted her to believe that her daughter's marriage was *allt i lagi*, or all right."

His smile lines creased next to his light brown eyes. "I love it when you speak Icelandic."

"Most people do. In addition, I can get away with saying anything behind people's backs, because the words resemble nothing that can be construed as troublesome!"

"I'll remember that."

Back to their table, the waitress moved plates and cups off her tray. "Enjoy. I'll be back to check on you."

Viktoria dipped a spoon into the red, dark soup. After a sample, she tried the hot, overflowing sandwich. "On both counts, this is what I needed," she remarked.

Jeff stayed with the soup, and continued on until the cup was empty. "Yes, excellent choice.

They chewed in silence, and then she said, "How is your dog, Mattie, and what did you do with her for this trip?"

"She's fine, except for the fact that she's right now in a kennel. What about your Millie? Is it by accident that you named your new dog like my Mattie? Sounds like they're twins."

"I realized that after the fact. Must've been some unconscious thing. It means they are bound to get along, like Mattie did with Buddy in Pennsylvania. When you drop me off later, I'd like you to meet her."

"Yes, I'd love to." He sipped his coffee, but admired her features as she wiped her hands on a napkin. It was one of the few times he'd seen her with her hair down. It was stunning, no matter how she wore it. Her full lips were delectable, he knew, and he tried his best not to imagine them on his own. For today, it would be distance only, for that he was sure.

Viktoria left only a bite of her sandwich, otherwise, they finished together. Jeff laid a bill inside the payment jacket, and the waitress brought him his change.

"Thank you," Viktoria said. "I could've paid, you know. After all, you are a guest in my little town."

"I wouldn't dream of it." He rose and let her step in front of him. "How about we stop at your mom's place and you can break the news to her? I can wait in the car."

Viktoria turned her head. "That would be too much to ask."

"You didn't ask, and I don't mind. You would be rid of that one more thing that you need to do."

They stepped off the curb outside and meandered to his rental car. At the door, she nodded while looking at him directly. "Make a right out of the parking lot."

Jeff parked by the front entrance of the multi-complex retirement facility in a visitor's spot.

"I won't take too long," Viktoria announced. "She should be finished with the early dinner they serve, and back in her room. This place houses independent living, assisted-care living, and a nursing section. My mom's in the assisted-care section—not too sick to be in the worst area, and not in the independent section where all they do is play cards and dream up clubs for this, that, or the other. The men even have a golf club, although all they really do is putter around on a range."

"Can you putt on a range?"

"Ha! Shows you how much I know about golf."

"Well, if you don't play, you don't need to." He laughed and patted her hand on her lap.

"Okay, I'm off." Viktoria edged out, signed the visitor's book inside, and made her way down the brown-plaid carpet to her mother's room.

CHAPTER 23

Viktoria knocked on her mother's door and waited for a response. The woman's voice sounded from inside. "Come in." It carried a perkiness to it, her joy apparent because some visitor had come to call.

Her mother, Elisabet, fixed her eyes on the doorway from a dark recliner against the back window. Her living space was one big room with a bathroom to the side. A refrigerator and sink was to the left, and the rest of the space held a TV table, bookcase, her chair, and her bed and nightstands. It was scanty for "assisted living" but, then again, any space whatsoever on Long Island wasn't cheap or plentiful.

"Viktoria, what a surprise." Elisabet fumbled for the TV remote between her leg and the armrest, and muted the television.

"Ma, how are you doing?" Viktoria stepped close, bent, and gave her a gentle hug. Like she always did when visiting, she scanned her mother up and down, her astute physician eyes monitoring her for any obvious physical changes. Since she was presently working on Long Island, she felt better being able to check on her more often.

But Viktoria noted that her hands were turning bony and her waistline thinner. Her high cheekbones were still the same, but the skin over them was losing its moisture and softness. However, the hair stylist at the facility didn't need to make her mother's hair any more striking than her natural 50/50 black hair interlaced with gray.

"My wonderful daughter, what a delight to see you, on a Monday no less. At least I think today is Monday, according to the day-of-the-week rug they put out by our common area." She lit up with a smile, her teeth still well taken care of and not artificial replacements.

"It is Monday, Ma, and you don't need any rug to tell you that. Did you eat in the dining room today, or did you have something here in your room?"

"I went for the chicken in the dining room, like the hockey pucks that they are, but I'm not complaining, honey. Some people in this world don't even eat dinner."

"Ma, I'm sorry. I'm back more than a week, and we're overdue for me to spring you out to wherever you'd like to go for dinner."

Elisabet patted her daughter's hand. "Your job is stressful. We'll go when it's convenient for you and Rick."

"I have bad news about Rick. It happened all at once in the last few days."

"You *do* look tired, and you're wearing a sad film over your eyes. What's going on?"

"He was admitted to the hospital over the weekend with a new type of lung illness. They put him on a breathing machine in the intensive care unit because it was necessary, but the doctor couldn't turn around his pulmonary problem. It only grew worse.

"He passed away, Ma."

Elisabet's head nodded just enough to be perceived, and the wrinkles on her forehead grew worse. "News doesn't get any worse than that, dear. No, he is too young for that." She placed her hand by her heart. "Did he have some kind of infection?"

Viktoria looked down, not wanting to tell her mother the truth. But she knew it came down to honesty being the best policy, and trying to cover up her husband's history with marijuana would only make her mother pry more.

"Ma, I don't think I ever told you that Rick was smoking marijuana. Lots of people do that, but with Rick, he became more and more addicted, and was getting his grass from suspect places. In essence, marijuana can get tainted with other dangerous products, causing a bigger problem to evolve."

"How sad. My son-in-law a drug addict. I wondered why, in recent years, he didn't seem like the nice man that originally married you. He became more aloof. And in the short two years I've lived in assisted living, I felt like whenever he visited, his foot was half out the door."

Viktoria squatted down and put her head in her hands. "You recognized the changes in him. The worst part was that he became terribly moody, and would sometimes become very nasty. The mood swings made me want to divorce him all the time."

"But you didn't." She sighed. "I didn't know it was that bad. You should have confided in your mother."

"Mom, getting older is hard enough, I'm sure, without listening to your daughter's relationship woes. You did enough for me already."

"But a mother has that right and desire with her children—to be there for them in any way—until the day of death, Viktoria."

"Your sons too?"

"Absolutely. And I barely see them every two years."

Viktoria read the sadness in her eyes. "Alexander, Bjorn, and I should make a point to change that."

Elisabet stroked her daughter's cheek. "Don't worry about that right now. What are you doing in your husband's memory?"

"Why don't you come to the memorial I'm having for him next weekend and then I'll take you out to eat."

"Yes, I'd like that. And Viktoria, whether you're burying him or cremating him, fill the service or celebration with lots of pictures of him when he was happy and before he did that terrible drug. That was his real spirit before being plunged into an existence based on puffing someone's idea of heaven."

Viktoria climbed back into Jeff's rental car with more despair written on her face than when she'd left.

"Are you okay?" he asked.

She shifted towards him as much as possible. "I think my mom understood my marriage was in the gutter all along. However, now I have a sense of something else. I believe she misses her sons more than she lets on, and probably misses Iceland just as much. I never thought of it before, but she launched herself and her daughter into a better life than what we had in Iceland. Life there was more difficult then, but my brothers situations have also changed over time for the better. Maybe now she'd like to go back."

Jeff furrowed his brow. "And so…"

"I need to do a better job of fulfilling her needs. After all, there's no crystal ball to tell me how long she'll be around. And you alluded to me telling my brothers about Rick's death. Maybe that can force all of us into a visit."

"There *is* nothing like a funeral to get people together."

"How ironic. Death may breathe life back into us."

Jeff shifted his eyes back to the steering wheel and started the car. He found his way back to her house, and parked in front.

"Millie needs a walk. Are you going to stick around?"

"If you want me to."

"Come on. You must meet my little girl."

Rick waited on the front step while Viktoria accepted Millie's greeting inside the door and hooked her to her leash. Stepping out, the dog barked with interest at him, rather than as a concerned watch-dog.

"She's lovely," he said, crouching down. It took but a second, and she was licking his hand. "Let me better check you out." He picked her up in his arms, Viktoria let go of the leash, and he cuddled her like a baby. "How old is she? How much does this feather-weight weigh?"

"All thirty pounds of her is nine-months old."

"Oh my. If you ever need a baby-sitter…"

"You're not the first person to say that."

"She and Mattie would enjoy each other."

"Yes, they would."

Jeff placed her down, she grabbed the leash, and the three of them began walking.

"Do you have much business tomorrow?" Viktoria asked.

"Most of the day will be busy. How's it going for you at that plastic surgery center? Are you dreading going back on Wednesday?"

"I am beginning to wonder if Amour is as creepy as what happened at Masonville General."

"Really? That bad?"

"Jeff, a patient died under my care last week. The circumstances are convoluted, starting with the woman's first plastic surgery days before. As you are aware, operative or perioperative deaths are rarer than an albino whitetail deer, unless the patient came through the trauma room to the OR from a massive MVA."

"Viktoria, your hometown on Long Island is not treating you well." He stopped, and Millie chomped down a few blades of grass.

She bobbed her head, they soon turned, and headed back to the house. Without discussing it, they both sat on the step. Millie put her head flat on the ground between her paws.

"Can we meet again before you fly back?"

"I was hoping you'd say that." He put his arm around her shoulder and inched her upper body to his until they touched. She pressed her head against him for a moment.

"What's a good time tomorrow?" she asked. "I'll call."

"Text me anytime, and we'll figure it out." Jeff rose. "I better let you get some sleep."

"You too. Thanks for tonight. I needed this."

"You are tougher than you think, but you're welcome." He leaned in and covered her lips with a kiss. "I hope none of your neighbors are watching."

"Let them watch. Sincere, thoughtful kisses are meant for anyone, whether they're grieving or not."

Jeff smiled. "And this little girl…" He put his head near Millie's snout and looked her in the eyes. "You take care of each other."

Tuesday morning, Viktoria prepared the coffee pot for the first time with Rick's ashes on the overhead shelf. She grinned at the artistic urns, and opened the blinds to the rising sunshine filtering up through the neighborhood. There were too many immediate details to take care of during the day, but she didn't feel pressured. She would do them, sooner or later.

Millie scarfed down her kibbles while Viktoria sipped coffee and ate instant oatmeal. Jeff's words from the night before resonated with her, and she grabbed the portable landline phone. It was later in Iceland, and she called her older brother first. After a few rings, he answered.

"Alexander, it's Viktoria. We need to talk. Is it a good time?"

"Fire away, sis. Uh-oh. Is Mom alright?"

"Yes. She's the same, except that I believe she misses you and Bjorn more and more as time goes by."

"And we her as well. It is up to one of us to do something about that."

His voice was robust, and she could picture him outdoors with a horse's rein in his hands like the last time she saw him.

"I agree. I have other news, however. Somewhat of a shocker. Rick passed away."

"What? No way."

Alexander waited for her to correct her statement, but she didn't. He softened his voice. "What happened?"

"He died in the hospital on a ventilator from a pulmonary problem which stemmed from vaping marijuana. The by-products these days can cause EVALI, a newly named medical issue."

"You told me before that he went around sneaking that stuff, but I had no idea."

"It has been a big issue in our marriage because it made him a different person, and now this…"

"Well, he obviously didn't care about a damn thing to be so self-centered. I'm sorry sis. Now's not the time to speak my peace." He pushed his brimmed hat further back off his forehead and continued stabling the horse next to him. "Listen, what are your plans for him?"

"I'm having a service this weekend. He was cremated yesterday."

"Why don't I tell Bjorn? We will correlate between us and one of us will fly down. Somebody needs to stay with the business."

"Are you sure? That's a lot to ask."

"You didn't ask. Plus, like you mentioned about Mom—it's been awhile since she's seen either one of us."

A heartfelt smile crawled across her lips. "She's going to be ecstatic."

"Why don't you spring her out of assisted living by the weekend, and she can stay at the house? Either of us visiting you can help out with whatever she needs. And did I mention nobody's staying at a hotel?"

"You did just now. No problem. We'll figure it out. Keep me posted."

"Okay," Alexander said, and added "Elska þig," which meant "Love you."

Viktoria hung up, and thought out plans as fast as she could. She called a restaurant on the north shore which had private rooms and booked one for Saturday. Afterwards, she dialed Rick's dad again and solicited his help in inviting family and friends to an early dinner and memorial on his behalf. The remainder of the afternoon, she made her own calls regarding Saturday.

As she set down Millie's dinner earlier than usual, a text message dinged from Jeff.

"Hey there, you faring okay? Here's a suggestion. How about I bring you dinner or let me take you out?"

She stood tall, stretched her arms overhead, and didn't think twice. *"The contents in my refrigerator are getting low. You'd be a lifesaver. Bring it on. No, better yet, I'm overdue to leave the house. I'll meet you at your hotel and we can decide where to go."*

"You sure?"

"Absolutely. I'll be there in an hour."

Viktoria picked up Millie's bowl. "Let's go, girl." They headed out, and basically trotted along the sidewalk for most of the walk. A van cruised down the street and pulled into her driveway when they returned. The paint job on the side said, "Island Flowers."

A young man stepped out. "You live here?"

"Sure do."

"I've got a delivery."

"My husband passed away. I suppose flowers are to be expected."

He opened the sliding door and changed his expression from a smile to a responsible frown. "Sorry for your loss. Here you go."

Viktoria dropped Millie's leash and accepted a pastel vase with an assortment of spring flowers. A large ribbon circled its neck and was tied in a pretty bow.

"Thank you."

"A note card is attached in the foliage." He slid back into the vehicle and backed out.

"Let's go in the house, Millie."

Millie tailed after her owner, her leash dragging along. Inside, Viktoria unclipped her and pulled out the florist's card.

"A little something for your spirits as you go through this difficult time, Jeff."

Wow, she thought. They were the perfect touch. Not only was she going to see one of her brothers at the end of the week, and have her mother closer than usual, but this man who worked in the health care industry like herself, was starting to put a dent in her heart.

CHAPTER 24

Viktoria had passed the hotel on the north-south road for years, but never before had a reason to stop there. The parking lot was almost always full due to a stellar location, and it gathered groups of event-goers for annual meetings. The sign outside said "Welcome American Legion."

She parked and unbuckled her seat belt. After walking Millie, she had changed out of the sweat pants she'd worn at home all day, and put on high-end cargo pants and a silky-looking V-neck top. She touched up her lipstick in the rear view mirror, and grabbed her cell phone and purse.

The inside lobby proved to be more decorative and formal than what she expected. She slipped to the left, picked one of the cozy sitting areas, and called Jeff.

"I'll be right down," he said.

He appeared from the elevator area around from the registration desk, and planted his eyes on her. With a casual stride, he registered a smile, and waved for her to keep seated.

Viktoria's breath caught in her throat, he was so damn handsome. His sandy-colored hair was a bit untidy, more unkempt, making him even more enticing. With a barely perceptible shake of her head, she admonished herself. She needed to curb her ill-timed thoughts because her husband was fresh ashes in a box.

Jeff sat in the circular, cushiony chair across from her, and laid his phone on the round table between them.

"Thank you," Viktoria said.

"For what?"

"For the flowers."

"Ah, yes," he nodded. "Even in grief, one must smile."

"How was your day?"

"Productive. And my hospital group wants me to stay longer because I'm making headway with the nitty-gritty details of the merger."

"Are you happy about that?"

"Yes, for two reasons. The business part makes sense and, secondly, I'll be in the same vicinity as you—whether or not you can make time for me or not."

"We can try. I suppose the week will unfold the way it's meant to."

Jeff nodded. "How about talking over there in the restaurant? They have a bar, and we can order a drink."

"Let's go."

Several restaurant tables were busily occupied as they stepped to the mahogany bar and sat on stools.

"How about a whiskey sour?" Viktoria told the bartender.

"A Johnny Walker on the rocks," Jeff said.

"The week's plans are perking along," Viktoria said. "One of my brothers is going to fly down by the end of the week, we are bringing my mom to the house for an interim duration, and I've booked a spot for a celebration of Rick's life on Saturday."

The bartender placed their drinks on cocktail napkins, slid the mixed nuts between them, and turned to the overhead sports channel.

Jeff raised his scotch. "Here's to a better week."

Viktoria obliged by tapping her glass on his and then fished for the stem of the cherry. "There's nothing like an alcoholic red cherry," she said, popping it in her mouth. "And I'm overdue."

"Better or worse than that, have you ever tried cherries stuffed into a wide-brimmed bottle of moonshine?"

Her gaze went to the ceiling. "Get out. No kidding?"

"Really. Someday we should take a trip to the Smoky Mountains in Tennessee. Those people there know how to do it."

The remnant of the fruit slid down her throat, and she nodded.

"And/or go to Nashville and bar hop downtown where they carry the same moonshine. There, we can not only bar hop, but we can listen to each venue's version of country music."

She turned to him and couldn't keep a straight face. "Here I am with a dead husband from a drug addiction, and you're trying to turn me into a lush?"

"You're too serious to ever let loose that much."

"Damn it, but you're right." She swirled the whiskey sour around in her mouth. "Just for that remark, I'm going to drink two of these."

"Be careful. You do need to go back to that awful outpatient surgery practice tomorrow."

She glanced behind them. "Then let's get a table here. The food's probably decent, and I can give my second drink something to land on in my stomach."

"Your wish is my command." Jeff took her drink, as well as his own, and stood. "Bartender, what's your entrée suggestion if we eat here?"

The man turned his head. "Chef comes from New England. He makes the best clam chowder. Then order the veal Parmesan. You won't regret it."

"Thanks, we'll take these with us." Jeff put down a few singles, and they moved to a booth against the wall. A waitress noticed and walked straight over.

"We'll take another Johnny Walker and whiskey sour when we're finished with these." His eyes landed on Viktoria. "Should we order the bartender's suggestions?"

She nodded. "We'll take one bowl of clam chowder that we'll split, and two veal Parmesans with French fries and mixed vegetables."

"It comes with spaghetti."

"That too," Viktoria said.

The waitress left, still holding the menus, and Jeff raised an eyebrow, "Spaghetti and French fries?"

"What the heck. You just said I'm too serious."

"Are you sure you're doing okay?"

"It's like this, Jeff. Never ask a woman who is eating ice cream straight from the carton how she's doing. And if she wants to eat French fries and spaghetti, don't ask her about that either."

A humorous smile crossed his lips. "Point taken."

As she pushed away her empty glass, and the waitress brought the second drinks, he wondered if he needed to drive her home when the time came.

An hour turned into two, and then Viktoria insisted on paying the bill. "Most of this food was my fault," she said, although she mostly put down the veal Parmesan and not much else except the soup.

Jeff sighed and sat back against the brown leather while she paid by credit card. They scooted out and reluctantly walked to the lobby. Neither of them spoke. He took her hand and held it.

In the same circular area that they had linked up in, they faced each other. "If needed, I am offering to drive you home in your car. I can Uber back here." He paused. "That is, if you want to leave."

He let his feelings surpass any societal norms that one might assume, and he took a gamble. Viktoria was a grown woman, and she could make up her own mind. He leaned into her ear and whispered. "Would you like to stay for a while... we can go upstairs."

She squeezed his hand in answer to his question.

After riding the elevator upstairs and entering Jeff's room, they grinned with mischief while taking off each other's shoes. They sprawled on the Queen bed and began kissing, slowly at first, and then with the intensity they'd missed since their last encounter. Wrapped beneath him after they shed their clothes, she let the moments simmer with pleasure and let everything else go.

The culmination of their night was just what she needed, and she had no regrets as, dressed again, she kissed him at the door and insisted on driving herself home.

"I wish you could stay," he said.

"Me, too. Not this time though. Millie is waiting for me, and sleeping at home is a better idea. I must be bright and early at Amour Cosmetic Surgery. Sleeping with you would be too much of a physical, longing distraction." They kissed again, and she scurried down the hallway.

Her alarm buzzed at 5 a.m., and Viktoria groggily planted her feet on the floor while Millie jumped off the bed.

"That was a super sleep, Millie. Maybe I need to drink whiskey sours more often or, better yet, jump in the sack with Jeffrey Appleton more frequently. But don't tell anyone I told you so. I'm supposed to be in mourning." Whatever that is, she thought, but then reconsidered.

But she did mourn, she decided. She mourned for the way Rick had taken the path he did and, in doing so, ruined their marriage. And she agonized over the fact that he jeopardized his health by buying tainted marijuana when he really knew better. The pleasure he received from the stupid vaping was not worth dying over.

After dressing hurriedly into trousers and a plain blouse, she turned the coffee pot on, and took Millie for a spin. She fed her and poured a cup of coffee to bring in the car, and left.

Viktoria made a left turn into the strip mall without scanning the familiar billboard signs mounted at the entrance. Her cup of coffee was in her hand, and she slid down the last French Roast and smacked her lips. She was prompt at 6:45 a.m., and pulled around to the back of the building and parked in her usual place towards the back. It was always more considerate to leave front spots for patients.

Stuffing loose items into her purse, she left her vehicle and sauntered with her head down across the two aisles. She stepped up on the curb near the landscaping and the outside bench.

She looked forward and reached for the door handle.

That's strange, she thought, noticing something different. The fancy blue lettering of the surgery center was missing from the glass door.

Amour Cosmetic Surgery was scraped off like it never existed, and the entire see-through door was spanking clean from a superior cleaning job.

Viktoria took two steps back and glanced up over the door, where the wood inscripted business name was mounted. At least last week it was.

"What the ...." she said aloud.

The plaque now said "Long Island's Surgery and Cosmetic Beautification."

Dumbfounded, she stood motionless. What was going on here? And if this was a different practice, technically, she was not hired to render anesthesia services to the surgery center inside.

She'd only been gone Monday and Tuesday, she thought. If the previous group went out of business, why didn't they inform her? But Amour going out of business seemed unlikely due to the cash payments they received and their sheer volume of cases. Actually, they were a gold-mine.

Being trained in medicine and not business, she was not business savvy like the professionals in that field. However, the next thought slapped her in the face. Bonnie Sandler's death may already be detrimental to their image and maybe there could already be a fallout of negative reviews on their website from her deadly result. Thinking further back, she'd seen irate customers complaining about refunds for cancelled surgery not being refunded, and patients hiring attorneys against Amour because of unacceptable results.

Totally puzzled, she opened the door. She ignored the scattering of people in the waiting room, and glanced at the scrolling advertisement on the wall. The sheer notion of it was mind boggling—the same screens moved on with pretty pictures of surgical results—however, the name on the first slide had been changed.

Long Island's Surgery and Cosmetic Beautification.

Damn, they worked fast, she thought, but giving them the benefit of the doubt, perhaps the name change had been planned for some time.

She peeled her eyes off the wall and pranced straight to Lucy Murray. The woman wore her dark blonde braid to the right today and, with a pen in her hand, stared at the paper OR schedule on the front desk.

"Lucy, what is going on here? Last I was aware, this was Amour Cosmetic Surgery."

Ms. Murray's eyes shot up. "Nothing's changed," she said matter-of-factly. "The little 'reorganization' doesn't affect you in the least. Your first case is waiting on you in the preop area."

Viktoria's feet seemed glued to the floor as she tumbled Lucy's words around in her brain. Yes, she didn't doubt her services would be paid for through her locum tenens agency, but the situation stunk of skulduggery.

"Well?" Lucy said as a follow-up, waiting for Viktoria to move away.

Dr. Thorsdottir stilled her tongue from saying a word, afraid she would say too much of what she thought, and not what was substantiated. Plus, there were patients with their significant others in the waiting area who need not overhear her accusations.

Lucy still fixated a glare on the young doctor, but suddenly realized she had forgotten to address the reason for Viktoria's two-day absence. "Regina, from the locum tenens agency, told us about your husband's death. Everyone was sorry to hear that. Was he ill for a long time?"

"No, he had a short, but critical ICU hospitalization," she responded, knowing that Regina had, rightfully so, not given Amour Cosmetic Surgery the details of Rick's death.

"If there is anything we can do for you, or if you need more time off, don't hesitate to ask us."

"Thanks. I think I can get through this. Working is the best method I use to keep my mind off of problems or, in this present situation, my grief." She scooted in the door to the back, and frowned. A person's day-in and day-out job, she thought, can help them maintain the mental denial they have about a personal problem which, in her case, was her marital situation for the last few years.

In the locker room, she quickly donned scrubs, and purposefully stepped into the kitchen before seeing her patient. It was not coffee she sought, but Rigoberto Castillo.

CHAPTER 25

Dr. Castillo stood leaning against the counter, his legs crossed, his hands cupping a mug of coffee. Her impression was that the short man's shoulders were weighted down with problems, and he wore a puffiness around his eyes. She had learned enough about cosmetic facial enhancement to realize it wasn't Botox creating that look but, rather, lack of sleep.

He spoke before she opened her mouth. "Dr. Thorsdottir, I'm so sorry to hear about your husband's death. He couldn't have been that old. Was it an accident?"

Viktoria suddenly realized that she better brace herself for the type of questions she'd already heard from Lucy. After all, they were correct. Rick's death was sudden, and he was too young.

"No. He had an acute medical illness, worse than anyone anticipated. Thank you for your concern, and I have a question for you. I'm puzzled to come back and find your center under a different name…"

"That doesn't sound like a question. My center? You can look at that two ways. This practice is legally a different one than the one sitting here last week. I worked at that one, and I've decided to work at this Long Island center as well."

That went over her head. No doubt, his answer was as cryptic as he was.

"I am only some temporary doctor sailing through here for one month, so most of what you do is none of my business. But, I was involved in a case with the worst outcome possible and want to know what the ramifications will be because of your name change."

"What ramifications? Why would you think there are consequences? In essence, Amour Cosmetic Surgery doesn't exist anymore."

"Exactly!" The man's answer sounded as devious as the expression on his face and, like a racehorse, her pulse bounded in her wrist.

"Miss Viktoria, a name change is part of normal business and marketing." He abducted his forearm and put the mug down on the counter. "Now, if you'll excuse me, patients are waiting, and I need to change into scrubs."

"Unbelievable," she mumbled as he left.

Viktoria spied two plastic containers of muffins, apparently left over from Monday or Tuesday. She grabbed a blueberry one with a glazed sugary top and sat down with it. Comfort food, she thought, kind-of like last night when she resorted to two whiskey sours. After pinching the puffy top off the rest of the muffin, she swallowed it down with a chase of black coffee.

The scheduling board showed Viktoria as the anesthesiologist in OR Room 2 with Dr. Kippy Saliner as the surgeon. In the preop area, she shed her contempt for Dr. Castillo, and opened the curtains to a couple sitting on either side of their seven-year-old daughter.

"They told us the anesthesiologist would be here in a moment," the mother said.

Viktoria introduced herself and gave an enthusiastic greeting to the young girl named Trish, whose ears were very noticeable and stuck out in front of her curly brown hair.

"You will be asleep when Dr. Saliner makes your ears prettier," she said, "and next thing you know, you'll be sipping on a soft drink when it's all over."

The timid girl bobbed her head.

"What grade are you in?"

"I'm in the second grade, but I don't like to go. All the kids make fun of me because I have big ears."

"You are special whether you have large or small ears. But after today, I'm sure you'll like them better."

"Mommy said the same thing." She smiled for the first time, and nestled back into the pillow.

After speaking with both parents to find out that Trish was a healthy patient, and explaining the anesthetic and what to expect, she set up her equipment and drugs in her room. The tech and RN also focused on their own jobs as an OR door swung open and the anesthetic tech hobbled in.

"Anything I can get you?" Lola asked Viktoria.

"No. The cart in here is well supplied. How is that baby growing?"

"Just fine. But how are you? I heard there was a death in your family."

"Yes. My husband died in the ICU over the weekend," she said in a quiet tone. "Life sure throws punches at all of us, Lola."

"I'm sorry, Dr. Thorsdottir." She took off her glasses and wiped a lens off on her scrubs. "One more thing, in case someone forgets to tell you, make sure any paperwork you use has the new name of 'Long Island's Surgery and Cosmetic Beautification' on it. Sometimes the old documents hang around in unexpected places. I do my best to weed them out, but I'm not perfect. Yesterday I found an old unused postop instruction sheet from two years ago that said 'Go-2 Aesthetic Plastic Surgery Center.'"

Viktoria's tilted her head. "That was also a previous name of this place?"

"Yes. In essence, that one lasted pretty long."

She exhaled with a whish, as if trying to expel the bad taste in her mouth. Lola adjusted her glasses back on the bridge of her nose, and came closer, right against the other side of the red anesthesia cart.

"I'm not going to work for a while after my baby is born. But then I'm not coming back here. On my resume, all these different names of plastic surgery centers makes it appear as if I constantly change jobs and can't stay in one place."

Viktoria nodded. "I can see where that would be a problem, you job hopper, you." She patted the cart. "Lola, in the future, if you need a job reference, you can count on me."

"Thanks, Dr. Thorsdottir." She stepped out the door with a hand resting on her abdomen. "Besides, this month was the last straw. Dr. Castillo asked me if I'd like some instruction on how to use chemical filler stuff like Botox. He said he would let me inject the faces of patients to remove wrinkles. There's another unqualified, unlicensed person here who does that, and I don't want to be like her."

Viktoria's mouth fell and she heard voices approaching. Digging into her scrub jacket pocket, she quickly pulled out a notepad. Not wanting to forget it, she scribbled the name Lola told her—Go-2 Aesthetic Plastic Surgery Center.

The doors swung open with Trish being wheeled in on a stretcher. She scooted straight over to the OR table when the time came, and wasn't phased by the monitors or the medical environment. Viktoria safely put her to sleep and the surgeon walked in after scrubbing. She was glad it was her taking care of the young girl, as well as Kippy.

"Perfect age for her otoplasy," Viktoria acknowledged.

"Yes, it certainly is. Anytime after five years old is advised, since that is when a child's ear reaches full size. I'm happy they brought her in to see me because she's a perfect candidate. She will have good results and be able to shed the ridicule problem at school."

"She's a sweet kid." Viktoria watched as Kippy soon made an incision in the crease behind Trish's right ear.

"Dr. Saliner, do you do cases here very often?"

"I mostly work at another plastic surgery center and the hospital down the road. Only if my patients request this strip-mall outpatient center, do I come here." She rolled her eyes above her mask. "And certain things bother me, like finding out this morning about an organizational change. I never can figure out the business practices around here. I'm more comfortable doing cases at the other facilities. My colleagues won't even come here, but I cave in and want to accomodate my patients." She scanned the eyes of the tech and RN.

"I'm not saying a word," the tech said, her hands resting on the tray table.

The RN stood at the bottom of the table. "I'm with a locum tenens agency, so I'm no loyal full-time employee, just passing through."

"I am with an agency as well," Viktoria said.

"A percentage of our staff is temporary help all the time," the tech added.

"See?" Kippy said, looking straight at Viktoria. "Not your most stable surgical practice."

"Seems like that's the way they want it," Viktoria said.

"You've got that right." The tech straightened the instruments on the tray table and waited for Kippy's next request.

It was stress-free working with Dr. Saliner for two otoplasties in a row, and then Viktoria was given the green light to fetch lunch. The muffin had tied her over, but she yearned for a substantial sandwich next door. First, however, she personally discharged Trish from the recovery room and also talked to her parents. The young girl sipped through a straw from an apple juice container, and was no worse for wear with her ears wrapped with sterile dressings.

"Thank you so much," the mother said. "We gambled to let Trish undergo this elective procedure when we were worried about her safety under anesthesia and what kind of results she'd have. So, the anesthesia part is behind us."

"You are welcome," Viktoria said. "And I believe Dr. Saliner did a fine job. Once Trish's bruising heals, I think the three of you will be happy with the outcome."

Trish's father rose, grasped Viktoria's hand, and shook it.

She smiled at their heartfelt gratitude as she left the recovery room and donned a long, different scrub jacket to step away to the sandwich shop. The Long Island sunshine was in full bloom, and she hated to go back inside the strip mall. But she did, and within minutes she had a paper-wrapped sub-sandwich and a large iced tea.

The sun was too inviting to not be outside, she thought, so she carried her lunch to the bench on the sidewalk outside the surgery center. The warm rays warmed her spirit as well as her face. A car parked in an empty spot to her right and a young man popped out and grabbed a camera from the passenger seat. He threw its strap around his neck and then held the camera in front of him as he positioned himself away, but in front of, the prestigious center for beautification.

After unwrapping the paper, Viktoria sunk her teeth into the loaded veggie sandwich with cheese as the perky young man aimed the camera at the sign above the door. He moved to the right and left and took the same type of shots from different angles. Although his presence was entertaining her lunchtime, she preferred him not there.

"You're not putting me in any of those pictures?" she commented loud enough for him to hear.

"No, ma'am." He walked over and stood with one foot on the curb. He wore a black shirt and the high-end camera blended right in. "Don't mean to disturb your lunch. Just taking pictures of the sign, and I'll take a few farther away—of the whole front of the business. Then, you might want to move away."

"I sure will. What are you taking pictures for?"

"Ads and social media. The surgery center uses a marketing company and they hire me whenever. I'm a freelancer."

"Ha, you could say I do the same thing. However, I better get out of your way."

"Thanks. Lucky for me, today is sunny, and these photos are going to turn out well. Big media blitzs' need dazzling pictures to bring them to life."

Viktoria nodded. The real business heads behind this plastic surgery site knew how to proceed every step of the way. She gave up finishing her lunch outside and went back into the sandwich shop and finished there.

Lucky for Viktoria, she only had two shorter anesthetic cases when she returned. It was after three o'clock when she went to the locker room and readied to go home, but she didn't mind. Her cases had gone well for the day, and she had no more run-ins with people she didn't want to talk to, especially about things which made her shudder about where she was presently working.

Lucy Murray slipped into the rest room as Viktoria pulled out her purse from the locker, and left. She passed the front desk and nodded at the last family members and significant others waiting on patients. When she stepped out for the day, it was warmer than before, and as lovely.

As she headed towards her Honda, another man was in the parking lot—with a camera, no less. Older than the man earlier in the day, the small man wore a well-pressed gray business suit, but his camera didn't need a neck strap and it easily fit in one hand.

"I thought you all would have finished taking your pictures by now," Viktoria said, with an abrupt stop.

"I'm just getting started," he said, and narrowed his eyes at her. "Why, has someone else been taking pictures of *that* place?" He spoke loudly and had a deep voice, and his Long Island accent was strong, so he was no outsider to the area.

"A fellow was taking pictures today for their high-end advertising." She nodded her head toward the building.

He scowled. "You work there?"

"Last week was the first time I set foot in there. I'm temporary, and there will be no love lost when I finish at the end of the month. Can I ask you what you're doing if you aren't associated with the marketing company?"

He transferred the camera to his other hand, and extended his dominant hand. "I'm Jonathan Stewart, a partner of Stewart and Klein, working on legal matters for a client."

Viktoria shook his hand which was no bigger than her own. "And I'm Dr. Viktoria Thorsdottir. Let me guess. Your client is or was a patient of the plastic surgery establishment, whatever it's name may have been, in the middle of this strip mall."

A grin formed on his lips.

"May I ask you your client's name?"

"Dorothy Flores. Her considerate sister, Marilyn, was the one who made the initial call to me on her sister's behalf."

Viktoria raised her hand to her mouth in surprise. "Oh no, is Mrs. Flores okay? I did her anesthesia last week. Victor Reed was the surgeon who did her abdominoplasty."

"No, she didn't do too well after her surgery, but I'm glad to find out you were not one of the surgeons. As a matter of fact, she complimented the anesthesiologist doctor who put her under."

"Mr. Stewart, please tell me what happened to her."

"That butcher, Reed, caused her to have an abdominal perforation, and even though she tried to straighten out her postop course with Amour Cosmetic Surgery, she got the run around. She ended up in the hospital. I already took the deposition of a Dr. Woodson, the surgeon who had to bring her into an emergency surgery."

"How terrible. I hope she's on the mend, and please tell her that I send her my best wishes for a speedy recovery."

"I will."

"Why are you taking pictures?"

"I drove by to see the place, but I never expected this. My client is suing Amour Cosmetic Surgery and Dr. Victor Reed. But fancy that, by the looks of it, Amour no longer exists. Dirt bags. By the time I finish with them…

"Anyway, I always have a camera in the car. I try not to use my cell phone for lawyer-related work. Now I have evidence of the new name and name change." He chuckled. "Otherwise I will forget a long name like that."

"I don't blame you. For your information, I wasn't here but two days when I stumbled upon a scene at their front desk. A woman with her attorney son were complaining about not being reimbursed her money after her surgery was cancelled. Plus, a patient died within the last few days after two surgeries in one week."

Viktoria glanced at the ground, and closed her eyes for a moment. "There is nothing worse than truly unnecessary deaths."

She looked back up at him. "After getting a botched-up plastic surgery result, I hope Mrs. Flores gets the justified legal result she deserves.

"And, would you mind giving me your card?"

Mr. Stewart pulled out the firm's business card and handed it over.

CHAPTER 26

Viktoria and Jonathan Stewart went their separate ways. As she drove home, she calculated what she still needed to do for Saturday's event to commemorate Rick. Her biggest blessing was that her former father-in-law was helping out with invitations because in two more days, her brother and mother would be house guests.

But her day-to-day practice of anesthesia and the patients who relied on her were extremely important as well. She may go place-to-place, she thought, and not consider one hospital or outpatient surgery clinic her own, but the moral codes of conduct and upholding of the Hippocratic Oath were still held sacred to her no matter where she rendered an anesthetic.

By the end of the month, she'd be gone from Long Island Surgery and Cosmetic Beautification. She didn't know if she could stand finishing her assignment at that dreadful place. However, for the patients that were being suckered into having their surgery there, better that she take care of them than perhaps someone else, especially since she was eyeing the surgical procedures that much closer for complications. Resuscitation was right up an anesthesiologist's alley. Although, she frowned, Bonnie had been so botched up, she couldn't even prevent her death.

She pulled into the garage at home and, inside the house, reciprocated Millie's exuberant greeting. The dog's stunning eyes bore a hole in her heart as she picked her up, sunk into a chair, and cuddled her.

"I missed you today more than you know. And although one of your human beings is now permanently missing, you're going to meet some new ones this week. So far, your life has been filled with people coming and going like in a revolving door, but your newest mom is still here, and she isn't going anywhere without you." Viktoria bent closer and planted kisses on her snout. The dog lay spreadeagled, receptively loving it all.

"Let's go for a walk, girl." She stood, put the dog on the floor, and sprinted to the door. Once Millie was leashed and they walked down the street, Viktoria called Jeff.

"Hey," he said. "How's your day?"

"Can you talk?"

"I'm sitting outside somebody's office just waiting to meet with them, but this shouldn't take too long. Want to meet when I finish?"

"Absolutely. There was a turn of events today at work."

"I'll be all ears."

"How about popping over here?"

"Sure thing."

"Want me to bring take-out?"

"How about I scrounge around in my refrigerator and come up with something edible, but that's all I can promise."

"Viktoria, forget about it. I'll bring something. Quick, no mess to clean up, and hopefully tasty. You have enough on your plate."

"You do too. After all, you're not here on vacation."

"But being able to see you is the best part."

"Thanks. I'm happy you're here too."

"Okay, gotta go."

"I'm walking Millie. Take your time."

With Millie fed, Viktoria cinched the drawstring on her sweatpants, went to the mirror, and let her hair settle on her shoulders. She was becoming that much more comfortable with Jeff, and wanted him to feel the same way at her house. The doorbell rang in an hour, and she opened it with a grin.

Millie said hello to him first by stepping in front of her. By the looks of it, the dog liked Jeff a lot more than she did Rick.

"You've made a friend," she said.

"I hope that means she has excellent taste."

"She's a smart little girl, so..." She gave him a smile.

Jeff stepped through the doorway, held up a brown bag, and off to the kitchen they went with Millie leading the way.

"She tends to have this routine figured out. Do you always have men show up at your doorstep with parcels of food?"

"No. She's a fast learner, or makes up the household routines herself."

Jeff unpacked the two Styrofoam containers. "I didn't bring drinks, however."

"We can fix that right now." Viktoria turned to the refrigerator and pulled out a bottle of white wine on the lower door shelf. "I don't have any beer. Wine okay?"

"Perfect." He uncorked the bottle while she peeked in the containers to find grilled chicken breasts on top of salads. The mixed greenery was peppered with mushrooms, tomatoes, cucumbers, and blue cheese, and she nodded her approval.

They placed the containers and cutlery on the table, and Viktoria bent one leg and tucked it up on the seat. Jeff poured the wine into two glasses and sat.

"I'm glad you changed out of business clothes," Viktoria said, eyeing his soft, fitted Henley shirt, the top button undone, "especially since I'm wearing sweat clothes."

"Yes, I dressed casually and I'm unwinding already." He held up his wine, and they both tapped their glasses. "So, what turn of events happened at the Mommy Makeover or Man Alterations Center today?"

Viktoria shook her head. "Funny you should say that. I'll make a note of those names because maybe they can use them in the future. I went back to work today at a different place. Amour Cosmetic Surgery no longer exists."

He held his fork without using it. "What do you mean?"

"The name is dead and buried, as in they buried the hatchet."

He tilted his head to the side. "You gave me a whiff of what that place is like, so do you think their purpose is to leave no trace of Amour Cosmetic Surgery?"

"Exactly, and the same facility is now called Long Island's Surgery and Cosmetic Beautification."

Viktoria swirled her glass around. "Jeff, I tell you, I can't stand to sit by. This is awful. Plastic surgery is a gift to modern society, but this practice? The entire place is a business shrouded in deceit and money-making practices, unskilled surgeons, and wretched results."

"And I thought you and I found problems in my hospital!"

"Well, I must say that the surgical practice has at least one fine plastic surgeon, but she is rarely there compared to the rest of them. I think she's the only pearl they've got."

Viktoria sampled the chicken and Jeff did the same as he pondered what she'd told him. "When I was leaving this afternoon, I bumped into a lawyer in the parking lot who has taken on one of their patients as a client. The woman was hospitalized and had emergency surgery due to an abdominal perforation last week after a tummy tuck. And, of course, the breast augmentation woman just died. And I've overheard and seen things from patients, lawyers, and a factory-like business office that would make you want to turn them into the National Enquirer."

"The next few days will be a lighter work load for me, and I'll still be around. Should we dig deeper?"

"What you mean is should I become another whistle-blower? The problem with that is I need to work the rest of my life and can't afford to carry along that kind of baggage postscript to my name."

"Maybe we can keep your name out of it…somehow."

"Although, lately, I am becoming disenchanted with the corruption and bad people I'm running into all the time. Makes me want to get up and leave Long Island."

"Long Island?"

"Problems existed in Pennsylvania too, Viktoria, and I'm sure they're all over the U.S. There are good and bad people everywhere. You know that. The grass is always greener…"

She leaned over her plate. "It just seems like it's more entrenched anymore in American society. Even politics. I better not get started…"

He gave her a small frown. "No Shangri-la exists."

"Lately I've been thinking about going home." She eyed her salad, and then looked down at Millie sleeping beside her chair.

"Home? As in Iceland?"

She nodded.

"Sounds like you are *very* disappointed with your current affairs. Can I help you with the current surgery center debacle? Honestly, we can dig deeper and see what we find."

"With my husband's death, this is a lot to handle. It would be like me trying to push a boulder up a mountain."

He inched his hand over and cupped hers for a moment. "I will help, and I bet when your brother shows up, he'll be helpful to you too."

"Yes, and he can help with my mom. And my father-in-law is a nice guy, and he's handling most of Saturday's activities. He's always understood my work situation since he was a hard worker himself. Worked as an engineer until he was seventy."

"Okay, there you go. Let's finish eating and tell me everything you know and have heard about Amour or Long Island's new surgery center."

She gave him a prolonged frown. "The anesthesia tech also told me that before Amour Cosmetic Surgery, it was called Go-2 Aesthetic Plastic Surgery Center."

Jeff widened his eyes. All he could say was "Wow."

Viktoria and Jeff finished their meals and moved inside where Jeff leaned forward from the leather chair and Viktoria sat on the floor with Millie cuddled up next to her. The square coffee table was between them, and Jeff had requested paper where they could both jot down notes.

With a steaming hot cup of coffee in his hand, Jeff listened to the chronological sequence of events that Viktoria had been privy to since her arrival at the surgery center. They filled the sheet with dates, names, surgeries, and outcomes, as well as all things notable about their business practices. Viktoria wrote down lawyers names.

"We make an excellent team for this type of thing," Jeff noted. "With my medical business background and your keen professional eye, I vow right now that we put a bump, if not a huge dent, in their operation. And by 'operation,' I mean their physical operations as well as their business operation."

Being both tired, yet hopeful, Viktoria sighed. "Let's say you do, or you don't, dig up more unscrupulous facts about them. Exactly...*who* do we go to with this, or *what* do we do with our information?"

"We will tell the New York medical disciplinary board, particularly referencing specific physicians. We can talk to legal experts and state officials. States should be able to suspend the operations of clinics, or centers, when they pose a threat to the public."

She stroked Millie's fur and nodded. "I better tell Regina at the locum tenens agency not to schedule me next month for another assignment. I would rather end up with some resolution to this matter and also let the dust settle as I contemplate what to do next with my personal life."

Jeff set down his coffee and cocked his head. His light brown eyes stared at her with tenderness. Millie whimpered in her sleep, and Viktoria stretched over and gently caressed the hair on her neck.

"Okay, then," he said. "I best be going." He rose and she followed his lead. With a mischievous smile, he added, "Plus, we had a late night last night."

She returned his grin. "And it was worth every minute of it."

"No regrets because of your husband's passing?"

"No, Jeff. It's okay. There's a reason for everything, and I think you were meant to be here at this time."

Millie stretched her limbs while still lying on her side, but then scurried up on all fours. She followed them to the door and Jeff crouched down. He went head-to-head with her, and planted a kiss on her snout. "See you soon, girl."

When he stood, they sunk into each other's arms and held steady. The seconds ticked by, and they didn't let go. "Good night," he finally said.

"Talk to you late tomorrow," she said. "Thanks for the take-out."

They kissed, slowly, and without intensity. And then he also kissed her forehead. "Hang in there Icelander."

CHAPTER 27

Jeff pulled onto the main drag and headed south to his hotel. He had drunk the one glass of wine with Viktoria, but he wanted a smooth beer to take back to the room and think things over before sleeping. He deviated from the lobby into the bar where the same bartender was on duty.

"Do you have any craft beers?" Jeff asked.

"Sure do. Our supplying brewery's bestseller is an earthy blend. Want to try it?"

"If I can take it to my room."

"No problem," he chuckled. "I trust you to bring back the glass." He slipped a pint glass under the keg puller and poured. "Where's your pretty date tonight?"

"I just left her. She is attractive, isn't she?"

He nodded. "And don't mind me. Working this job, I can always tell what the relationship is of people sitting across from me even if it isn't blatant."

"I bet. I bar tendered a few months myself, and it's quite entertaining."

"Frightfully so." He handed the beer to Jeff and took the bill on the counter.

"Keep the change."

"Thanks. And continued luck with your relationship, wherever it goes."

"I'm going to give some thought to that very subject."

"In my opinion, the two of you look suited for each other." He took a cloth from below and wiped the counter. "Have an enjoyable night. You can leave the glass on the end of the bar tomorrow."

Jeff left, and took the elevator. At the end of the hallway upstairs, he eyed the sprinkler system overhead and headed to his room. One thing he appreciated about this particular hotel chain, was that the rooms never smelled heavily of cleaning products. Yet, the rooms always appeared to be free from dirt or stains.

He put a local news channel on the television, but kept the volume low in the background. While sipping the beer, he caught up on emails at the desk where his laptop was stationed. On purpose, he refrained from diving into Viktoria's subject which had hooked his interest—that of the plastic surgery site with the revolving door of new names. Tomorrow he would devote every possible minute he could spend on it, separate from his own work with the local hospital.

He finished the beer, changed, and slipped into bed. The sheets still smelled of Viktoria, making it easier to think about her. Then again, the bartender downstairs had voiced his impression of her, like a second pair of eyes to corroborate what he thought. And he had been thinking of her a lot.

At forty years old, and a bachelor by default, he had been meticulously careful about forging ahead with any serious relationship or one ending in marriage. The only reason he was single was because he had not found the right woman.

Some men he knew were single because they had witnessed colleagues or relatives in marriages that had turned way too sour. In essence, they were trying to avoid the bad examples.

He, on the other hand, had witnessed one of those rare marriages where both partners simply adored each other. It was like they lived in a cocoon together, living and breathing the same desires and happiness. They were practically inseparable.

The couple in question had been his own parents. The remarkable companionship he had seen in their relationship as he grew up as an only child and later when he had witnessed them as "empty nesters," had and could exist. He wanted nothing more than to emulate them.

However, the reality of that dream, he knew, may not ever come to fruition if the two individuals never cross paths. And all along, he accepted that possibility. He was content in not accepting anything less than true love. He refused to be half-way miserable like many of the skiers he hung out with in winter, or the colleagues in the medical and business field—the ones he crossed paths with during work.

His parents had been his role model. Up until their deaths, they were still enthusiastic and displayed affection for each other. And the closest thing he'd ever seen them do if they were annoyed at each other, was to shake their heads.

Jeff believed he was a good judge of character. Usually, at best, his approximate three times a year attempt to "find" someone for a long-term relationship ended up in three dates or three months of "seeing" each other. Either way, he called it his "three tries." When the three tries were up, he knew there was no future in going any farther. Occasionally, the other person felt the same way, which was a blessing for Jeff. Other than that, he usually just backed off calling the woman.

Dating Viktoria was already different. They weren't up to three months yet since he'd met her on her assignment last month, but they were certainly past three dates. And he'd seen and talked to her countless times last month, besides dating, while they were both in the hospital where he worked. He was not prone to making rash decisions but, so far, he felt the most comfortable being with her than any woman ever before.

Of course, that was in addition to having the strong physical and sexual desire for her that experts say dies away over time. He believed experts in their fields, like counselors and therapists, and knew there had to be a super foundation underneath a relationship—like his parents—for when the lust petered out.

As he drifted off to sleep, he turned his attention to her problem at her locum tenens assignment. The situation there was definitely making Viktoria sound despondent about not only work, but the whole country she had immigrated to. He understood her viewpoint about escalating corruption, despicableness, and meanness from people all over. It seemed like her point was that the scale in the U.S. was tipping more to the side of degeneracy than the upholding of truth, decency, and lawfulness.

Tomorrow he would help Viktoria—the first woman he believed he loved—dive deeper into the surgery center and their doctors. He inhaled deeply and soon drifted off into a solid sleep.

Jeffrey rolled over and opened his eyes to the alarm clock radio on the nightstand. The digital red numbers showed 5:30, and he blinked twice. His first meeting wasn't until ten a.m., so this gave him even more time than the 6:30 time he'd set to wake up. He rolled out of bed, put on the room's mini-pot of coffee, and brushed his teeth.

He remembered the days when he traveled and hotels often didn't have reliable internet services. Not so anymore, he thought, as he opened his Mac computer. Hotel chains competed against other hotel chains, and working on one's computer was key for just about everyone anymore.

Jeff spread out the folded paper with a list of names which Viktoria had given him—the people at the beautification center whom she'd dealt with, those she believed to be downright unsafe and Machiavellian. He pulled up the ABMS or the American Board of Medical Specialties site, logged into the member portal, and clicked on "Is My Doctor Board Certified?"

Based on what Viktoria had told him, the most important player at the Long Island Surgery and Cosmetic Beautification practice was Rigoberto Castillo, so he plugged in the man's first and last name, the state, and his specialty, and clicked on "Find My Doctor."

The next page, "The Physician Search Results," appeared and it said "No Results Found."

Jeff stood and grabbed the rich coffee he'd made and brought the cup over. The internet search result gave him the creeps. If the head doctor who 'ran the place,' was not board certified, then maybe he was not picky about who he hired, confirming Viktoria's suspicions. There was nothing very contemptible about not being board certified because some doctors were poor test takers and yet were clinically adept. But, in Viktoria's opinion, this "business" had too many demerits against it.

After a gulp of coffee, Jeff plugged in the remaining names of all the doctors Viktoria had on the list. Only two of the twelve physicians were board certified—one of them was Kippy Saliner whom Viktoria thought highly of.

Jeff started a document on his computer to compile his findings, then he deviated to the center's present and past websites and searched every single doctor's name listed not on Viktoria's sheet. Overall, he learned that over two-thirds of all the doctors Rigoberto recruited were not board certified. He frowned as the specialty was one which required six years of residency, as well as safety training.

With Jeff's medical business experience, he was well accomplished at searching people's backgrounds. As he drained the mini-coffee pot, he discovered that some doctors had no training whatsoever in plastic surgery. It made him think of the "olden days" when doctors did one year of a medicine internship, followed by practicing whatever the hell they wanted. Sometimes back then, however, that was the way it was.

A scarier thought came to mind. Viktoria had told him that sometimes Brazilian Butt Lifts were on the surgery schedule. He researched plastic surgery sites and found out that even some board certified plastic surgeons won't perform those dangerous procedures.

And non-board certified physicians were doing them at Long Island's Surgery and Cosmetic Beatification!

Jeff checked the time, grimaced, and closed his computer. He had a business meeting to hurry to and, hopefully, would be able to grab a bite of eggs in the breakfast nook downstairs before driving to the hospital.

By one o'clock, Jeffrey was finished with his meetings, and multiple walkthroughs of the hospital's OR's to point out specific points regarding the model of care they used where he came from. Since the Long Island hospital was being acquired by the bigger health care facility, they wanted uniformity in their standard of care. He had no issues, however, with the hospital he was visiting. The care was good, and he believed Viktoria's husband had been well taken care of.

Jeff excused himself when they finished and declined their offer for lunch. He itched to get back to his own online investigation of Viktoria's present work place.

It had been a big blow to Viktoria, he thought while driving, that her recent patient had died after a breast augmentation which followed a forehead lift. The poor woman's sons had helped her with her decision and finances, and the outcome had ruined an entire family.

The surgeon responsible for that had been Ernest Pinto, who he already knew was not board certified.

Jeff arrived at the hotel, bought a generic sandwich and soda from the lobby's small snack machine, and headed upstairs. Absentmindedly, he opened both and ate and drank while he opened up his computer and notes.

He started by carefully reading the last website which was more thorough than the new one—which the center seemed to be still beefing up. He focused on Dr. Pinto and read.

"Ernest Pinto, M.D. is a board-certified physician with an impeccable history of providing the highest quality outcomes to his patients."

Jeff's blood boiled at the first outright lie at the beginning of the sentence, staring at him in black and white. Now he needed to dig into the doctor's past. He doubted any truth to the second part of the sentence, especially since last week his patient died.

Due to his experience searching online, Jeff learned Dr. Pinto had relocated to Rigoberto's practice three years ago. Before that, for six years, he had practiced in Chicago.

"Damn," Jeffrey said, putting down his dry sandwich on a napkin. While in Chicago, Dr. Pinto had three lawsuits filed against him for malpractice. Jeff shook his head, figuring there could be more states where he had practiced and more lawsuits.

In one case, Ernest had settled for half a million dollars, and another one he had settled for two-hundred-and-fifty thousand dollars. An undisclosed monetary figure had settled the third case.

Jeff jotted down one of the patient's names and immersed himself into finding medical lawsuits from public court records. Within a half hour, he found the case. The woman patient claimed Dr. Ernest Pinto's use of an electrocautery device during her surgical procedure burned her so intensely, that she was badly scarred for life. Her claim was supported by the support staff in the operating room.

He leaned back in his chair, ready for a break. It was terrible, he thought, and Viktoria realized it as much as he did. Almost all doctors, nurses, and health care personnel are in their chosen fields because they care about patients and the safe and best delivery of care that they can provide. It only takes a few, but those few workers can sometimes be dreadfully dangerous.

After chewing another bite of the sandwich, Jeff wiped his hand across his mouth, and dialed Viktoria's number.

"Hey," he said when she answered after a couple of rings. "How'd it go today at work?"

"Ha! I disrupted Dr. Castillo's assignments for me today and insisted on doing anesthesia in Dr. Saliner's room. She was on the schedule, and I refused to work with Dr. Pinto. Rigoberto's not too happy with me, but he'd rather have my services than not."

"Good for you. Especially if you are going to finish out the remaining two weeks after this, you had better look after yourself and the excellent standing you have earned in your specialty after years of practice. Patients have a tendency to blame all providers in an O.R. case when things go downhill."

"So true, Jeff. And how was your day?"

"My meetings are going well and the hospital here is still amenable to our changes. It's refreshing that it's going this smoothly."

"Nice. Were you able to research some things we talked about last night?"

"Did I ever. Researching these culprits is like walking through a minefield. The more I dig, the more explosive it gets."

Viktoria was staring at Millie, perched on the ottoman in front of her. She nodded at the dog and into the phone. "Tell me, especially since tomorrow will get crazy with my brother flying in, and both him and my mother staying here at the house."

"Yes, but you know I'm here for you in body and spirit."

She patted Millie on the head. "I sense that you mean what you say. How lucky I am."

"Are you ready for what I've found so far? But I'm warning you, I'm not finished yet."

"Tell me."

Jeff launched into his morning and afternoon's worth of discoveries of Amour Cosmetic Surgery and Long Island's Surgery and Cosmetic Beautification. When he finished making her skin crawl after learning more about where she worked on her present assignment, he said, "This Rigoberto Castillo is behind the whole sordid business model. I'm going to focus on digging up dirt on him tomorrow."

"Thank you so much, Jeff. The worst thing is that innocent patients are being hoodwinked and hurt. And do you know what?

"Dr. Castillo doesn't care, and he doesn't care that he doesn't care."

CHAPTER 28

Viktoria finished giving a report to the recovery room nurse on Friday. Her last patient wore a half-smile on her face with the residual effects of anesthesia as she walked away, ready to grab a cup of coffee in the kitchenette. Her next patient was a no-show, so she expected Rigoberto to come up with a plan for her. After all, he needed to get his money's worth out of her and put her in an OR room delivering anesthesia.

The aroma of coffee filled her nostrils as she walked up to the fresh pot. One of the techs nodded as she began leaving, heading back to set up for her next case.

"Thanks for putting the coffee on," Viktoria said. "Good timing on my part."

"You're welcome."

Viktoria poured and pulled out a chair as Dr. Castillo walked in and unsnapped his scrub jacket. He slipped it off his sloped shoulders and hung it on the chair opposite her.

He filled a mug to the brim with coffee, placed it down, and sat. "Until your next patient shows up, go around and give every anesthesia provider a break."

"I'd be happy to."

"Of course, finish your own break."

"No problem."

He scratched a sideburn and tilted his head. "Where are you going on your next assignment, Dr. Thorsdottir?"

"I have not spoken to the locum tenens agency yet about that. I suppose I'm dragging my feet, not sure about jumping into another assignment so soon. With the death of my husband, I may take a breather. I'm new at this, and I bet there are details I'm overlooking."

"Yes, like cashing in on insurance policies." He tapped a finger on the table. "If you're not jumping back into some OR, you might want to consider the wonderful discounts I give staff to get plastic surgery done here."

Viktoria had to keep from gagging on her coffee. "What? And have the same nose, implants in my cheeks, or gigantic lips like all the women walking around on the nearby beach? Women who have been to Amour Cosmetic Surgery?" The displeasure was evident in her voice.

Rigoberto straightened and let out a huff. "Why not ridicule beach-y blonde hair and little Chicklets for teeth as well? We don't do those things here."

"Do *any* of the aforementioned body additions really make women any prettier?"

"Most of the time they do."

"I would argue that many times they don't. Don't get me wrong. Plastic surgery has a wonderful place in some people's lives, when said patients are the correct candidates for the proper procedures, and in a rigorous facility, and under the care of well-trained and specialized physicians."

Rigoberto eyed his coffee and then glared at her. "And I would argue that you should veer away from doing plastic surgery cases in the future if you despise them that much."

"No, I only despise doing them here."

Dr. Castillo's mouth fell open, but she stood, rinsed out her cup, and gave another anesthesiologist a coffee break.

The bellows on the anesthesia machine cycled up and down as Viktoria sat on the rolling chair at the head of the table and Kippy Saliner did a beautiful job with a patient's face lift later in the day. She considered herself lucky that Rigoberto had put her in Dr. Saliner's room again. In essence, Viktoria was starting to wonder if she wanted to work at Long Island's Surgery and Cosmetic Beautification even one more day.

As it was, after that morning, Dr. Castillo would be hard-pressed to leave any compliments about her to Regina at the locum tenens agency. However, Regina considered Viktoria to be one of her prize anesthesiologists, and his critique of her would not hold water.

Viktoria worried more about whether Jeff was able to unearth more past corruption in the very place she was working in, and whether her upcoming weekend would run smoothly. For some odd reason, it seemed as if Rick had died weeks ago. The passage of time was behaving strangely, and she could not understand why.

With the facial surgery case finished, Viktoria transported her patient to the recovery room, and gave a report to the nurses. Her patient's vital signs were perfect and the woman nodded appropriately when asked how she was doing.

Viktoria strolled over to the desk where Dr. Saliner finished writing her intraoperative note.

"You did an excellent job with that face lift."

"Thank you, and I appreciate your anesthesia." Kippy closed the chart and her hazel eyes looked sorrowfully at Viktoria. "By the way, I was sorry to hear about your husband's death. I imagined myself going through a similar problem, and I can understand why you finished off your week with a few days of work. Our medical practices are fantastic at diverting our minds from other problems."

"This is true, although the opposite can occur as well. Sometimes our private lives can divert us from thinking about problems at work."

"The death of your anesthesia patient last week must also be weighing you down. That's a lot to handle in such a short time."

Without thinking about it, Viktoria walked behind the desk and sat next to Kippy. They swiveled their chairs to face each other and, since she was done for the day, Viktoria untied her surgical mask and dropped it in the wastebasket.

"Thanks, Kippy. I'll manage." Leaning forward, she lowered her voice. "To tell you the truth, I'm pessimistic about this place. I live here on the North Shore, and I'm disgusted to find a surgical practice so insensitive to the safety of patients."

Kippy squirmed in her chair. "I feel the same way. We just took care of the last patient I'm ever doing here. Walking into this last name change this week was the last straw."

Viktoria glanced around. "That does it. I needed a confirmatory boost, and you just provided it."

The plastic surgeon raised her eyebrows. Leaning forward with her elbows on her knees, she rested her chin in her hands and gave Viktoria her undivided attention.

"My time's up—two weeks early," Viktoria continued. "I'm telling the agency that this was my last day here."

Both women rose and headed to the women's room where they changed into street clothes.

"Let's walk out together," Viktoria said, clasping her things from the locker.

Without a good-bye to Rigoberto, and a mere wave good-bye to Lucy at the front desk, both women exited the front door.

"I won't miss the coffee in there," Kippy said, stopping at the bench to say good-bye.

"Or anything else," Viktoria emphasized and laughed.

"I enjoyed meeting and working with you," Kippy said. "My number's in the book if you need me for anything."

"Thanks. Likewise."

The two women went separate ways to their cars and Viktoria, due to her decision, felt a weight lifted off her shoulders.

"Millie girl!" Viktoria opened the house door to her Miniature American Shepherd who immediately pranced up on her back legs and greeted her. "Yes, yes, Mommy's home."

She dropped her things on the spot and picked Millie up in her arms. "You're right at the tipping weight for me being able to pick you up, but I can and must do so once in a while. Now is one of those times. Your mommy is taking off from work, at least for a short time." Viktoria cuddled her despite being licked in the face, and then carefully placed her on the hardwood floor.

After hooking Millie to her leash, they headed out for a walk, passing the marigolds and holly bushes in the front of the house. Viktoria took in a deep breath, and as the dog squatted, she brought up Regina's phone number, slipped in her Bluetooth earbuds, and called.

"Dr. Thorsdottir, how are you holding up?"

"If you have a few minutes, I have a lot to tell you. But first, and foremost, I am cancelling my contract to work at Long Island's Surgery and Cosmetic Beautification anymore."

"What happened?" she asked after a silence, her voice soft and understanding.

Viktoria filled her in, and then added. "Knowing my friend Jeff from Pennsylvania, I don't think what I told you is the end of it. I'm also too afraid to work with those surgeons anymore—afraid of bad patient outcomes as well as lawsuits."

"Viktoria, I understand. I will call there immediately and catch them before they close, so that they're armed with that knowledge for next week. However, I won't be sending them any other anesthesiologists I know in the locums tenens system looking for work. I'll make some kind of excuse."

"Perfect."

"In a way, I'm glad you're 'taking off.' These two weeks and last month were difficult enough but, on top of it, your husband passed. Grab some sunshine."

"My sunshine is with me right now. Her name is Millie."

"I bet she's lovely. Give me a call when you're ready for another assignment. In the meantime, your check will be in the mail."

"Thanks, Regina. And be careful zipping along in that wheelchair breaking speed records."

"I'll try."

They both laughed and hung up.

Back at the house, Viktoria cut chicken tenders into smaller pieces, sliced carrots and an onion, and threw it all into a slow cooker with sauce and herbs. She set it on high so that it would be cooked in a few hours instead of all day. Not knowing what and when her brother and mother would have eaten, she wanted to be prepared.

Within a half hour, her phone rang. "Viktoria, I'm at JFK Airport," her brother announced. "I've picked up my skimpy luggage, and I'm at the car rental place."

"How was your flight?"

"A snap. Can't say I remember the last time I napped during the day."

"Ha. You need to come see me more often."

"No. You're the one who needs to head back to Iceland once in a while."

"Alexander, I plan on talking to you about that."

"Sounds like a serious discussion, otherwise you would have called me Alex."

She took a deep audible breath. "Listen, I really appreciate you making the trip. I'm going to go pick up Mom. Why don't you come straight here?

Get a car with GPS so you can drive around Long Island and not get lost."

"I plan to. Sjáumst fljótlega."

"See you soon as well."

Viktoria fed Millie her dinner and, before leaving for the retirement and nursing home facility, she listened to the messages on her land line voicemail. As she expected, she needed to return calls about Rick's memorial luncheon set up for the next day.

Ready to open the door to the garage, Viktoria saddened as Millie cocked her head and slithered flat on the floor. "You actress. I suppose you want to come along for the ride.

"Let's go," Viktoria said. Soon Millie's snout was sniffing near the partially opened car window, and they were on their way to get her mother, Elisabet.

Viktoria put her signature in the guest log at the facility and strolled the hallway with the usual clutter of medicine carts, wheelchairs, residents, and workers. At the desk, she waited patiently to speak to someone.

"Dr. Thorsdottir, your mom will be overjoyed to see you." The red-headed nurse stopped what she was doing, and ushered Viktoria towards Elisabet's room. "The doctor saw her yesterday and there is good news. He said she still qualifies for assisted living when she returns from visiting you. He's very pleased with her blood pressure which has stabilized nicely." She dodged a patient with a walker coming out of a room, and looked at Viktoria. "He's much less worried now about her having a stroke."

"Excellent. I hoped her being in assisted living was going to continue. This is wonderful news."

"She's happy too." They pushed open the door where Elisabet sat expectantly on a cushioned chair.

"My dear daughter," the woman said. For seventy years old, she was distinguished and elegant in her own way, and Viktoria scrutinized her on every visit, both from a daughter's perspective and as a physician.

"Hi, Mom." Viktoria hunched over and kissed her. They grasped each other's hands and squeezed. "You look nice. You could model that dress."

"You gave it to me about two years ago on Mother's Day."

"Yes, I remember. A lavender color like the flowers you used to keep."

Viktoria turned to the nurse, who pointed to a wheelchair in the corner of the room. "You are welcome to escort your mom out in that, especially since sometimes it's a safer way to travel in the hallways."

Elisabet shook her head. "No, I'm fine. I'll walk with my daughter."

"I have some of your things at the house, Mom, so we don't need to bring anything if you don't want."

"Wonderful."

Viktoria thanked the nurse, and her mother rose.

"Has Alex arrived yet?" Elisabet asked.

"Yes, he's driving to the house as we speak. And I heard the doctor is happy with your medical status."

Elisabet beamed. "God is showering me with good fortune. However, my daughter is not doing as well." She leaned into Viktoria as they exited the automatic doors and into a gusty breeze and cool temperature.

CHAPTER 29

Viktoria opened the passenger door and her mother's face lit up like a gleeful little girl. "This must be Millie!"

The dog had climbed into the front seat and wiggled back and forth, trying to plant her wet tongue on either face. "Yes, meet my little girl, who shouldn't be in your seat." Viktoria picked her up, held her tight, and let Elisabet pet her. Then she placed her in the back while her mother got in as well. Viktoria shut the passenger door, hopped into her side, and started the ignition. "I am so looking forward to seeing Alex."

"Too bad our family doesn't get together more often than for funerals."

Viktoria nodded. "That is the way of the modern world, Mom. People work, and live long distances away. Think of your own situation and what happened when you immigrated here with me."

"I understand, but it doesn't mean I like it that way. We all only live once. Think about your father. I hadn't seen him in more than a year before he passed, which is all my fault. Maybe if I had stayed in Iceland..."

"No, Mom. You and Dad made the correct choice for yourselves and your children at that time. Don't beat yourself up about that. Bad situations at home have historically caused millions of people to move somewhere else throughout history. You're no different."

Elisabet crossed her age-spotted hands on her lap and sighed. "I suppose. One thing I'm sure about. Whether in Iceland or on Long Island, I have some intelligent children."

"You're smart too." Viktoria glanced over and appreciated the worried frown dissipate from her wrinkles.

With her mother bonding with Millie on her lap, Viktoria set the table without getting too fancy. A knock sounded, and she scooted over and saw a car in the driveway through the open glass pane beside the front door.

As a smile curved on her lips, she opened the door. Her lean, tall, yet muscularly defined brother grasped her into a hug. "Hey sis."

"Hey yourself." They separated, and she scanned him, wondering how he was holding up after the long day. He had the family's dark looks, and eyes, and he was earthy and vibrant. She decided he looked no worse for wear. Being the only child in the family who never married, Alexander thrived just fine.

"Is Mom here?"

Viktoria stepped aside and motioned. "We'll grab your stuff from the car later."

Alex had been to Viktoria's marital home one other time, so he knew the layout. However, Millie had pursued the knock at the door, and showed up at his feet.

"Meet Millie," Viktoria said.

Alex scooped her up like a toddler, his hands wrapped around her chest, and extended her in front of him. "Glad to meet you little Millie. Aren't you a pretty thing?" He swaddled her into him and went straight to Elisabet.

"Mom, how wonderful to see you, and you look gorgeous as ever!"

Elisabet squeezed her eyes shut and swept away a tear. "Thank you for coming."

"No, Ma. I should visit more often. Life back home is difficult to break away from, but there's no excuse."

He let go of Millie, and the dog sat without being told. Alex leaned in and gave his mother a gentle hug.

"We have encouraging news today," Viktoria announced from the sideline. "Mom's recent bout with high blood pressure is under control. The doctor is now less concerned about her having a heart attack and stroke."

"We are thrilled, Mom, but you must be the most happy with that news." He turned his head and winked at Viktoria.

"Yes, I am." Elisabet patted his hand on the armrest, and also turned to Viktoria. "When are we going to feed this young man?"

Viktoria dished out large ladlefuls of her crockpot concoction onto three dinner plates and bused them over to the table.

"Rick's Dad and brother have been tremendously helpful in the guest list for tomorrow's luncheon. I don't think I could have arranged it all myself." She frowned as she set down the salt and pepper shakers. "And my assignment since returning to Long Island ended up being a major problem. So much so that I basically 'quit' going back on Monday."

Elisabet stared at her daughter and Alex uttered a grunt. "That's not like you, sis. What the hell happened?"

Viktoria slowly shook her head, and darted her glance to her cell phone. "I'll explain, but I hope you don't mind my calling someone quickly. I should have done it before."

"Please do," Elisabet motioned.

Viktoria called Jeff. "Hey there. I meant to call you earlier. Would you like to come over for dinner, meet my brother and Mom, and spin me up to date if you've found anything new?"

"Are you sure?"

"I asked you, didn't I?"

"I'll be over. Do I ever need a break."

"Jeff, I hope I haven't burdened you."

A silence ensued. "Never. Plus, someone has to take the bull by the horns with this group."

"I agree. Also, I am not going back there on Monday."

"Just like that?"

"Yes, just like that."

Viktoria, Elisabet, and Alex lingered over their meal, their conversation revolving around Viktoria's marriage, Rick's marijuana habit, and his hospitalization the prior weekend.

"It is too bad Rick's life ended this way, and way too early," Elisabet said in the end, "but I also don't believe your marriage would have stayed intact had he not succumbed to this EVALI you spoke of."

"I agree with mom, Viktoria. After you work through your grief, your personal life may become less stressful because you won't be worrying about him and what he's doing or not doing."

"Isn't it terrible we're talking this way?" she asked.

"Sis, this family has always spoken out with what we're thinking. It was, and became, a bad situation for you. Damn, but he should have left the weed well enough alone. Didn't he know, or did he deny, the lung problem which caught on with users like wildfire? However, I am happy for whatever good times and happy memories you made with him." He paused, and continued. "Memories are what you need to hold onto now."

Viktoria sighed, bobbed her head as the door bell rang, and padded to the front door. With Millie at her heels, she turned the knob.

"Hope I didn't disturb your dinner," Jeff said.

"Appease Millie and say hello, and come in. Dinner's still hot in the crockpot."

"Hold this while I grab your girl." He handed her a folder, picked Millie up and received a wet tongue of kisses as he walked up to the dining table.

"You men are both alike, and can pick up Millie like she's five pounds," Viktoria said at the table. "But, forget that. Alex and Mom, this is Jeffrey Appleton, who I met on my last assignment. He's here on his own work, but is helping me out with the trouble I've become aware of at the plastic surgery facility."

Jeff placed Millie on the floor and Alex rose and shook his hand. "Happy to meet you," Alex said.

"Likewise." Jeff moved to Elisabet, gently took her hand into his, and gave it a small squeeze. "And I'm glad to meet you too, ma'am. Viktoria has talked about you, and her brothers, very fondly."

A tiny glitter showed in her eyes and she nodded. "And she's my darling girl."

"I'm breaking up the mutual admiration society," Viktoria said. "Jeff, let's make you a plate. I bet you're famished like the rest of us were."

Elisabet used the upstairs bathroom, changed into pajamas, and stepped into the second bedroom where Viktoria waited on her.

"Let me know if you need anything, Mom." She pulled down the bedspread and let her mother climb into bed.

"You need rest as well. Tomorrow will be taxing and emotional for you. How long are you going to stay up?"

"Jeff and I have things to discuss. It may be awhile."

Her mother grasped the end of the bedspread and pulled it high on her chest. "I think he likes you."

"Hmm." She tried not to roll her eyes at her mother's wisdom.

"It may be mutual. In difficult times, sometimes God sends us help or new love in unusual ways."

"Let's not talk about that."

"Okay. Go check on your brother. Good night."

Viktoria switched off the lamp and closed the door behind her. Alex stepped up the last step to the upstairs carrying two luggage bags.

"You'll be in Rick's office room, which is also a bedroom." She stepped into the room where the curtains were closed, a computer was open on the desk, and a single bed was made up with a dark afghan on top.

"Thanks, sis. This is so much better being here than in a hotel."

"Of course."

"I enjoyed talking to Jeff. He seems like a nice guy."

"I believe so."

He placed the duffel bag and suitcase on the bed and turned. "Perhaps he will end up being more than a 'nice' guy." He winked at her.

"Here I am burned from the last relationship, and you're suggesting I start anew? I don't see you getting hitched."

"Now, now. What did mom say?"

"How did you know she said something?"

He shrugged his shoulders. "She's perceptive. Mom never was comfortable about you marrying Rick."

"All right. Point taken," she said, and grimaced. "Listen, you must be dead tired. See you in the morning."

"Likewise."

Viktoria left and quietly went downstairs. Jeff was in the kitchen putting the clean dinner dishes away.

"I hope you don't mind me stacking these in your cabinets," he said.

"Thanks. I'm sorry it's getting late. Are you sure you want to tell me what you learned today?"

"I do, unless you don't want me to."

"I would hate to postpone putting together the facts, especially since I definitively 'quit' today."

He closed the cabinet and, after ushering inside where they sat by the coffee table, Viktoria lowered to her favorite spot on the floor where Millie curled up beside her.

"Your two weeks at Amour," Jeff said, "or whatever you want to call them, is but a snapshot. There have been other deaths of women, but each time the clinic changes its name, the harder it is to find information."

"And each time there's a name change, they blast promotions of their newly named clinic, making their business skyrocket. They have no shortage of patients, that is for sure. Did you manage to focus on Rigoberto Castillo today?"

"Did I ever." Jeff inhaled deeply. "Get this. After several bad patient outcomes, with sparse details that I could find, Go-2 Aesthetic Plastic Surgery Center changed its name to Amour Cosmetic Surgery and Rigoberto began the process of transferring the title of his multi-million dollar home east of here to his wife. Of course, she has a different last name than his. Along with that, I learned, Amour did not list him in any of their corporate records, at least that I could find."

"I'm not the brightest bulb when it comes to business shenanigans. I understand that people change ownership to protect their assets. So was his purpose to become a ghost? Disappear on paper so as to not be tracked down and sued?"

With pressured speech, Jeff went on. "Not only that, but Dr. Castillo was named as the president of the Go-2 Center, but get this. When they changed to Amour, he was no longer listed as the President—someone else was."

Viktoria squinted and stopped petting Millie. "Uh-oh."

"Viktoria, I had help today, otherwise at this point I would have hit a dead end. I called the lawyer you met in the parking lot, Jonathan Stewart."

"That was clever. Go on…"

"Anyway, the president's name of Amour was Timothy Bundet. Stewart tracked the guy down and got him on the phone. Bundet rents an apartment in Jamaica, New York, and is an auto mechanic. Stewart said the man never heard of Amour and didn't know what he was talking about."

She shook her head emphatically. "Castillo's actions are more inconceivable than I ever imagined. Where did he learn such despicable methods?"

CHAPTER 30

Jeff took a sip from the mug of instant coffee Viktoria had made for him, and placed it back down on the table. "It's entirely possible Rigoberto has been doing this for several decades, and he may have learned these maneuvers all by himself. However, his methods are fairly common in Hollywood where they make a production company for each movie. If the movie flops, they bust the company and make a new one the next day. Each movie is a different corporation. Dr. Castillo figured out how to do it with plastic surgery centers."

"And he won't stop because there's too much money in it for him."

"Exactly."

"But this isn't like a movie firm because in this business people can, and are, being hurt."

Jeff bowed his head and sighed. "What would you like to do?"

"Want to go after him with me?"

"I was hoping you'd say that."

The atmosphere at the funeral home was subdued, more so than for many of the more modern 'celebrations of life' that Viktoria had attended in the last two years. She wondered if it was because Rick had died due to something that he could have prevented. But, nevertheless, the room was set up nicely with flowers, two memorial side tables with pictures, and a short stage where she had placed the three ceramic urns with his ashes and green wreaths around them.

"Pete, I couldn't have done this without your help," Viktoria told Rick's father one more time, pointing to the tables. "Combining pictures from you and me, when he was young, an adult, and married, makes the portrayal of his life complete. But I feel terrible every day that I did not succeed in turning him away from marijuana."

"Viktoria, no one is blaming you. My son always had an addictive type of personality. If it had not been the marijuana, something else would have taken its place." He was dressed in a black suit and a crisp white shirt, and patted her arm. After standing and greeting people for some time, he sat next to Elisabet, who consoled the man in her own way, telling him about her fond memory of him—which was taking her out once in his dinghy on the Long Island Sound. The weather had changed quickly into a threatening sky and blustery winds, and he skillfully maneuvered the little sailboat straight into shore for her safety.

"He always liked the water," Pete said. "I should have done more to steer the boy into hobbies when he was growing up."

Elisabet rested her hand on the man's sleeve, and they sat in silence while Jeff walked in and paid a moment of silence in front of Rick's wreathed memorial spot.

"Thank you for coming," Viktoria told him when he was finished. "You did not have to, you know."

"I wanted to come, but I hope I'm not an imposition."

She waved his comment off, took him to the side, and pointed out Rick's father and brother so that he knew who was who. "You are coming to our luncheon, aren't you?"

"Yes, thank you. I haven't told you yet because we've had enough going on. After you mentioned that you 'quit' going into work the rest of the month, I called my hospital and told them I'm taking two personal days on Monday and Tuesday. We, or I, can work undisturbed in seeing the Rigoberto Castillo case through."

Viktoria bent her head. "I don't know what to say." Slowly, she brought her face up to make eye contact. "Are you sure the hospital administrators are okay with you doing that?"

"Yes, particularly since my assignment here went well."

A woman lingered a short distance from them, and then stepped over. Smartly dressed, with a dark sweater over a maroon dress, she spoke with a soft voice. "Dr. Thorsdottir?"

"Yes. Thank you for coming. Did you know my husband?"

"Yes. I'm Paula Spinner, a Psychologist. Rick had recent appointments with me for his smoking problem."

"He spoke of going to see you. Thank you for trying to help."

"I obviously didn't do a decent job. He quit, you know. Called me one day and flat-out stopped coming." She grimaced.

Viktoria nodded. "You, more than anybody, understands. You can't *make* someone do something if their mind is dead set against it. Rick was using marijuana for years. He kept his addiction so secret, I married him without knowing about it at first."

"Still…"

"We all have failures at work. Don't dishearten over the few who slip by, because they are the ones who seal their fate with a hammer on a box." She sighed. "We are having a luncheon after this, please join us."

"I wish I could. My schedule is full back at the office. I'm sorry for your loss and wish you all the best going forward." She turned and her long, slender figure made its way through the sparse crowd and out the door.

The restaurant Viktoria had chosen for the lunch gathering was one of Rick's favorites, one by the water which could accommodate the twenty-seven people who responded to the invitation affirmatively. The back room filled up with the guests. Most of them were family members, but a few had been Rick's friends, insurance colleagues, and prior workers from the gym where he'd worked.

The wooden building sported seafaring decorations and the tables were all wood as well, with benches instead of chairs. The pictures on the place mats were all lighthouses and once Rick and Viktoria had tried to guess their locations, which were printed on the back.

Viktoria and Pete greeted each person after they signed the guest log and sat down, and then they went to their own tables. She sat down, her mother and Alex beside her, and was glad to see that Alex had invited Jeff to their table. He was directly across from her.

Since several people at the funeral home had given miniature speeches about Rick, including herself, she decided to forego further formality during the luncheon. The waiter made sure everyone had something to drink, and then she rose her glass of iced tea, thanked everyone for coming, and said, "And may Rick rest in peace."

With three entrée selections available for the luncheon, Viktoria and Elisabet chose a spinach quiche and salad. Jeff and Alex both ordered Greek kabobs. To Viktoria's approval, the tone of the luncheon became happier than the gathering at the funeral home, and she felt more relaxed.

"I wish Bjorn could have come," Alex said.

"He's our brother," Viktoria said to Jeff. She glanced sideways to Alex and held her fork. "I've been thinking. It would be stupid to make rash decisions at this time, but I can't help but think that the handwriting has been on the wall—that each job I've taken lately is an example, or a sign of things to come."

"What are you talking about?" Alex asked.

"There are negative events, and unscrupulous people, in the world, but recently I'm wondering if there is a downward spiral in the United States that is presently deeper than most places. I can't explain it, but I am pretty fed up with dishonesty and lousy people. Of course, my personal situation just took a turn for the worse. Besides the fact that Rick made his own bed, losing a spouse is still sad."

She focused on Alex's dark eyes. "I'm wondering if, in fact, I should return to Iceland."

Elisabet let out a little squeal and Viktoria turned. Her mother smiled, but then tried to suppress the growing grin.

"Of course, I'd want to take you too, Mom, if you were amenable."

"Amenable? I'd be packed before you."

Alex swallowed the pork he'd been chewing. "You're wondering about moving back? Sounds to me like you've given it a lot of thought. Bjorn and I would welcome you and Mom back with open arms."

"We'll talk. But I have a lot to talk about with Jeff before he leaves on Wednesday. We want to take down a plastic surgery center and their king pin."

Jeff tried to suppress his sadness over her announcement about relocating, and faked keeping a straight face. "Viktoria, once we hand over our details to the correct persons, the case is in their hands."

She nodded. "Listen, I wanted to tell you my initial thoughts about moving before today, but things have been crazy."

"I understand."

The volume of the voices in the back room had ramped up, and there was even laughter. Viktoria gasped a big breath. "Honestly, only in the last two days did I decide definitively that I need, and want to go back to Iceland. You must put it on your bucket list of places to go, especially after I get settled. This is a formal invite."

Jeff considered her invitation. At least, he thought, the conversation was off to a start—one which he wanted to be more in-depth. Her leaving was a new development, and he harbored some serious thoughts on the matter.

Viktoria looked down at her mother's almost empty plate as Elisabet steered a serving of the moist quiche into her mouth.

"Mom, do they feed you in that place?"

"I don't tell you how miserable I am there. Now, since there is a possible new beginning to the tail end of my life, I'll speak my mind. The biggest event of the day where I live are the meals, but what we are served, I wouldn't feed to Alex's horses back home. For instance, the amount of 'salad' they serve us in two weeks would barely be the serving of salad I am eating here right now. However, there is no shortage of starch—hash browns, French fries, and fish sticks—I've been served all in one meal."

Appalled, and feeling guilty, Viktoria and Alex stared at her.

"Okay, but if I am to be honest, the assisted living food is a tad bit superior to the 'nursing' home side. Folks in assisted living have better mental faculties left, so the kitchen has to do a better job with our food, otherwise we'll tell on them."

"Oh my," Viktoria grumbled. "It took the death of my husband to find out how miserable you are. I'm sorry, Mom."

"You are working like a fiend, and with a responsible career. Isn't that the way I raised you, however? To fend for yourself and make a living. Don't be sorry. You can't give up working to look after me now or in the future."

"Nevertheless."

"Mom," Alex said, "your three kids are going to dream up a plan back in Iceland, and we'll make sure you're comfortable, get decent medical care, and eat a balanced, nutritious, and tasty diet."

"I second Alex's idea," Viktoria said. She rose her iced tea, and they all tapped their glasses together, including Jeff.

Elisabet clinked her glass gently, put it down, and wiped the moisture from her eyes. "Then I'll hold you to it."

Her home seemed like a different household. The presence of Elisabet, Alex, Jeff, and Millie on Sunday warmed Viktoria's heart like everyone else's. The sun beamed down in full force on the house and yard, making it easier for any of them to move from the inside to the outside with Millie making her own choice to follow or not.

She believed Saturday had been a success and the best possible send off for her husband, and she had given Pete and Trevor huge hugs when they all went their separate ways carrying their own separate urns with Rick's ashes. Even though they promised to keep in touch, she suspected that, over time, contact would dwindle down until it was left to two phone calls a year or a birthday or Christmas card. She had also not mentioned to them that her plan may be to leave the country.

Viktoria and Jeff concentrated on a plan against the surgery center. They wanted to waste no time and, although they wanted quick results, they knew that would be impossible.

She leaned back in a cushioned yard chair, their papers stacked and accessible in front of them, and she put a foot against the lip of the wrought iron table.

"Tomorrow's Monday," Jeff said, "so we'll contact the New York medical disciplinary board."

"And I'll contact Jonathan Stewart with Stewart and Klein and arm him with more incriminating data he can use in the Dorothy Flores case."

Jeff nodded and put numbers next to their list. "In the meantime, we must set off some kind of firecracker at their front door."

"To jump start the investigation?"

"Precisely."

She shrugged her shoulders. "Let's go to the police."

"What would make them kick off taking a look at them right away, though?"

"Perhaps it won't even take the death of Bonnie Sandler, or their advertising and media gimmicks, or their doctor's lack of board certification, or changing their name, etc. Maybe it can be simpler than that."

CHAPTER 31

Two officers were manning the front desk when Viktoria and Jeff walked into the police station on Monday morning. After hearing the reason for their visit, one of them escorted the two medical professionals into a stark office down a hallway and left them in two visitor's chairs to wait.

Jeff tugged at his collar, and he turned his head to face her. "If getting up and leaving the United States is really what you want, I admire your decision, but isn't credentialing in Iceland going to be a nightmare for you?"

"Not as difficult as the reverse—leaving Iceland to work as a physician in the U.S. But, of course, I did all my training and residency here in the states. I am still a citizen back home, and I plan on keeping my foot in the door, so to speak, in both countries."

Jeff rolled that around in his head. "Is there a need for medical workers in most areas and specialties?"

"For sure, like everywhere else, the population is growing. And, fortunately or unfortunately, tourism is booming. There are plenty of patients to treat."

A slender, uniformed man hustled in with a cup of coffee, and stopped between both their chairs. "Officer Massey." He set his mug down, shook Jeff's hand, and nodded at Viktoria.

After introducing themselves, the officer went around his desk and sat. When he smiled over at them, the dimple to the side of his lip created a dip like a hole from a pencil point.

"We came in," Viktoria started, "to report a plastic surgery center here on the North Shore. They practice dirty business and jeopardize patients' safety. I am a physician and I've seen it first-hand."

Within minutes, Viktoria and Jeff suspected they'd struck a nerve with Massey who seemed to take the matter personally. "My cousin is worse off after plastic surgery than before," he mumbled up front.

Soon, the three of them had a fresh cup of coffee in their hands, and Viktoria explained the xeroxed notes she and Jeff had written up.

Massey gasped at Viktoria's description of their advertising and marketing methods, and the description of the business center above the surgical suites. She explained they would pursue legal avenues as well as through the state's medical board. He swallowed hard when they appeared to be finished.

"You two are like gold-star whistle blowers dropping off this information. At this precinct, we take crap like this seriously." He rubbed his chin, and looked past them. "I'm wondering which of your tips I can nail them on immediately to put a bump in their drive."

"Rigoberto Castillo asked a tech working in his facility if she'd be amenable to injecting filler into patients' faces. In other words, he's using non-medically trained, unlicensed workers, to inject chemical fillers like botox and injectable gels into the faces of people. Those procedures can cause blindness if someone doesn't know what they're doing. Which they don't!"

Officer Massey tapped his pencil. A flicker of a smile shot across his lips, and he stood. "Thank you for coming in. I am going to look into this. Actually, rest assured, we'll be doing more than 'looking into' this."

"Thank you," she said.

"A double thank you," Jeff added.

"Can you find your way out?" the Officer asked.

Viktoria rose. "Sure thing."

"I have your phone numbers. I'll give one of you a buzz if we put a dent in this doctor's business."

Viktoria smiled at Jeff, and they took off for the parking lot.

In her Honda, Viktoria turned to Jeff. "How would you feel about stopping at my mom's retirement facility with me? Before I move, I'll be home for a while, so there is no sense in letting her go back there. She can stay with me."

He squinted his light brown eyes at her and then looked forward. "Man, when you make up your mind about something, you don't waste any time, do you?"

"Which is usually the case," she said, guessing he wasn't too happy with her. "Makes sense I went into anesthesiology because sometimes a patient's situation requires a split-second decision and action."

Jeff frowned. "I stayed for a reason, and that reason is you. I wouldn't miss going with you, but that means I'm buying you lunch."

"No way. Let's go back to a restaurant overlooking the water, just the two of us, but I'm buying, not you."

"Fine. Have it your way."

Viktoria laughed while putting the car in drive. "Sounds like our first fight."

"It's all your fault." He buckled his seat belt, and chuckled.

She tapped him on the knee, but Jeff grabbed her hand, squeezed it, and then moved it back towards the steering wheel. In a short time, they grabbed boxes she'd put in the back, and walked along the path to the front entrance of Elisabet's place.

Inside, Viktoria knocked on the primary executive's office door, and she and Jeff entered when they heard a "Come in." They left a stack of empty boxes in the hallway.

A dark-skinned man with glasses, and a crisp shirt and tie, stood.

"I haven't spoken to you in a long time. I'm Elisabet's daughter, Dr. Thorsdottir, and our plans have drastically changed. Jeff and I are here to clear out her things because she is moving with me."

"I'm sorry to hear we'll be losing her. Where will you be headed?"

"We are immigrating back to Iceland after practically a lifetime here."

"That's a big move. I wish you both well."

"Thank you."

He slid out a desk drawer and grabbed a folder. "I just need a few signatures. She'll officially be a nonresident at the end of the month."

It was a big, official step, taking her mother out, and she signed her name with a bit of trepidation. The man walked them to the door, and paused. "Let us know if you both need any help."

She nodded, they picked up their cartons, and walked to the assisted living corridor. As she and Jeff packed the boxes with framed photographs, hanging clothes in the closet, and a few items from the mini-kitchen, Viktoria felt her heart ache for the changes going on in her life. If only people weren't so despicable, she thought.

"I'll run out with a stack of boxes," Jeff offered, and disappeared to the car with her keys. After two more trips, they finished and Viktoria drove straight to a small café in the historic district. She parked in the rear lot, and they went in a side door. The inside was rustic and spacious, and a waitress escorted them to a corner table with a water view.

"What's good?" Jeff asked Viktoria as the waitress handed them menus.

"I suggest fish, but you'll be happy if you like and order the best southern catfish, hush puppies, and coleslaw north of Tennessee."

"Sounds like a winner," he said, glancing at the waitress. "Along with coffee, of course."

"Make it two," Viktoria said.

The woman smiled in agreement and stepped away.

"When we go back to your house," Jeff said, "let's make the call to the New York medical board."

"I bet it will be a long process if they decide to investigate what I have to say."

"That will be fine. In the meantime, I believe Officer Massey will fill in the gap." He pulled out a sugar packet as the waitress arrived with their coffee and left. "How long should I wait to visit Iceland after you leave?"

She darted her eyes in his direction. "Waiting for me to be all set up may take months. The most important thing I need to do is find a job or start doing locums again. However, your visit depends on you."

He tilted his head. "In what way?"

"Whether you can take time off when you want, and whether you prefer to stay with me in whatever confusion I'm living in, or a hotel. And depending on a work schedule, if I have one—how much time we can spend together." Her tone was soft as she leaned in as much as possible.

"Available days for vacation have been stacking up for me because I'm chintzy with taking time off for myself. Now I have a justification. You're that reason, Viktoria."

Searching his eyes, she nodded. "I am so grateful I met you."

He inched his forearm forward and he squeezed her hand.

"You leave on Wednesday," she said with displeasure.

"The king-size bed in my hotel room has plenty of space for you."

"How about tomorrow night?"

"Now we're talking," he said with a mischievous grin.

Hunkered over the cocktail table at home, Viktoria and Jeff had their call to the New York state licensing board on speaker. Elisabet and Alex sat on the couch, their ears attuned to the interesting call, listening to Viktoria's explanation and chronological sequence of events which occurred at Amour Cosmetic Surgery.

"You've done tremendous homework for us," said the woman on the line. "I want you to send as many of your notes and documents to us that you can."

"I will be happy to," Viktoria said. "I will scan the information and you'll have it by this afternoon. Perhaps you can shed some insight into what may happen from your end."

"Are you aware that our courts have found that medical facilities are also directly responsible for the deaths and injuries of patients like Bonnie Sandler? In other words, it is not only the doctors like Ernest Pinto and Rigoberto Castillo who are liable?"

Jeff gave Viktoria a thumbs up while she responded. "Then I am optimistic something can be done."

"You bet. Dr. Thorsdottir, I assure you that the board will jump on investigating these cosmetic surgery safety issues."

After the call ended, Viktoria grinned.

"Do you realize," her mother said, "you may be saving someone's life or terrible surgical outcome in the future?"

"I hope so, Mom."

"You're doing the right thing," Alex said. "We sure are proud of you for not looking the other way."

"For me, there's nothing to lose. I'm out of here anyway." Copycatting her brother, she winked at him, and then turned to Jeff. "Besides, Jeff egged me on and is helping."

Viktoria untucked her legs from under her and rose from the leather chair. "Now, you all talk about Iceland, and I'm following through with sending paperwork to the New York licensing board."

With Millie at her heels like a little shadow, Viktoria gathered her papers, padded away, and closed her office door behind her.

Officer Massey shunned away from most doctors. He hadn't been to one in years and didn't intend to in the foreseeable future. Maybe when he turned into an old man with a limp and chest pain, he'd make a lifetime check up with some old doc with experience nearing his dream goal of retirement. But it looked like a trip to a plastic surgery doctor's office and surgery suites was needed due to his job. How the hell regular people not needing medical care put themselves under the knife to look better, he had no idea.

He'd brainstormed his plan of action after the anesthesiologist and hospital business man had paid him a visit, so the first thing he did in the morning was to request help from one of the female officers he often worked with. After that, he picked up the phone and called Dr. Castillo's office.

"Long Island's Surgery and Cosmetic Beautification, Lucy Murray here. How can I help you?"

"Good morning. My name is Mr. Massey. I am wondering if I can get my girlfriend in there today for some of that stuff that gets injected into people's faces to make them look younger."

"Injectable gels to fill in her wrinkles and make her appear ten years younger?"

"She would love that. Me too."

"We are booked solid today, Mr. Massey. However, we could try to squeeze her in at lunchtime."

"That'll be great. We'll be there."

"By the way, we only take cash or credit card for that. No personal checks."

"No problem. What's it going to cost?"

"It depends. Anywhere upwards from seven-hundred dollars."

"Not a problem. See you later."

Loretta Wilshire stood leaning against the door frame of his office, listening to the whole thing, and twisted her lips. She was a forty-eight-year-old police officer with two decades on the job and a healthy love of her job. "Girlfriend, huh?"

"Yeah, aren't you flattered?" he joked.

"It could have been worse. You could have told them I'm your wife."

He rolled his eyes. "Finally, your past years of smoking, which has promoted wrinkles around your mouth, is coming in handy. You'll be a believable patient for them."

"You better quit while you're ahead, Massey."

"I'll try. Let's go over there at noon."

Officers Massey and Wilshire drove to Long Island's Surgery and Cosmetic Beautification in an unmarked car, parked, and scrutinized the surroundings as they went to the front door. They were dressed in plain clothes with their holsters hidden from view. Loretta wore stylish fitting pants and low flat heels, and her hair was pulled back from her face.

As usual, the waiting room had an abundance of patients, and the two officers lingered to watch the advertising screen on the wall, and to surmise the people on their digital devices, reading magazines, and talking. Loretta stepped to the counter where Lucy anticipated them signing in.

"My boyfriend called earlier. I'm Loretta Wilshire."

"Sign in, and we'll bring you in to be evaluated. My beautifier normally takes a quick lunch, but she's going to forfeit most of her time to help you out."

Loretta signed as Officer Massey stood close.

"Come around," Lucy said, and handed her a clipboard.

They walked through the door, and Lucy led them to the small conference room where she moved the sample breast size boxes to the end of the display table. "Fill out that form, so we know a little about you. After your evaluation with Margie, she'll tell me how much it'll cost you today—no doubt a super deal to make you more beautiful than you already are."

Lucy laid a strong smile on both of them and left.

The door pushed open again quickly and a petite, young woman walked in. Her pitch black hair was cut squarely at her chin, and she had clear, unblemished skin and not in any need of the promoted services where she worked.

"Hi, I'm Margie." She sat in the cushiony solo chair while Lucy said hello and handed her the clipboard.

"I'll be doing your injection. Not allergic to anything?" She barely glanced at the form which had few questions.

"No, nothing that I am aware of."

Margie leaned across the space and wiggled her finger at Loretta to do the same. "We can eliminate these baby wrinkles all above and below your lips, and a few areas around your chin. I would advise filler into your upper lip as well."

"You're the professional at what you do. I must rely on your expertise. How much is this going to cost?"

"We charge not only for the procedure, but for how much product we use. One bottle should do it."

"A whole bottle?"

"There is enough liquid in each bottle, but you need your own."

"Even though you may not use the whole thing, you then dispose of leftover contents? I mean, you wouldn't use somebody's left overs from a bottle on another patient, would you?"

"That would be double dipping. Uh, no."

Officer Massey let the women talk and didn't interfere. "Double dipping" rolled off Margie's lips so easily, he figured it was a regularly used term in the facility—one that the head doctor, Castillo preached and wanted the employees to practice.

Margie reached back into a drawer and pulled out a sheet. "If you're ready, here's the consent form, and the procedure will cost a thousand dollars total, including the vial."

Loretta waited for a further explanation, such as a detailed description of what would happen and, in particular, a discussion about the risks involved. But nothing else escaped the young lady's lips. The officer signed the sheet.

"We'll go straight to my room after you pay."

Officer Wilshire glanced at her partner, he dug his hand into his pocket, and pulled out a wad of cash. After counting out the necessary bills, he handed them over.

"By the way, what are your credentials?" Loretta asked.

"I took a plastic surgery course. After that, of course, Dr. Castillo showed me how to do it in more detail."

"Like see one, do one?"

"'See one, do one' is common in the medical field."

"I hope that doesn't happen with heart surgery. However, where was the course you attended?"

A muscle twitched on one side of her face. "Texas, yes, San Antonio."

"I hope you strolled the riverwalk."

Mystified, she shrugged her shoulders. "Let me leave you in the other room and I'll give this to Lucy at the front desk."

They walked two doors down, and Margie guided Loretta to the procedure chair, wheeled a tray table over, and grabbed a blue wrapped package from a cabinet above the counter. She also took down a vial and placed it behind the packet. "I'll be right back."

CHAPTER 32

Margie stepped to the front desk and handed Lucy the thousand dollars.

"Productive lunch break." Lucy smiled, and jammed the bills into an aluminum box in the top drawer. "Inject your patient and then grab lunch in the kitchenette. Dr. Castillo ordered in some sandwiches from next door."

As Margie headed back to the procedure room, Officer Massey and Wilshire did more than wait. Loretta stepped off the leather chair for patients and scrutinized the aluminum tray table. Beside the packet lay a syringe and the vial of injectable contents, the brand name on the label. The round metal seal was off, and the rubber part of the top was exposed, indicating that the vial had been opened before and used. Sure enough, the glass bottle held only about half its original contents.

"How's this for 'double dipping,'" Loretta said, and handed the vial to her colleague. "This bottle has been used on a previous patient."

Massey nodded and placed it back on the tray. Loretta popped back into the chair as the doorknob turned and Margie stepped in.

"Let's get started," the young woman said to Loretta. "I'm going to wipe around your mouth with an alcohol pad, smear on some local anesthetic gel, and then inject."

"First I'd like to see your credentials."

"I thought we went through that before?"

"Not to my satisfaction."

Officer Massey pulled out his identification from his back pocket. "We do want to evaluate your qualifications, Miss."

Margie's eyes grew round with fear. "Uh... I think I better get Dr. Castillo."

"Let's all go do that," Loretta agreed.

As Margie walked out, she kept turning her head back at the cops masquerading as a patient and her boyfriend. Her hand trembled. Rigoberto was not going to be happy with her.

Dr. Castillo and Lola were both at the table in the kitchenette, starting their sub sandwiches.

Loretta jutted in front of Margie, and Rigoberto sneered. "Patients are not allowed in our kitchen," he said. "Margie, head back to..."

Massey pushed his official badge in front of him. "This is a police sting, sir. Show me the credentials which allow Miss Margie here to perform facial filler injections on people."

He didn't miss a beat. "She was given instruction here at Amour, I mean Long Island's Surgery and Cosmetic Beautification. Well, it used to be Amour back when she learned."

"Or maybe back when you were named Go-2 Aesthetic Plastic Surgery Center," Loretta said. "But none of that matters, because she isn't credentialed. Is she?"

Rigoberto shrugged his shoulders and waved his hand at them as if proper training didn't matter.

"You might as well wash down the awful taste you're going to have in your mouth as you ride to the station with us." Loretta handed him his iced tea.

Officer Massey turned to Margie. "You're coming, too."

Margie wrung her hands into a ball so tight, her wedding ring dug into her finger.

Massey practically herded them out the door as Loretta lingered. She watched Lola half frozen with a sandwich in her hand. "Who are you?"

"I'm Lola. I'm just the anesthesia technician here."

"I heard about you. Not to worry, you're not in any kind of trouble. You should start looking for another job right quick, however. This is only the start of Dr. Castillo's downfall, as well as his cushy, dangerous business operation."

"Thank you. I plan to. Perhaps after the baby comes. "

Loretta plucked a wrapped sandwich off the tray and a filled plastic cup with iced tea. "Do you mind?"

"Not at all. I'm lucky I didn't do those face procedures like Margie. He wanted me to, but I'm busy enough being an anesthesia tech."

"I'm glad you didn't either." She went to the door, but turned back. "Enjoy that newborn when it arrives."

As Loretta passed the front desk, she popped her head around the corner. "Lucy lady, did you give my partner back his money for my procedure?"

Lucy Murray's mouth still hung open, and she shook her head.

"He'd forget his gun if it weren't for me. Hand over the cash."

Lucy plucked out the thousand dollars and counted to make sure she didn't pay back more than she'd taken.

"Thanks, and don't mind my comment. Officer Massey had his hands full with your ring leader." She hurried out the front door, while the people in the waiting room whispered to each other, wondering why Dr. Castillo's leaving seemed odd.

On purpose, Viktoria and Jeff not only wanted to sleep in extra on Tuesday morning in their own beds, but they wanted Alex and Elisabet to as well. They all planned on getting together and going out to eat late in the morning. The place Viktoria chose served mostly breakfast food, and it was far better for meeting up than a coffee shop.

Jeff wore summer slacks and a cotton Oxford T-shirt and picked a table against the wall. The waitress poured him black coffee while he waited for Viktoria and her family. Although he was a bit of a workaholic back in Pennsylvania, and enjoyed his job, he was already saddened about his departure the next day. He and Viktoria had made progress against Rigoberto Castillo and his center, and he wanted to continue through with that as much as possible, but he felt heavyhearted to leave Viktoria.

He must visit her again, he thought, and the sooner the better—even if that meant returning to Long Island before she made her big move.

From the front of the restaurant, Viktoria, her brother, and mother showed up, and approached his table. Jeff stood, and pulled out Viktoria's chair, while everyone greeted each other. Alex saw to Elisabet, and the waitress soon turned over their ceramic coffee cups, and filled them to the brim. She parceled out a menu to each of them and stepped away.

"This is a no brainer," Viktoria said. "Bacon, eggs, and pancakes."

Alex put down the menu. "You'll get no argument from me."

Elisabet sipped her coffee, and then chimed in. "I'm skipping the pancakes." She'd worn lipstick and a smear of it rubbed off on her coffee cup.

"I'm going for the bacon and everything omelet," Jeff added. "I studied the menu longer since I've been sitting here. I'll need to come back for the pancakes. Maybe before you leave for Iceland?" He turned to Viktoria to the left of him.

She tilted her head. "I don't want to burden you with these trips.

Jumping on a plane to Iceland in the future will suffice."

"Viktoria, give a guy a chance," Alex mumbled. "Jeff wouldn't say that if he didn't mean it, and his goal is to date you in the foreseeable future."

Jeff nodded. "So true."

The waitress arrived again and flipped out her order pad. "Who's first?"

"We're easy," Alex said, and spouted off the orders they'd decided on.

She tipped her pink cap and left as Viktoria's phone rang.

"Hello?"

"Dr. Thorsdottir, do you have a moment? Officer Massey here."

"Absolutely."

"I promised to update you. The North Shore Police Department ran a sting yesterday on your infamous Dr. Castillo and his plastic surgery operation. He's still in custody, but I expect supervised detention soon."

Viktoria glued her eyes on Jeff, smiled, and nodded. "All because of the non-trained technician?"

"Yes. Like you informed us, patients have been disfigured there, some have died, and he and much of his personnel are crooks, but we started the process on your littlest tip—the most insignificant of his atrocities."

The phone fell silent.

"Are you there?"

"Tjá algjöra hamingju," she said as her eyes moistened.

"Which means?"

"In my language, it means I couldn't be happier."

"Okay, then. You keep delivering safe anesthesia, *and* keep practicing beyond your job description, because patients owe their safety to you."

"Thanks for the call, Officer, and I'll tell Jeff as well. Good-bye."

Two waitresses brought out their food as Viktoria relayed the information Massey told her. She turned to Jeff and congratulated him too. "And after I finish this mound of bacon and eggs, I'm making the last call to wind up our part in this."

After washing down her breakfast with one more cup of coffee, Viktoria scrolled through her contacts for Bonnie Sandler's oldest son's number. The twenty-seven-year-old answered after a couple of rings, and she glanced at Jeff.

"Andrew, this is Dr. Thorsdottir. How are you and your brother doing?"

"We are living one step at a time. It's mighty difficult cleaning out our mom's personal possessions, but we're still forging ahead."

"That can't be easy. You were clear that the two of you were going to hire a lawyer regarding your mother's surgery and death. I called to pass along another attorney's name in case you have not settled on someone. This man is working for another one of the surgery center's patients who had a bad result. I can't give you the patient's name, but her attorney's name is Jonathan Stewart with Stewart and Klein. He is also privy to other information about Amour, so I believe he would be a great asset to you in building a full and detailed case against them."

"I'm grabbing a paper and pen at the moment." He repeated the law firm and name. "We'll call this guy today."

"And Andrew, the cops paid Dr. Castillo a visit yesterday. Fingers crossed, okay?"

"Wow. You've made my day."

"Bye Andrew, and good luck."

"Thank you so much. Same to you."

She placed her phone down.

"What did he say?" Jeff asked.

"He'll call Stewart and Klein today."

The waitress came along to top off their coffee cups, but Viktoria put her hand over hers. "I've had enough."

"No more for me," Elisabet said.

Jeff and Alex let the waitress top off their cups, she placed the bill face down on the table, and left.

"My treat," Alex offered, reaching his hand into his pocket for his wallet.

"No it's not," Viktoria said. "You and Bjorn are going to put mom and I up at your sprawl outside of Reykjavik, until we figure out where home will be. I've told you before, when you're on Long Island, only my money works."

"All right, but you and mom can stay as long as you want at home. There's no shortage of space."

"We'll figure out the situation when the time comes."

Jeff's hand darted out for the bill, but she beat him to it. "And you keep your hands to yourself too."

Elisabet shook her head. "Don't you men realize she's in charge?"

Viktoria scurried into the hotel lobby and turned into the bar. She spotted Jeff's sandy-colored hair and fit, lean upper body from the back where he sat on a stool facing the counter.

"Would you like to buy me a drink?" She slipped next to him, and placed her overnight bag on the floor.

He rooted a kiss on her cheek. "Wine?"

"Sure." She asked the bartender for a Pinot Grigio.

"Going simple tonight? No whisky sour?" His eyes flirted with her, and she took a deep breath. He'd dressed nicely, like her, and their knees touched as they fully turned.

"For right now. After all, the best is yet to come."

Jeff widened his eyes. "I have no doubt about that."

The bartender placed her wine glass on a napkin and stepped away to another customer.

"A toast," he offered, "to our last evening for a while. Too bad I must fly back home tomorrow."

"Yes, let's leave it at that."

"But, I take it we'll try to see each other sooner than later?"

"Yes, Jeff Appleton, for sure."

"In the meantime, let's quit talking and finish these. We have business to attend to up in my room."

"Business?" she asked softly with a mischievous smile.

He stood for emphasis, and whispered into her ear. "More like hanky-panky. Better yet, making love."

"Förum."

"Let me guess. Does that mean something like 'let's go' in Icelandic?"

"You're learning fast."

"Don't forget your wine glass."

He grabbed her bag, she rose from her stool, and they took off for Jeff's hotel room.

EPILOGUE

The sights and sounds of New York's John F. Kennedy Airport permeated Viktoria's senses as she and Elisabet arrived at Terminal 4 for their international flight. Although an hour and a half remained before their departure to Iceland, passengers already dotted the black vinyl chairs and younger people's hands were busy with cell phones or laptop computers. A mixture of fast food and Asian food smells wafted down from the center court, and a nearby coffee shop pulled a gate across their front entrance to close up for the day.

She picked two end spots nearest to the window, and Elisabet sat without any coaxing. Her mother held a small pocketbook with all her travel papers, and Viktoria helped her place a compact duffel bag in the empty seat beside her.

Viktoria traveled light, a flat shoulder bag with travel documents hanging in front of her chest, and carried a business bag which held her computer and two pockets with important papers other than for travel. Major luggage was checked, and seven shipping cartons had been sent ahead with everything they were bringing along. All other things in her house had been sold or given away and, although she had contemplated auctioning off her home, she left it in the hands of a competent Realtor who said it should fetch a decent penny in a reasonable amount of time.

Most importantly, Millie was squared away with the airline in a crate in a holding area, and she was slightly sedated. Viktoria carried the veterinarian's travel papers with her. Her dog was calm and well-mannered and she believed her trip to Iceland would go smoothly.

Twilight grew darker outside. She decided not to sit just yet and walked to the window to peer at the Icelandair plane parked outside. The catering truck was up against one of the doors as other airport personnel walked around the periphery. She glanced at her watch and realized they'd start boarding the nighttime flight in one hour.

In the last two months, Viktoria's focus had been geared towards going back to her original country. Since she could now relax, she wanted to address the medical skulduggery she'd seen and been privy to on Long Island at Amour Cosmetic Surgery. Then she hoped to put it in her past.

Viktoria stepped to the row of chairs, and settled next to her mother.

After pulling out her laptop computer, she established a network connection, and brought up the NY Board of Medical Licensure Newsletter which came out every quarter. Enough preliminary time should have elapsed, she thought, for initial findings against some plastic surgery doctors she'd worked with. Plus, all the information she had gathered against Amour, she had been careful to leave with the proper authorities.

Taking her time, she read three pages of medical news. On the top of Page 4, it said "Board Action Report." All current and new orders taken against physicians by the board were listed, and the names set up alphabetically.

Scrolling through the "A" and "B" last names, she read all types of dated orders against physicians—*"Second Amended Agreed Order, Amended Agreed Order, Order Terminating Agreed Order, Order of Probation, Agreed Order,"* etc. If she wanted more specific information, she could go to the Board's website and view under the particular Physician's Profile.

She quickly thought of the most important offenders she wanted to check on, and alphabetized them in her mind. Rigoberto Castillo was first, so she scrolled to names under "C," and found him:

"Rigoberto Castillo, M.D., North Shore, Long Island, NY, License #XXXX
Order of Probation issued, and effective immediately."

Like reading a miracle, she let out a gleeful, muffled "yessss!" Elisabet turned her head to her daughter, and Viktoria patted her hand. "I'll fill you in, mostly later on the plane, Mom."

Her search was not complete, and she scrolled through several more pages looking for the last name of Pinto, and he popped up as well:

"Ernest Pinto, M.D., North Shore, Long Island, NY, License #XXXX
Order of Probation issued, and effective immediately."

This would not help Bonnie Sandler after her forehead lift, breast augmentation, and death, she thought, but at least her sons Andrew and Jack would derive some comfort that the medical board had implemented action.

Clicking further to the last names with "R," she also found Victor Reed who had botched up Dorothy Flores abdominoplasty. Her happiness at finding a probation order against him as well made her eyes moisten, and she spoke to her mother. "A triple win if I ever saw one, Mom. I'm referring to three doctors, ones I worked with. They received disciplinary actions by the New York Board, so it's now official. They violated the New York Medical Practice Act."

"Congratulations are in order for my dear girl. You started the ball rolling, especially when you set in motion that police sting two months back."

Viktoria took in a deep breath. "Thanks, Mom. I love the support you give me, all the time."

"That's what mothers are for."

"So true. You are the backbone of my life."

She focused back on her computer, scrolled a bit more, but didn't spot other obvious physician names from Amour. After putting away her laptop, she pulled out an unopened letter from the side pocket of the bag.

The last few days had been chaotic due to the iconic trip back to the northern continent, and she had saved the letter. Wanting to open it when she could better absorb its content, she hoped that it contained gratifying news about the private legal courses underway against Rigoberto Castillo and his charade of deceptive practices.

After glancing at the return address of "*Stewart and Klein,*" she ripped open the envelope's back closure. The letter from Jonathan Stewart was dated several days ago and, as she began reading, she could almost hear his loud, deep voice giving her the update she wanted.

Dear Dr. Thorsdottir,

After I was contracted by Dorothy Flores to prepare her lawsuit against Rigoberto Castillo, Amour Cosmetic Surgery, et al., I was hired by the Sandler boys, Andrew and Jack, after the death of their mother, Bonnie. I thank you for recommending me to them.

I believe working for both these clients gives their cases a much better chance of receiving excellent results. Through our lawsuits, I believe they will receive substantial monetary compensation. At least they will have that, although nothing can bring back Bonnie Sandler, nor the medical result sustained by Mrs. Flores abdominoplasty.

In addition, since I am following through with finding out the actions of the State Attorney General and the NY Medical Board (which you may also be doing yourself), I believe it will only be a matter of time that Rigoberto and some other physicians, particularly those without board certification in plastic surgery, will have their licenses suspended. A total suspension of their licenses, I believe, will be the final result after the probation that the Board recently ordered.

The Attorney General is going to argue that these medical professionals are a danger to the public, and that they be ordered not to practice any aspect of medicine or surgery, nor should they be allowed to supervise other medical caretakers, prescribe or deliver any kind of drugs, etc.

I don't think, Dr. Thorsdottir, that a next generation name change into another plastic surgery center in the North Shore strip mall will be forthcoming. Maybe Long Island will be lucky enough to get a new bookstore instead.

Thank you again and all the best on your journey and new lifestyle back in Iceland.

Sincerely,
Jonathan M. Stewart, Esq.

Viktoria's heart warmed, and a calm swept over her. She folded the letter back up and slipped it into the envelope. Justice would be served, she was sure—like the outcome which had occurred in Pennsylvania with her other assignment at Jeff's hospital.

She did not regret her decision to leave the United States, although she knew that the deception and corruption she'd seen in medicine was but a sliver, a fraction, of the whole field. Almost all the people working in the medical field had chosen their individual path because of their love to help patients, and not to scam the medical system or to hurt others. She'd come across the worst individuals and situations but, just like in everything else, there were good and bad people everywhere and in every field of work.

It would be best if she not only go back to Iceland and be with her two brothers, she thought, but to also bring her mother back to her original roots. Life would not be as difficult for her now in her motherland as it was years ago—she and Alexander and Bjorn would see to it.

The only regret she had regarding relationships, however, was Jeffrey

Appleton. He would be a continent away. He was a special man, one she hated to leave. Would he visit her in Iceland like he mentioned? They had not seen each other again after his big, helpful trip during Rick's funeral week, but they both ached to spend time again with each other in the near future.

Viktoria and Elisabet boarded the 8:25 p.m. nonstop flight to Reykjavik and, smoothly, the plane took off and climbed in altitude. She then felt a sudden turbulent bump because of a change in wind direction due to the airport's location on the Atlantic coast of Long Island.

She looked down on the waters of Jamaica Bay, and silently said good-bye to the United States of America.

— End —

FROM THE AUTHOR

I hope you enjoyed Wretched Results and, if you did, please consider writing a review. Thanks so much!

If you'd like a release alert for when Barbara Ebel has new books available, sign up at http://eepurl.com/cKrn0D   This is intended only to let you know about new releases as soon as they are out.

Barbara Ebel is a physician and an author. Since she practiced anesthesia, she brings credibility to the medical background of her plots. She lives with her husband and pets in a wildlife corridor in Tennessee but has lived up and down the East Coast.

Visit or contact her at her website: http://barbaraebelmd.com

The following books are also written by Dr. Barbara and are available as paperbacks and eBooks:

The Outlander Physician Series:

Corruption in the O.R.: A Medical Thriller (The Outlander Physician Series Book 1)

Wretched Results: A Medical Thriller (The Outlander Physician Series Book 2)

EBook Box Sets:

The Dr. Annabel Tilson Novels Box Set:
Books 1-3 (The Dr. Annabel Tilson Series)

The Dr. Annabel Tilson Novels Box Set:
Books 4-6 (The Dr. Annabel Tilson Series)

The Dr. Danny Tilson Novels Box Set:
Books 1-4 (The Dr. Danny Tilson Series)

The Dr. Danny Tilson Series: (Individual paperbacks and ebooks):

Operation Neurosurgeon: You never know… who's in the OR (A Dr. Danny Tilson Novel: Book 1).

Silent Fear: a Medical Mystery (A Dr. Danny Tilson Novel: Book 2). Also an Audiobook.

Collateral Circulation: a Medical Mystery (A Dr. Danny Tilson Novel: Book 3). Also an Audiobook.

Secondary Impact (A Dr. Danny Tilson Novel: Book 4).

The Dr. Annabel Tilson Series: (Individual paperbacks and ebooks):

DEAD STILL: A Medical Thriller (Dr. Annabel Tilson Novels Book 1)

DEADLY DELUSIONS: A Medical Thriller (Dr. Annabel Tilson Novels Book 2)

DESPERATE TO DIE: A Medical Thriller (Dr. Annabel Tilson Novels Book 3)

DEATH GRIP: A Medical Thriller (Dr. Annabel Tilson Novels Book 4)

DOWNRIGHT DEAD: A Medical Thriller (Dr. Annabel Tilson Novels Book 5)

DANGEROUS DOCTOR: A Medical Thriller (Dr. Annabel Tilson Novels Book 6)

Stand-alone Medical Novels:

Outcome, A Novel

Her Flawless Disguise

Nonfiction health book:
Younger Next Decade: *After Fifty, the Transitional Decade, and What You Need to Know*

Children's book series written and illustrated by Barbara Ebel:
Chester the Chesapeake Book One
Chester the Chesapeake Book Two: Summertime
Chester the Chesapeake Book Three: Wintertime
Chester the Chesapeake Book Four: My Brother Buck
Chester the Chesapeake Book Five: The Three Dogs of Christmas

Made in United States
North Haven, CT
14 June 2022

20146797R00146